The Two Faces of Love

Laura Thrash

First paperback edition December 2024

Book design by Abby Thrash

ISBN 979-8-9916215-0-2 (paperback)

Chapter 1

Ada should never have swiped right. She regretted her decision to sign up for the dating site at all, but her group of teacher friends were relentless. It had been two years since her husband was killed in a helicopter crash, and she was approaching another birthday without him. She missed the joy that she had felt before she had kissed him for the last time that fated day, and the longing for him never seemed to lessen. Ada couldn't imagine moving forward without him, but she knew that she also couldn't keep only looking back.

On their first date Calin had taken her to a restaurant in town. Evidently, she was over-dressed, as he had pointed out in place of any compliments. He had reserved a table in the corner,

1

and the meal that he had preordered was served soon after they were seated. Ada had never cared for seafood, so the clam and mussel linguine rather turned her stomach. She moved the main dish around with her fork but was grateful for the mixed greens with honey vinaigrette. Calin noticed and waved the waitress down to remove her seafood plate.

"Sorry, just assumed anyone living along the coast would like seafood." Ada thought she detected a bit of irritation in the half-apology.

"My parents tried their best to get me to like something—grilled salmon, scallops, lobster, you name it. I have just always preferred chicken or vegetables," Ada tried smiling.

"Do your parents live here in town?" asked Calin, being polite.

"They still have the home I grew up in. I'm an only child, so after retiring a few years ago they've done nothing but travel the world. It was the plan from the beginning of their marriage. I just talked to them two days ago, and they called me aboard a yacht in the Mediterranean."

"Geesh!" Calin said a bit loudly. "Sounds like they do okay for themselves."

"My father was a general surgeon for over forty years. My

mom was the head librarian at the University library. She kept vivid notes over the years from travel books," Ada laughed.

The waitress came back to offer choices on desserts or more drinks, which they both turned down. Calin suggested that they take the bottle of wine he had brought from his personal collection and go sit at the beach on the boardwalk instead. Ada wasn't sure at this point if she even wanted to spend any more time with Calin but didn't want to appear rude. They drove the twenty minutes in awkward silence.

"Better grab your sweater since we're on the water. It's getting cooler," Calin said once they arrived.

Ada reached in the back seat and retrieved her pale blue cardigan. She noticed a packet of stapled papers with the Hertz logo at the top. *Calin was renting a car?* Ada thought. *Strange, he hadn't mentioned anything earlier.* Come to think of it, Ada had no idea where he even resided in town. She was beginning to doubt her ability to make wise choices.

A lot of young people were walking along the boardwalk. Afterall, the seniors had already graduated, and everyone else had only one week left. Calin and Ada finally found an empty bench, but another couple sat fairly close on the sand, holding hands and laughing.

The conversation consisted of Calin telling her about his high-level accounting and acquisitions position with a company, something Ada had to totally feign interest in. He wasn't altogether braggadocious about his career but did have Ada feeling like she needed to respond as though she was impressed.

Calin finally switched the focus back to Ada and was particularly interested in what she was planning to do during the summer months.

"Must be nice to have the entire summer off and not even have to think about work!" Calin scoffed.

Ada felt the heat rise in her cheeks and was glad that it was dark outside. The last thing she wanted was for Calin to know that he had struck a chord. She wanted to respond calmly.

"Well, that's something people say when they have no idea what we do," Ada began. "For starters, we're only paid for a nine-month contract. So, when you see us staying late after school, coming in on weekends to work, or painting our rooms and preparing for the new school year during the summer—we don't get paid for that." Ada raised her eyebrows and smiled slightly.

"Yikes, sorry I said anything," winced Calin. "You made your point. Although, I'll have to say, I find this spunky side of you quite attractive."

Calin moved toward Ada quickly, put her face in his hands, and kissed her firmly on the lips. Ada was too stunned to move. When Calin pulled back, he merely laughed.

"I just really couldn't resist," he commented. "How about some chocolate from the sweet shop over there to end our first date?"

Humph. Ada thought. *You mean our first and last date.* She was still reeling from the unwelcome kiss.

"No thanks. It has been a long week, and I'll be working in my classroom tomorrow to prepare for the close of school next week. Of course, I'm not getting paid for that." Ada couldn't help the dig. She simply got up and walked ahead of Calin toward the car.

"I didn't mean to piss you off, Ada," Calin said softly. "I do apologize."

The drive back to her apartment was once again silent.

"Thank you for dinner, and enjoy your weekend," said Ada as she opened the car door and tried to hurry away. Calin quickly got out, ran around to her side, and walked with her up to the apartment entrance.

"I am sorry if I came on too strong tonight. Just wanted to impress you, but I realize I may have taken things too far."

Oh, ya think? Ada thought to herself.

"I just don't think this is going to work with us, Calin."

"How can you say that after only one date? You've got to give me another chance." Calin grabbed Ada's hand and gave it a quick kiss, then hurried off.

"I'll call you next week, Ada!" he exclaimed.

Ada could say with certainty that there was no spark between her and Calin. Maybe it had been too long since her last date, or she had really lost that lovin' feelin', like the Righteous Brothers song says. Sure, Calin ordered her dinner without asking her, hadn't paid her any compliments, and kissed her a little aggressively, but were those reasons enough not to see him again if he asked? Ada was too tired to even think about it any longer. She made it to the second floor of her apartment building where she quickly slipped out of the cute black dress and into a comfy worn-out t-shirt, washed her face, brushed her teeth, and fell into bed.

Ada squinted her eyes and realized she hadn't even closed the blinds the night before. The sunshine was illuminating the entire room, and it was only 6:30 in the morning. Today was Saturday, but she was planning on working in her classroom to get things organized.

Afterwards, some of the other teachers were planning on attending a festival in town to celebrate the beginning of summer break. She threw on a cotton shirt dress and tennis shoes, and then put jeans, a top, sandals, and a cardigan in her bag for later. Ada locked the door behind her and headed to the school. Daisy was the only one there when she arrived, which was not surprising. Daisy was always the first one to get to school and the last to leave. Since Ada taught 2nd grade and Daisy 3rd, their classrooms were across the hall from each other.

"Of course, you beat me here!" Ada called out.

"Hey there! Just thought I'd get a head start so we can get out of here sooner. You know how I am." Daisy laughed and so did Ada.

After unlocking the door to her room, Ada headed down the hallway to get some empty boxes from the supply room. She had decided it was finally time to clear out the accumulation of excess materials she hadn't used for the last two years.

From the corner of her eye, Ada thought she spotted a figure moving in an adjacent hallway. Nobody she knew in that area of the school, all male teachers who shared a love of golf, would be here this early. She knew where they'd be on this sunny Saturday morning, and it certainly wasn't the classroom! Trying to shake her feeling of unease, Ada decided that the five boxes she was able to carry would be enough.

Ada found herself spacing out several times while deciding on what to keep. Some of the new math they were supposed to be incorporating into their teaching was exasperating even for the parents, so she tossed that stack into a box. It seemed that every year at this time Ada questioned her decision to teach school. Her real dream was to be an artist, particularly creating charcoal sketches. She'd often daydream about having her own studio and being invited to showcase her art in various featured exhibits throughout the country, but who was she kidding? Very few people in the arts make their dreams a reality. The eight-week art course she would be attending on Hartlyn Island in a few weeks was actually serving two purposes: one was working toward a graduate degree in art history and the other satisfying a professional development requirement, although it took a bit of convincing at the administrative offices that this should count towards credit for elementary education since she wasn't necessarily an art teacher.

"I'm over this!" Ada yelled across the hall to Daisy three hours later.

"Right back at ya," she called. "Let's leave in five."

Ada stacked the last box of recycling by the door and

headed to the restroom to freshen up and change into the clothes she had brought. Fortunately, the weather was comfortable, so she hadn't gotten too gross cleaning and didn't require a shower before heading downtown to the festival. After applying a new coat of mascara and some lipstick, Ada again thought she saw a shadow pass by the frosted glass in the restroom door. *Why am I being so paranoid all of a sudden,* Ada mentally asked herself. Lots of staff could be doing the same thing she was today.

Daisy rounded the corner to the restroom, and Ada let out a little scream.

"Wow! You scared me half to death, Ada," Daisy said, placing a hand over her heart. Ada laughed, "Same here, sorry. Meet you at the car."

Daisy and Ada were lucky enough to find a parking spot on the street about three blocks from the center of town. As they walked over, they waved to several people they knew. There was music blaring from a local band, all throwback songs from the 90s.

The girls were starving and made their way to the food trucks. There was an overwhelming number of choices, but they decided on tacos with fresh Pico de Gallo and craft beer. The sun was shining directly overhead at 3 o'clock in the afternoon, so they chose a picnic table with an umbrella.

"Cheers to another exhausting year," laughed Daisy.

"Are we just getting older or are the kids becoming more intolerable?" added Ada.

"A bit of both!" a voice behind them said. It was Donny, an 8th grade math teacher at their school.

Ada spoke up quickly, "Noticed your end of the hallway was quiet this morning. No sign of anyone working."

Donny swung his arms like he was holding a golf club. "Are you kidding me? No way on a day like today!"

Ada thought about mentioning the two incidents she had this morning but thought it probably would sound silly. She hadn't even said anything to Daisy.

"See you gals later. Enjoy the beer!" Donny shouted as he ran to catch up with his girlfriend.

"Okay, spill. I want to hear about your hot date last night. I knew I couldn't ask earlier, or we wouldn't have accomplished anything." Daisy laughed, and Ada thought about what a good friend she had. She loved how Daisy approached life with such enthusiasm.

"Hmm . . . I haven't given myself much time to process

things, but I guess it was fine."

"Uh oh," Daisy tilted her head to the side, "What exactly does that mean?"

"Calin was nice enough. I'm not sure how I feel about a guy preordering our dinner on the first date. It involved seafood." Ada stuck her fingers in her mouth and made a gagging noise.

"Oh geez, Ada. Anything else interesting happen?"

"I tried on about seven outfits after he told me that it would be someplace special. I ended up deciding on the black dress that I bought at that little boutique you and I shopped at last summer in Santa Barbara."

"I love that dress!" Daisy smiled.

"Well, he was quick to inform me that I was way over dressed! Not even a mention of my looking nice, so that didn't make me feel too great. And thank goodness for the salad that came with the seafood, or I wouldn't have had a bite to eat." Ada looked down at the rest of her taco and pushed the plate away.

"I'm so sorry, friend. The girls and I were just hoping you'd find someone to enjoy being with after these last two years. You deserve a good guy." Daisy reached over and put her hand on Ada's.

"I do appreciate you all thinking of me, but I probably shouldn't have agreed to a dating website to start over again. It just feels too risky."

"Most relationships are, though." Daisy said quietly. "Did you do anything after dinner?"

Ada took a deep breath and looked up at Daisy and then toward the band. "We took a bottle of wine down to the beach and talked a while. I had to pretend I was interested in hearing all about his boring accounting job." Ada rolled her eyes. "Then, he made some maddening comment about teachers and our summers off."

"He didn't," gasped Daisy. "Please tell me you set him straight?"

"You know it! Guess what, though? It turned him on so much that he grabbed my face and kissed me!" Ada stuck out her tongue and made a face of disgust. "I was ready to go home after that. Oh, but he promised to call me next week! No, thank you!" yelled Ada.

"Good riddance to Callous Calin is all I have to say! Don't worry, there is someone perfect for you out there. I just know it!" Daisy said as she put her arm around Ada's shoulder and started walking. "Let's go get some of those ice cream tacos!"

Ada burst out laughing. "Oh, why not?"

Chapter 2

Ada was relieved that she had made it to the last day for teachers and had yet to hear from Calin. By now, she and Daisy had shared the entire nightmare of a date with the other teacher friends, and they all had a good laugh over Ada setting him straight about teachers! She had already closed her account on the dating site, even though several requests to meet her had come through her email. She sent kind regrets to those and blocked her email from the site. Never again would she attempt to meet someone in this way. She had heard of other couples developing a relationship from swiping right, but this just wasn't going to be for her.

"Hi, Miss Cameron," she heard a sweet voice say. "I haven't seen you for such a long time."

"Well, hello, Layla; what a nice surprise! You look so grown up. 7th grade, right?" asked Ada. Layla was the secretary's daughter and had been a former student of Ada's.

"Yes, well, 8th grade now!" Layla giggled. "These flowers just arrived for you, so the office asked me to deliver them to your room."

"Thank you, Layla. Have a wonderful summer!"

"You, too," Layla said and bounced out of the room.

The mixed flower bouquet was not only beautiful with its tulips, lilies, and roses, but filled the room with such a fragrant aroma. *Who would send me flowers?* thought Ada. Maybe her mom and dad, although how would they remember school was almost out when they were in the middle of the Mediterranean? Possibly Daisy and the girls felt sorry for her after the disaster date last Friday?

Ada opened the envelope and took out the card.

"Looking forward to our second date. C"

Ada's heart sank. *Are you kidding me?* She was so in hopes that Calin had realized, as she had, that they were completely incompatible. She didn't want to have to turn him down again. Her main goals this summer were to attend the graduate classes and forget about a relationship. Just focus on art, and maybe even get a few more sketches under her belt.

The classroom was finally ready to close for the summer. Ada looked around at the organized shelves, the chairs stacked on top of desks, and the cute black and white checked curtains hanging in the windows. It hadn't been a particularly bad year with students, although, there had been a couple of run-ins with parents who thought their children should automatically receive top-notch grades in everything, even without putting in the effort. Also, the principal wasn't the sharpest and had his own way of doing things. If you didn't at least appear supportive, he could make your year miserable.

Ada let out a loud sigh and thought how nice it would be to do something else with her life for a change. These last few years had taken a toll. She was so fresh and enthusiastic at twenty-one, thinking that she could make such a difference in young minds, and perhaps she had, but now she just felt tired.

Oh well, what choice do I have? Ada thought to herself. *It's too late to change course now. I'll be ready for a new school year after some time off.*

The girls had all decided to meet at Charlie's Bar to have some dinner and drinks to celebrate the end of the school year. Ada had decided on a whimsical gauzy mint green dress and chunky sandals. She hadn't saved enough time to do her hair, so she did a quick updo which turned out rather cute.

Ada and Daisy arrived at the bar at same time and walked in together.

"Look at you all hot and sexy!" Daisy said, snapping her fingers and shimmying her shoulders.

"You're too funny," Ada giggled under her breath.

Their other teacher friends were already at the table with drinks. "Hey, ladies!" one of them shouted over the music, "What's your pleasure?"

Taking a seat, Ada ordered a Cosmopolitan, and Daisy went with a peach mango margarita on the rocks. As they sipped, the girls reminisced about the year and some of the more comical things that had occurred.

"Remember when Greg—" one of them began before getting lost in a fit of laughter. "Oh my gosh, yes!" Another picked up, gasping through her own laughter, "When he locked himself in the cafeteria freezer, and the janitor had to let him out?"

The drinks and appetizers of loaded nachos had them almost filled completely before their entrees had even arrived. Ada was able to take several bites of the delicious Cajun chicken linguine she ordered but had to ask for a box to take the rest home. It would make a good lunch for tomorrow. She then excused herself to go to the restroom to freshen up.

Heading around the corner, she glanced to her left for just a second, which caused her to run directly into the person walking out of the hallway. When she looked up, the person was smiling slightly.

"In a hurry?"

No, Ada thought. *Not Calin.*

"Oh, sorry. I wasn't paying attention to where I was going." Ada said sheepishly.

"You and your teacher friends seem to be partying big time tonight … someone's birthday?" Calin asked.

"No, end of the school year," she quickly responded, looking around Calin toward the bathroom.

"Ah, I see. I've been meaning to call you, Ada. It's just been a hectic week. The corporate boss was in overseeing the latest projects."

"Oh, no problem!" Ada fake accepted his apology, sounding much more sincere than she felt. "I've been busy myself with organizing my classroom for the start of the new school year, plus I'll be leaving soon for my summer courses." Ada sidestepped Calin, walking quickly away. "Nice to see you again, Calin." Ada hurried off and went inside the ladies' restroom.

Shutting the door behind her, she breathed a sigh of relief. *Of all places in town, why did he have to end up here and now?* Ada took her time in the bathroom and hoped he wasn't waiting for her outside the door.

After carefully peeking out of the door and checking he wasn't there, she rushed back to her table and sat down.

Daisy looked up, a little startled. "Are you okay?" she asked. Ada simply nodded and tried to brush off the strange run-in.

After another hour of drinks, the girls were trying to twist her arm to do karaoke. Ada decided then it was time to leave. As she closed the door to Charlie's, she could hear them singing with the crowd, "You Lost that Lovin' Feelin'."

The spring nights in Riverton could be a little chilly, but the weather had been beautiful this week. As she walked toward her well-lit apartment building, Ada was thankful for the glow emanating from the light posts; the security of the apartment helped her feel safe, especially with the lingering anxiety she had from unexpectedly seeing Calin earlier. There were two main building doors to unlock and then two flights of stairs before she reached her apartment, unless she took the creepy elevator. Considering, Ada picked the stairs. She felt uneasy enough already.

As she exited the stairwell, Ada saw there was something sitting in front of her apartment door. Leaning against the bottom of the door was a package wrapped in ivory paper with a simple bow.

Once inside, Ada anxiously opened the box. There was a sketch pad with a box of charcoal pencils. No note. *Who could have left this?* she thought.

The only person who came to mind was Calin, but she couldn't remember saying much to him about her passion for drawing. Maybe she had during the date but just didn't remember within the strangeness of it all?

Mulling over the mysterious parcel, Ada let herself into her apartment and moved toward the bathroom to shower and get ready for bed. Before stepping into the shower, she lingered by the door, eyeing the lock. Then she did something she had never done before. She locked the door to the bathroom.

She felt a sense of unease as she washed her hair, the feeling only growing when she closed her eyes to rinse out the shampoo. She felt like a horror movie character waiting for the killer to storm in and knife her down in the shower, Hitchcock *Psycho* style. *Damn it*, Ada thought. Something about locking the door was making her mind go crazy, making her itch with paranoia. Skipping the conditioner, she turned off the water and grabbed a towel. Once her hair was wrapped up, she stepped out and dried off before slowly opening the door and walking into her bedroom.

I really should get a dog, or at least turn the television on while I'm home. This quiet is unsettling, she thought. Opening her dresser, Ada took out the first shirt and shorts in the drawer. They didn't match, but she didn't care.

No conditioner meant more work getting the tangles out of her hair. Once that was accomplished, she grabbed her hair dryer. As she dried, the air from the tool droning, Ada's anxiety increased once again. Even with the hair dryer turned on low, she was surrounded by the white noise and unable to hear anything else. She shut the dryer off and listened to the night around her, trying to calm herself. *You're just imagining things*, she thought. She turned the dryer back on, but the anxiety returned. Ada decided not to finish drying her hair and to go to bed with it semi-wet.

She double checked the front door lock, left a light on in the living room, and even left the touch lamp in her bedroom on low. Ada turned on her side and stuffed the pillow under her neck. *I hate this,* she thought. *Why can't I relax?* Ten minutes later she was out of bed, opening her closet door to peer inside and checking under her bed. She had thought the higher mattress frame that left room for storage underneath had been an answer to an uncluttered apartment but now she was not so sure if she felt comfortable with that much dark, open space beneath her while she slept. She kept imagining monsters lurking in the depths.

Tomorrow she would order the door thing she had seen on TikTok. The one that braced between the inside of the door and the floor and prevented the door from opening. It might provide some comfort while she was at home alone—but it wouldn't help when she was out. It installed from the inside, so she had no way to set it up from outside the apartment. A security system could be a good option but investing in a security system seemed ridiculous in this smaller coastal community. Plus, she didn't exactly have the funds for it on her teacher's salary. Maybe she could get a set of cameras online for cheap? It wouldn't be the whole alarm, instant access to a security company and police kind of thing, but maybe it would provide some peace of mind?

Sometime during her fitful contemplation of home security

options, Ada must have finally fallen asleep, as she awoke the following morning to loud knocking on her apartment door. Her heart jumped. Prying her eyes open, she could see that it was already after ten o' clock. That was enough to nearly make her trip as she threw herself out of bed and scrambled to the door; she never slept this late. She looked through the peep hole and was immediately relieved to see it was Daisy standing with two coffees in hand.

"Seriously, girl? I knew you preferred sleeping in, but 10 am?" Daisy brushed past her into the apartment and flopped onto the papasan chair. Reaching a cup up to Ada, she recited her friend's go-to order: "white mocha latte, coconut milk, 2 shots of espresso."

Then she noticed the lack of coloring in Ada's cheeks.

"Oh Ada, what's wrong? Are you sick?" Daisy had jumped out of the chair and already set both of their coffees on the table.

"No, it was a long night I guess," Ada mumbled. "You didn't happen to leave anything at my door last night, did you?"

"Huh?" Daisy looked puzzled. "You mean after we left Charlie's?"

"Never mind, I didn't figure so . . ." Ada took her coffee, sat down on the sofa, and covered up with the chunky blanket her mom had brought back from Italy for her. "I had a wrapped package waiting for me at my door when I got home from the bar last night."

Daisy took a sip of her coffee and sat back down, tucking her legs beneath her. "Do tell."

"It was a sketch pad and charcoal pencils, but there was no note. If you weren't the one who put it there then I have no idea. Except for . . ."

"Except for . . . ?" Daisy motioned with her hand for Ada to continue. "Calin. He was at Charlie's last night."

Daisy gasped, "You saw him when you went to the restroom, didn't you? I knew something had happened but didn't want to question you in front of everyone. Did he say something to upset you?"

"No, we exchanged a few words after I accidentally ran into him, and I hurried into the bathroom and shut the door. I didn't see him after that."

"Is he still thinking that the two of you are going to go out again? I mean, that guy can't take a hint." Daisy rolled her eyes. "Okay, well Calin and weird package aside, gulp the rest of that coffee and let's go run around! After all, it's the first day of summer freedom! My only request is that we drive at least thirty minutes in some direction to avoid seeing any of our students, or should I say parents?" Daisy giggled.

"I do need to pick up some things for my upcoming classes this summer," Ada considered. "Okay, sounds fun! Give me ten minutes to get ready."

Ada drove them to their favorite shopping boutiques about forty-five minutes from town. The historic waterfront town housed wine-tasting rooms and art galleries. It was quaint, charming, and classy, but without the air of snobbery you sometimes find in similar places.

The girls had their arms full of shopping bags when they finally plopped into a seat at Ella's Cove, their favorite lunch spot that served the best crab salad and croissant sandwiches.

Sandwiches, homemade pickles, and iced teas were followed by a piece of peach cobbler. Ada grabbed her stomach and slouched in her seat. "Why do we do this every time we're here?"

"Some things are worth the pain," commented Daisy as she patted her own stomach and smiled.

The girls spent the next half an hour chatting about Daisy and her husband, Jackson, who was due back from a business conference later that day. Daisy also tried to assure Ada that Mr. Right was out there somewhere for her. Ada let her.

On the drive back, the windows of Ada's car down, they listened and sang along to Coldplay's "Something Just Like This." As they pulled up to Ada's apartment building, a figure was sitting on the steps. Daisy was the first to spot the man and, under her breath, said, "I wonder who that is?"

Before Ada had even a moment to ask Daisy what she was talking about, she saw him.

Calin. He looked up and waved to them both, stood up, and began walking toward the car. Placing his hands onto the passenger side door, he leaned in and looked directly at Ada.

"If I didn't know better, I'd think you were doing everything to avoid me," Calin laughed.

"I have no idea what you're even talking about," Ada said coldly. "You might want to remove your hands." Ada pressed the button to roll up the windows.

As she did, Daisy caught her gaze, "Yikes, Ada," she said, her eyes wide.

Ada popped the trunk so she and Daisy could retrieve all their purchases. Calin, undeterred by Ada's coolness, seemed to ignore her comments and went straight to the trunk, insisting on carrying everything.

"Oh, part of those go in my car," Daisy quickly jumped in. "Hi, I'm Daisy, Ada's best friend."

"Nice to meet you, Daisy. I'm Calin." Daisy opened the back door of her car so Calin could put the bags inside.

"Thanks." "I don't mean to run you off—" Calin began.

"Oh, I wasn't leaving," Daisy interrupted with a smile, and then headed upstairs to Ada's apartment.

Before Calin had a chance to respond, Ada quickly invented plans that she and Daisy had for the rest of the evening. He looked disappointed.

"I was really hoping to spend some time with you. Did you get my gift?"

Ada knew immediately that he was talking about the sketch book left at her door. "Yeah, about that . . . I'm not really a fan of those kinds of surprises. Also, Calin, I thought I made myself clear about our not seeing each other again. I would appreciate you not contacting me anymore." Ada was shaking inside but was determined not to let it show. *That stupid dating site,* she thought. She'd never again believe that was a good way to meet a decent guy.

Calin took off his sport jacket and folded it across his arm, smoothing the fabric with his hand. When he looked up at Ada, she couldn't read his expression. There was a hint of a smile but also a twinge of disgust within his features.

"I don't understand you, Ada. You can really string a guy along. I thought that our relationship was moving in a good direction."

Ada took a step back but stood her ground. Now she was feeling pissed off. What was he talking about? They didn't have a relationship, nor would they ever, for that matter. Why do some guys think women are so privileged to be in their presence?

"I have nothing more to say to you, Calin, except 'goodbye.' Please don't call or stop by again."

Ada reshuffled her two shopping bags and walked confidently upstairs. She was determined for Calin to see her as serious and confident in her decision.

Daisy was watching from an upstairs window, just about ready to head down and escort Ada upstairs herself, when she saw Ada move toward the building. Calin must have sensed her watching him because he glanced up to where she was. Daisy quickly moved away from the window, out of his view. *What a*

creeper, she thought. She was beginning to feel guilty about pushing Ada to set up a profile on the dating website. Ada deserved so much better than this weirdo.

Ada and Daisy had both married their high school sweethearts. They had all grown up together and figured they'd all grow old together. All four were graduates of the town's liberal arts college, with the girls both receiving degrees in education, Jackson a degree in business, and Troy a degree in psychology. Daisy and Jackson had broken up during their sophomore year and even dated other people for a while, but it wasn't long until the two found each other again.

It was Ada and Troy who had gotten married first, the week after graduation. Ada's parents had insisted on a destination wedding to St. Thomas and rented a large estate on the island. Not that Ada would have chosen this venue, but being an only child, she was used to everything in her life being planned for her. At least she had a say in the dress she wore, a simple, classic white satin gown with a strapless neckline, scoop back and full circle with pockets. The wedding and reception were beautiful, and dancing in Troy's arms to their favorite music made Ada's heart swell with gratitude. When Ada glanced over at her maid of honor, Daisy had her head on Jackson's shoulder; she smiled at Ada, mouthing the words, "I love you." Ada mouthed the same back to her best friend, and the four of them danced until no one was left except for the band.

Daisy and Jackson had planned for a July 4th weekend wedding that same year at a barn venue about an hour away from their town. For the following year and a half, life moved along as they had intended, with the girls teaching at the same elementary school across the hall from each other. Jackson was busy working for his dad's marketing company and Troy was working on his master's degree in counseling while coaching the high school baseball team. He had played during both high school and college, leading his team to victory at the Division II baseball championship, so going back to his alma mater to coach was thrilling for him.

Weekend game nights, golf outings, and beach barbecues were a way of life for the two couples, until one day in February brought everything to a screeching halt. Troy had taken a last-minute trip with the snowboard club he belonged to in town. They were driving to Vancouver and then taking a private helicopter to the top of a mountain where they'd be dropped off to make the harrowing journey down the side of a snow-capped mountain all alone. Ada really didn't want Troy to go, but he seemed so excited about the trip that she didn't have the heart to express her fears aloud, although, most likely, he already knew them. His lips seemed to linger on hers a bit longer than usual during that goodbye kiss.

It was Troy's father who had called her when it happened, in the middle of the last school day before winter break. Ada answered her phone even with students in the room because she had never received a call from him before. She instructed the students to continue working in their groups and quickly picked up the call.

"Tom? Hello, how—"

"Ada, my sweet girl," Tom swallowed hard. "I have some terrible news and wish I could be there in person to tell you."

Ada's stomach turned. "Oh no, is it Eveyln?"

"It's about Troy. We just received a call from the authorities up north." His voice broke and he exhaled hard.

Ada turned her back towards the students, who were beginning to sense that something was wrong. She pulled her phone away from her ear, swiped down the notifications, and saw two missed calls from an hour ago. They had been in the hallway for a restroom break. Ada's heart began to race. She put the phone back to her ear.

"I—I see that someone tried to call earlier. Is everything okay?" She gripped the cell phone with both hands for fear of dropping it.

"Yes, they tried reaching you first. Troy had our number as a second emergency contact." "Emergency? Please, Tom, this is scaring me."

"There was an accident, honey. His helicopter . . . it crashed."

"What?" Ada said louder into the phone than she intended. "Is he alright? Where is he? Did they take him to the hospital? I'll leave right away!" She began to grab random items, packing to leave.

"Ada," Tom interrupted her. "I'm so sorry." His voice broke again. "He's gone."

"Gone where?"

This time Tom didn't answer. There was silence on the other end of the phone for a few seconds before he proceeded to explain what had taken place on the mountain.

Everything suddenly went dark. Ada awoke with the school principal and Daisy on the floor beside her. Another teacher had taken the class across the hallway. Ada was in complete shock, staring blankly out into the classroom as she repeated what her father-in-law had told her. The helicopter carrying the group of five was changing course due to sudden blizzard conditions when the propeller got caught in a giant Sitka Spruce tree. The helicopter plunged over one hundred feet down to a cliff jutting out below, crashed, and went up in flames. By the time the crews were able to get any help to them, the area was smoldering with ashes. Nothing was left.

Ada's parents offered to have her come and stay with them, but Ada couldn't leave her house, or even her bed for that matter. So, it was Daisy who stayed with her for two weeks while she cried, slept, and had to be practically hand-fed.

Now, Daisy began feeling extreme guilt for adding unnecessary drama and stress to Ada's already vulnerable state. Even though it had been two years, Ada had never spoken about being with anyone else. She was so in love with Troy that nothing or no one seemed to interest her. After some prompting from a few of their teacher friends, Daisy presented the idea of a match-making website to Ada, but it felt like Ada had only gone along with it to please Daisy.

The door burst open, then quickly banged close. Ada leaned back against it and let out a huge sigh. She dropped her packages on the floor and shuffled to the couch. Hugging her legs to her chest, she rested her chin atop her knees and stared out. Daisy hurried over and sat by her friend without saying a word. She was afraid that Ada could be feeling upset with her over Calin.

"Before you say anything, I don't blame you for this. I don't blame anyone." Ada reached out a hand to Daisy, who clasped it with both of hers.

"You deserve so much better than this. I know I've said it like a thousand times, but I do believe there is someone out there who will love you with their entire being, just like Troy."

The girls sat in silence for a while as the evening sun gently guided streams of orange and red through the room. They heard melancholy piano music from the apartment next door. It seemed to go perfectly with the mood in the room.

"I can stay," Daisy spoke softly.

"You're such a good friend, Daisy. I promise that I'll be okay. I'm leaving bright and early in the morning anyway, since I have a reservation for the ferry over to Port Hartlyn. I'll call you when I get checked into the Airbnb, plus you can track me on your phone." Ada stood up to hug her friend.

"Okay," Daisy replied hesitantly. "Please drive carefully. Try to forget everything that has happened recently and enjoy diving into your art!" Daisy turned the door handle to leave, then stopped and turned around. "You know I believe what I said about finding another love like Troy, right?" Ada smiled sadly and shook her head.

Chapter 3

Ada figured she had overpacked, as usual. But the two courses would require a three-hour drive to Hartlyn Island and last almost the entirety of summer break, so she wanted to make sure that she had everything she might need in order to avoid any return trips. Ada surveyed the new outfits that she had bought during the recent shopping outing with Daisy. She had a total of twelve complete outfits, and all could be combined in different ways to make several more.

Seeing the coral and bright yellow tops radiating back at her, she was glad that she had fought the urge to go with only neutrals this time. Considering for a moment, she also threw in two pairs of leggings, a couple of sweatshirts, and her boots, just in case it was cool and rainy at all while she was there.

For her beauty and personal care items, the new toiletry bag she had ordered on a whim from Amazon fit everything perfectly and nestled nicely into her larger suitcase. Along with her suitcases, she grabbed a backpack. Not only would this help organize and carry her school supplies, but it easily allowed her to roll both her large and medium suitcases without requiring any help. Ada put an extra book for pleasure reading and a booklight clip into the backpack. She did one final check of the list she had typed—it was a habit before any trip. It was something that Troy had often lovingly teased her about, but he never failed to express how grateful he was when it helped her remember things for him as well.

Sighing and sitting down at the head of her bed, Ada rested her hand on the pillow next to her. What she would give to have her husband there looking back at her with those piercing blue eyes of his. He always looked at her with such love.

Just as Ada was about to drift off to sleep for the night, she thought she heard a noise in the living room. It was probably just the neighbor across the hallway or the closing of a closet door on the other side of her apartment, but Ada had become so hypersensitive to any little noise that even telling herself these things didn't alleviate her sudden, overwhelming sense of panic.

She blamed Calin. He had caused her to become suspicious of things that never crossed her mind before meeting him, especially after he entered her apartment complex and left that gift at her door.

She climbed out of bed reluctantly, feeling a little pissed off, which helped reduce the fear somewhat. The living room was dark except for the small sliver of light stretching under the front door from the apartment hallway on the other side. From the corner of her eye, Ada thought she noticed the light under the door leave for a moment, as though someone had walked by. She looked out her peep hole but didn't see anything except for the neighbor's door wreath. She waited, watching and listening intensely for any suggestion of movement in the hallway. After a few minutes, she decided she must have imagined it.

Unable to shake the unease, Ada did a sweep of the closets and under her bed, just to be safe. As she climbed back into bed, her heart still raced, so she left the nightstand lamp on low and asked Alexa to play her love song playlist. It was one that she had made for Troy and herself with all of their favorite songs. Comforted by thoughts of Troy, Ada finally drifted off to sleep thinking about him.

Thank goodness I'm not flying out, Ada thought the next

morning as she hauled her luggage out of her apartment to her car. Her larger suitcase was very likely over the fifty-pound limit. While struggling to get it into her trunk, her cell phone started ringing, her mom's face appearing on the screen. Hands full, she let the call go to voicemail.

After connecting to CarPlay and entering the ferry address, Ada called her mom back, and they talked almost the entire drive. Mainly it was her mom who did the talking. She couldn't wait to tell Ada about all the friends she and Ada's dad had met on their trip. They had even extended their stay in Barcelona. Other than filling her mom in on the end of the school year and upcoming art course, Ada didn't say much of her personal life, and she steered clear of the whole Calin situation completely. She knew her mom would give a lecture on the craziness of people these days, how you can't be too careful meeting strangers online, and she just didn't feel up for that. *Funny how she doesn't see the similarity of meeting strangers in different countries*, Ada mused.

Before they hung up, Ada promised to check in at some point during her first week of classes. Ending the call, she briefly wondered how long, if it ever happened, it would take her parents to genuinely understand her love of art. It wasn't that they didn't support her, Ada could tell that they didn't grasp the depth of her passion. *Maybe someday,* her thoughts comforted.

Ada got to the ferry in plenty of time and was instructed to head to lane five to wait for boarding. She decided to turn off the car and run into the ferry market to grab a Starbucks coffee. Ada had been to the island several times with friends and learned quickly that once you are queued up, you can turn off your car and are free to wander about until loading time. As Ada sat inside the coffee shop finishing her drink, she noticed people were starting to return to their cars. She took the last sip of her coffee, tossed the cup in a nearby garbage can, and joined them in migrating across the lanes back to her car.

Meandering through the rows of vehicles, Ada hesitated before crossing in front of one car that was idling. The driver motioned her on. She couldn't see the person very well except for the hat they were wearing, a blue Seattle Blue Jays baseball cap. The cap made her think of Troy; he often wore them, and there were still several in her front closet. Although they no longer were of any use, some things she couldn't part with yet, so they stayed in the closet.

Ada pulled up in front of the Airbnb and sighed aloud. It was perfect. The bungalow had recently been restored and sat right on the edge of the historic district with only a two-block walk to the pier in one direction and the University in the other. White stucco on the small home was framed in gray trim and encircled with black iron railings and fence. Clay-colored steps led to the cozy front porch adorned with soft pastel cushions on the wicker porch swing and additional chairs. Worn pillows and throw blankets were tucked neatly into a basket near the front door.

The lady who owned the house had left Ada detailed instructions about everything. She was visiting her daughter in Boston for a few months, so Ada was told that the place was all hers. Ada could already picture herself sitting on the porch with a morning cup of coffee and reading her book before class. The entrance to her suite was on the side of the house, next to a little garden area boasting a wall of clematis that clung heavily to the lattice, a faded mint green bistro table with chairs for two, and a bird bath surrounded by rhododendrons. The home was located within walking distance of the University, but the rental also came with an old Schwinn bicycle available for use.

Ada was in the process of putting away her clothes when the phone rang.

"Hi, Mom! I was just about to call you. Yes, I'm here and the place is lovely." She paused, listening, "Yes, it's safe—yes, plenty of outdoor lighting." Ada wasn't even sure about the lighting but didn't feel like drawing out that part of the conversation.

"Actually, the courses are four weeks each. Yes, I gain credit. Well, it counts toward my professional development requirements but also fulfills six hours toward my graduate degree in art history.

"Mom, we've talked about this many times. I don't plan on teaching elementary school forever. Of course, I love my students, but I just want an opportunity to spend more time on my passion for art." Ada was already feeling tired from her travels and didn't feel up to having yet another discussion about her future, especially with her mom.

"So, where are you and Dad headed next?" Ada asked, trying to change the subject. "Iceland . . . really? Oh, a trip with your new friends. Next week? That soon? Well, I hope that you and Dad have a great time, and I'm glad to know that retirement agrees with you! I will . . . take care. Love you, too." Ada hung up the phone and flopped down on her bed.

Hopping out of this bed in the morning might prove to be a challenge, thought Ada. The mattress seemed to fit her body just right, and the memory foam pillows conformed to her head as if they were made specifically for her. Maybe she would get a few minutes of shut eye and then she'd explore the town and walk to the University to get an idea of how long it took.

Ada jolted awake, sitting up quickly. *What time was it?* She groped around for her phone and saw the time read 6:30 pm. *Not too bad*, Ada thought. She freshened up and took off toward the University.

Tree-lined sidewalks and unique homes lined the street on both sides. One side of the sidewalk was newer, making it easy to gawk at the neighborhood without worrying too much about where she put her feet; the other, older side required attention so as not to trip. As she walked, she passed people out on their porches or mowing their lawns. One gentleman threw up his hand in a wave as she walked by, and she waved back with a smile. *I could get used to this*, Ada thought.

It took exactly twelve minutes to get from her front door to the front door of the University's main offices. Of course, Ada wasn't sure exactly where her class would be held, but the first day of registration would take place in this building, and she figured her classrooms couldn't be very far. As she explored the campus, she noticed that it was free of students for the most part. It was summer and a Sunday evening, so it wasn't terribly surprising.

Ada decided to roam a little further up the same side of the road and discovered a cute place called Sam's Diner. The sign said, "Open until 9:00 pm," so she went inside. Some kind of music, she couldn't quite make out what, played softly over the speakers, and the restaurant was mostly full, except for a couple of tables off to the side.

A waitress with a kind smile approached Ada to ask if she wanted to be seated, and Ada gladly accepted. Ada perused the menu, deciding on a chicken sandwich and house salad with iced tea. While waiting for her food, Ada decided to text Daisy and let her know that she had arrived, and all was well. Daisy replied immediately to say how happy she was that Ada had made it safely and that she couldn't wait to see Ada in two weeks when she came to visit.

Ada sat and enjoyed her meal and the peaceful comfort she had begun to find in her solitude; the meal was filling and quite good. After finishing her food, Ada left the diner and decided to head back toward the direction of her rental and perhaps walk down by the pier.

The smell of bay water lapping up on the rocks was familiar to Ada. She loved the Pacific Northwest. It had everything: mountains, forests, and water. What more would you want? As she walked along the boardwalk, Ada noticed a man struggling on a large rock that jutted out of the water about a hundred meters offshore. He was attempting to climb up as high as possible to escape the rolling waves but kept slipping back into the water. She stopped, watching, and was about to call an emergency number when she noticed what appeared to be the coast guard coming to the man's rescue. After a few failed attempts to pull the boat close to the rock without hitting it, one of the rescuers was able to jump out onto the rock with the man. He placed a silver blanket around the man's shoulders and helped get some boots on his feet. Ada stood and watched until the man was safely aboard the vessel. She shivered. *What was he doing out there? Crabbing or fishing or something?*

Brushing off the unusual situation, she yawned and figured it was probably best to get back, shower, lay out her clothes for tomorrow, and maybe even have a glass of wine on the front porch before turning in for the night. Ada was tired but also excited for what these summer weeks would bring. If her evening walking through the picturesque town and enjoying the local cuisine was any indication, it would be a fun and refreshing experience.

Just as she was about to reach her bungalow, Ada saw a man walking between her house and the one next door. *Maybe it was someone hired to care for the lawn?* She wondered. *But at this time of night?*

By the time Ada made it to the gate, there was no one in sight. *Damn Calin*, she mentally cursed. The whole encounter with him had increased her paranoia more than ever, and she had just finally been able to get used to living alone after Troy died. Now, those feelings of safety, comfort, and contentment, no matter how small, were gone. By the time Ada got her clothes and satchel ready for the next morning, she was too exhausted to even enjoy a glass of wine, so she opted for an early bedtime, falling asleep quickly in the luxurious bed.

Ada awoke before her alarm but felt too excited to lie in bed, so she jumped up, shuffled to the kitchen, and put on some coffee. She had decided on a cute blue skirt and white blouse with strappy sandals for the day. Wearing her long, highlighted brunette hair partly up and some light make up, Ada looked in the mirror and added some gloss to her lips. She grabbed a muffin and coffee and headed for the front porch. Birds were chirping, squirrels were darting up trees, and a mother was pushing a stroller up the street. She could get used to this type of living. This is what her life with Troy was supposed to be, along with a couple of little ones running around the yard. Ada didn't want to lose hope, but after her experience with Calin she seriously doubted there was a chance to meet anyone decent.

Ada glanced at her watch and decided to make her way to the University. It only took her ten minutes this morning; she must have been walking faster than yesterday, perhaps in anticipation. A long table was set up out on the front lawn of campus. There was a banner that read "Welcome to Summer Studies!" Ada approached the table and was met with a big smile.

"Good morning, welcome to the University! May I have your name?" asked a cute girl with a short bob hairdo. *I wish I could look that good in short hair*, thought Ada.

"Good morning," Ada smiled back. "Yes, it's Ada Cameron. I'm here for the art courses."

"Yes! We've got you right here, Ms. Cameron," the girl pointed to her paper.

The use of "Ms." made Ada feel old, like she was the one teaching the course instead of a student taking it. The girl handed Ada a folder with information about the class, a map of campus, and information about open food establishments. The right-hand side of the folder had a sticker with the course name and room number of her first class, so Ada followed some of the other students inside in search of her classroom. The main hall was open and airy with lots of windows. Several of the people seemed to know each other, gathering in small groups to talk.

Winding through the crowds, Ada found her classroom on the second floor. It was obviously an art studio but for now was set up as a traditional classroom with desks and chairs. Most likely, they would be spending time at the beginning of the course learning the history of art and viewing pictures on the large screen. Ada felt a surge of butterflies in her stomach, but this time it was pure joy. This is what she had been looking forward to for so long, being surrounded with art and those who loved it as much as she did.

"May I sit here?" An older woman with glasses and layers of clothes looked down at Ada.

"Of course, please do!"

"Thank you." The lady then proceeded to take off one of her sweaters, place it on the back of the chair, and rummage around in her bag, finally pulling out a notepad and pen.

Ada wasn't sure if the woman wanted to engage in

47

conversation and decided to wait a bit before saying anything. After a few minutes, a gray-haired gentleman with tanned skin and wire-rimmed glasses took position at the front of the classroom. Ada bet that he was probably younger than he looked but presented himself as older and distinguished. People in the art world tended to do that. A couple of the students, as they entered, stopped by his desk, speaking and laughing with the professor. Most likely they had already previously taken classes from him. She guessed there were about twenty people total in the class.

"'The object of art is not to reproduce reality, but to create a reality of the same intensity,'" spoke the professor aloud. "Who can tell me the author of this quote?"

One of the students up front quickly raised his hand and spoke at the same time. "Alberto Giacometti."

"Yes, good. Now, can someone tell me what he meant?"

Exuberance bubbled inside of Ada as she surveyed the room of eager students. She knew in that moment that she was right where she needed to be.

Chapter 4

The class paused for lunch around noon, and Ada was starving. She decided to check out some of the places on campus to grab a bite. Following some of the other students, she made her way to an area that reminded her of a mall food court. There were several offerings, although not all appeared to be open. Ada walked up to Just Like Home, a homestyle kitchen offering a variety of sandwiches and sides. She didn't need to look at the menu long before ordering an egg salad sandwich on sour dough with a side of potato salad and sweet tea.

The food was packed to go, so Ada thought she would check the seating situation outside. The sky was blue, the temperature just right, and a slight breeze stirred the air. Across the street there was a group of young men gathered inside a baseball field, appearing to be in a huddle with their coach. Ada saw an empty bench facing the players and sat down.

As she ate, the huddle broke, and the players began taking practice hits and fielding balls. She couldn't help remembering the days when she used to watch Troy play in high school. It was when she first developed a crush on him. Then, she thought about their college days, when after a game, Troy would drape his arm around her, sweaty and dirty, and kiss her on the cheek. Ada was so proud of him, and people often commented that they made a great couple. From this distance, the baseball coach across the street looked a bit like Troy. Well, at least his build. He was wearing a ball cap, so she couldn't tell if he also had Troy's piercing blue eyes, but it was fun to imagine it was him.

The sandwich was delicious. Ada had eaten every bite of her lunch and decided to take the iced tea back to class. The rest of the afternoon went by quickly, propelled by the professor's engaging and energetic teaching style. He was most definitely passionate about art, and Ada could tell he had taken his own studies seriously.

Before she knew it, Ada was done with class for the day and heading back to the house. Reaching the bungalow, she climbed the stairs to the front porch and sat down in the swing. Smiling to herself, she let out a soft sigh as she closed her eyes and continued to gently push the swing back and forth.

Ada heard some voices close by and slowly opened her eyes. Realizing she had fallen asleep, she checked her watch. It had been almost an hour! *I've got to snap out of this*, Ada thought to herself. *I don't want to waste such a beautiful evening!*

She climbed out of the swing, grabbed her backpack, and headed inside to scrounge up some dinner from the few groceries she had picked up last evening while she was out. Washing the dishes after eating, she looked up in time to see the neighbor across the street and the baseball coach from earlier talking. Both men noticed her and threw their hands up in a wave. Ada smiled to herself. *Everyone here is so friendly*, she thought.

The days flew by and soon the first week of classes had ended and Ada had the weekend ahead of her. Daisy wouldn't be coming to stay until next Friday, so she would need to find some entertainment on her own. One thing she was determined to do at some point was to take her sketch pad and pencils down to the pier and do some drawing. Taking the class had certainly renewed her excitement for art and pursuing something beyond creating lesson plans. Tonight, she decided, she would pick up a salad and garlic bread from the little Italian restaurant diagonal to the University and then settle in for a movie on the couch.

Ada walked across campus toward the Italian place. Looking around, a movement in her peripheral vision caught her attention. *Is that the baseball coach mowing the campus grounds?* thought Ada as she focused on the familiar baseball cap. It sure looked like him. Just about the time Ada was ready to look away, he was headed straight towards her, and she didn't want to appear rude. She waved to him, and he waved back and smiled. She couldn't see his eyes beneath the ball cap, but she was sure they were as beautiful as the rest of him. Ada almost tripped on the sidewalk when she realized what had just crossed her mind. What in the world was going on with her? She never thought things like that. Not since Troy.

Ada hurried across the street into the restaurant and ordered her meal to go. She sat on a chair by the window and realized she could still see the baseball coach mowing. She wasn't sure what drew her to him. Probably just the familiarity of the whole baseball thing. Either way, he definitely wasn't bad to look at.

"Number 31?"

"Number 31?" came the call again, slightly louder this time.

Ada looked down at her receipt. "Oh, sorry, that's me!" she apologized as she hurried over to pick up her meal. The young boy behind the counter smiled as he handed her the to-go bag.

"Thank you. Have a nice evening, ma'am."

Ma'am? Ada once again felt old.

After taking a relaxing shower and putting on her coziest sleep shorts and top, Ada grabbed her salad, bread, a glass of water, and settled down in front of the TV. She had already signed into her Netflix earlier account this week, so surely there would be at least one good movie to choose from on there.

She had finally narrowed it down to *Mission: Impossible – Fallout* or *Safe Haven*. Since Ada was so suddenly in a romantic state of mind, she chose the latter. It had a bit of everything: suspense, drama, intrigue, and romance.

Just about halfway through the movie, as Alex stepped into

Katie's cabin to see the new paint, Ada thought she heard a noise outside her kitchen window. She jumped, quickly grabbing the remote to pause the movie, and strained her ears in the sudden silence. She held her breath.

The seconds crept by, and then . . . nothing.

Ada exhaled loudly, "Are you kidding me?" She was feeling ticked at this point. "I can't spend my entire summer feeling paranoid," she said to herself.

Resolved, she shot up from the couch, stomped over to the locked door, unlocked it, and ripped it open angrily. She stepped outside and did a full 360 degree look around. The porch light and landscaping solar lights along the sidewalk illuminated the outside area, but she saw nothing out of order.

"Hmph," Ada pivoted around and walked back inside, closing the door with a bang. Determined not to let this ruin her evening, she went back to finish her movie.

Surprisingly, after some determined focus from Ada, she was able to enjoy the rest of it. By the end, going to bed sounded good, and she was too sleepy to think much about what had happened earlier. She shuffled to her bedroom, flopped on the bed, snuggled into the cotton quilt, and fell asleep.

Ada figured that some trail mix and a water bottle, along with her art satchel should be sufficient for her trip to the pier. She was anxious to see what she could produce with her charcoal pencils since the last time she'd picked them up, the day before Troy had been killed. She had been working on a piece for his birthday of a snowcapped mountain and snowboarder. It had stayed in a box under her bed at home after Troy's accident until just recently. She never had the heart to finish it but ended up bringing the piece along with her in case she became inspired in new surroundings.

The sun was radiant and warm today, but the light breeze cooled the air slightly, making it just right. Ada spotted the perfect place to set up as soon as she crossed the street. There was a sandy, pebble-strewn path that led down to some large driftwood resting by the water. She found a place to sit down, grabbed the sketchpad and pencil, and then did a sweep of the area with her eyes. There was a large rock jutting out of the water, a mountain to the right of it, and a sailboat appeared to be anchored slightly to the left.

"Perfect," Ada said aloud.

She first started sketching the mountain in the background, followed by the rock, the water, and, finally, the boat. Before adding the finishing touches, Ada set the drawing down and took the drink and trail mix from the satchel. Looking out at the water, Ada couldn't help but remember her honeymoon with Troy. They had rented a houseboat on one of the lakes close to home and had spent the week grilling on the open deck, soaking in the hot tub, swimming in the clear waters, and making love under the stars. It had been a magical week that neither wanted to end. They had always planned to celebrate their fifth anniversary the same way. It was so unfair. *Why did some people get to live their entire lives happily married with kids and grandkids?* Troy and Ada weren't even able to have three years together.

Ada brushed away her thoughts, retrieving the sketch. She held it out away from her in different directions. She smiled, pleased with how it turned out. Ada's phone rang and broke her artistic reverie.

The sun was too bright to see who was calling, but Ada answered, bringing the phone up to her ear. "Hello?"

"Hey, you! I couldn't wait any longer to get an update on your first week at art camp!" Daisy's cheerful voice came through the phone. She was always a breath of fresh air.

Ada laughed. "Art camp, huh? Well, my camp counselor is nice." The girls giggled like they always did.

"In all seriousness, is it everything you had hoped for?"

Ada let out a little sigh. "Yes! The place is so cute. Can't wait for you to see it! We have it all to ourselves because the owner is away. The street is like something out of a Hallmark movie with the tree-lined sidewalks and neighbors walking their dogs or pushing babies in strollers. I can easily walk to the University, plus some restaurants and stores, or go in the other direction two blocks to the pier—actually, that's where I am right now. Guess what I just completed?"

"A masterpiece?" asked Daisy.

"Well, I'm not sure it's a masterpiece," laughed Ada, "but I am pleased. I was inspired to pick up my sketchpad and pencil for the first time since . . . since . . ." Her voice faded out.

"I'm so proud of you, Ada!" Daisy jumped in. "You are the strongest woman I know. I'll be there in five days, and we can celebrate!"

Ada smiled softly. She had such a good friend.

The girls talked a while longer, with Daisy, between fits of laughter, trying to retell the fiasco that ensued the weekend before at her brother-in-law's wedding, when the maid of honor tripped on her dress and caused a domino effect, knocking down the entire row of bridesmaids. Fortunately, they were all good sports about it and laughed while the groomsmen came to their rescue. Daisy had to get off the call when she heard Jackson asking for help. They were finally filling the swimming pool after getting it resealed.

"I can hardly wait to get there! Love ya!" Daisy said as she quickly hopped off the phone. "Love you, too!"

Ada closed her eyes, feeling the warm late afternoon sun on her skin. She realized she hadn't said anything to Daisy about the grounds keeper/baseball coach or whoever he was. She wasn't sure why. Probably because she wasn't even sure what to say about him. All Ada knew was that her stomach got butterflies when she saw him. And that had to just be the baseball thing.

Ada planned to try out the Tidewater Grill down by the pier for dinner but decided that first she'd go back to the bungalow to freshen up and change clothes. On the way, she passed a couple jogging, the mother pushing a baby in the stroller. It was the same one she had seen the day before. This time she was close enough to see the cute little girl, about six months old with brown hair and eyes, wearing a pink and yellow sundress with white sandals. She was all wide- eyed, glancing up and smiling at Ada as they passed. The mother smiled too and said hello. Ada felt a little ache in her chest. Would she and Troy have had a baby by now? Maybe a girl?

What would they have named her?

I've really got to stop this, Ada thought to herself. *It's torture.*

After surveying her options, Ada pulled out a pair of pink and white capris with a matching crop top and some white tennis shoes. At the last minute, she grabbed her jean jacket off the rack by the door, just in case it was cooler on the walk back. Ada again appreciated the perfect location of her rental. She's been here a week and hadn't even needed to use her car. Not only was that saving her money, but she enjoyed getting out and walking everywhere. For that matter, her apartment back home wasn't as convenient or even as cozy either.

When she reached the restaurant, Ada's appetite was larger than she had anticipated.

After nachos, she ordered a glass of Graffigna Malbec to go with a chocolate tart. She wasn't in any hurry to leave. As she sat, she watched couples and families come and go on the pier. One older lady sitting by herself piqued Ada's curiosity. She was dressed in all red, including a hat, with a tanned attractive face.

"Here's your ticket but no rush," the young waitress interrupted Ada's pondering of the red lady as she brushed by the table.

Ada wasn't able to finish the last two bites of tart, but it wasn't worth taking with her.

She left enough money on the table for the bill and tip.

The walk home was quite breezy, and the darkness had settled in a little earlier than it should have this time of evening. Ada put on the jean jacket and made her way to the bungalow at a faster pace than she would normally.

Just as she stepped inside the entrance gate to the front yard, the rain began to come down in cold, heavy sheets. Ada ran to the side of the house and rummaged through her purse, struggling to find her key. Once finally inside, she stripped off her rain-drenched clothes, proceeded to hang things up, and figured she may as well jump in the shower. The rainfall shower head made her feel like she was still outside, except the water that fell in here was warm. Ada took her time washing and conditioning her hair, then stood for a while with her eyes closed while water continued to trickle down her body. She sighed. Life was good. At least as good as it could be without him.

Chapter 5

The rest of the weekend went by quickly, and Monday, Ada was back in class listening to a lecture on 19th century art, which involved the beginning of Impressionism, which happened to be Ada's favorite. She relished this creative movement in art in contrast to still-life portraits that always appeared so stiff.

She had learned that the lady sitting next to her was a high school art teacher from Nevada. Although a bit eccentric, Ada appreciated her whimsical flair for color, as exhibited each day in her clothing choices. In contrast to her loud wardrobe, she only said a few words from time to time. It wasn't enough for an invite to lunch, but that was okay. Ada was enjoying the solitude after the hectic year with students.

At the class break, she took her packed lunch of chicken salad, chips, and an apple out to her favorite bench across from the baseball field. About the time Ada was taking her last bite of an apple, she heard some yelling from the field.

"Heads up!" Several voices were shouting. Ada instinctively knew exactly what that meant and immediately scanned through the trees above for a ball. She saw it heading about a foot from her, stood up, reached out, and caught it with two hands. Cheers went up from the team.

One of the players ran over to retrieve the ball. "Wanna join the team? We could use another good outfielder! Coach said to tell you he's impressed."

Ada's face was turning red, and she hoped he couldn't see it through his sunglasses.

Ada laughed and gave the ball a toss to him, "Well, if you get desperate let me know!" The boy smiled and thanked her, running back across the street to practice.

Ada could see the baseball coach looking at her across the street. Her stomach did a little flop and a desire to meet him in person felt suddenly overwhelming. Too bad she had to head back to class when things were beginning to get interesting. They'd probably all be gone by the time she was finished for the day.

As she got back to the classroom, Trish, her seat mate, was organizing their table for a creative sketch that everyone would be doing in the afternoon. She smiled at Ada.

"Looks like you had a particularly beneficial lunch."

Ada almost choked. "Oh!" She cleared her throat, "the sunshine always does me good."

"Sure!" Trish said cheekily, then went on about her business.

The afternoon went fast as they were all so focused on the Impressionism drawings. The professor was very complimentary of Ada's work with shadowing, and this gave her the boost of confidence to know that art was more than a hobby for her. Maybe she really did have some talent, enough to leave behind public school teaching.

The students were encouraged to submit any of their work during the course for a silent auction on the last day. The proceeds would support high school students in the area who wish to major in any kind of art at the University. Since Professor Aglio had recognized her drawing, she felt it must be worth a few dollars at least, so she placed it in the submission pile.

The next day, Ada had her arms full since she had stopped at the Starbucks café to get an iced chai tea latte on her way to class. She started to push the door open with her back, but a gentleman was quick to open the door and motion her through. Ada thought she recognized him, and he glanced at her a second time.

"Ah, I believe you're the one living across the street in Marilyn's house. I've waved to you a couple of times. I'm Robert McGuire. Nice to meet you." The man smiled at her.

"Yes, I remember seeing you! I'm Ada Cameron. Nice to meet you as well." Ada smiled back.

"So, are you one of our prestigious students for the summer?" His smile was kind and sincere.

"I don't know about the prestigious part," Ada laughed, "but I am a summer art student, and am enjoying my experience immensely. I'm a 2nd grade teacher from Riverton and working on a master's degree in art history."

"Marvelous, marvelous. I'm a professor of psychology and have been here for almost forty years now."

"Oh!" Ada smiled, "My husband ..." Her face fell. "Um ...

my late husband ... he was killed in a helicopter crash—" She took a

deep breath and put a smile back on her face. "Troy had a degree in

psychology and was pursuing his master's degree in counseling."

"Ah, I see, and I'm so very sorry for your loss." He paused.

"Life is a great mystery and often brings with it unbearable pain.

Please, call me Robert."

"Thank you, Robert," Ada said softly. "I appreciate that, and

I must agree with you. I haven't been the same since I lost him."

"Say, my wife and I are having a little barbeque this evening

for a team from the college during their summer training. Please

come and join us. We'd love to have you!"

Ada blushed, "Oh, I don't want to impose."

"It's no imposition at all!" Robert assured.

"Are you certain that your wife won't mind?"

"Are you kidding?" He laughed. "She'd be upset with me if

I didn't. After all, she'll appreciate not being the only female!"

"What should I bring?"

" Absolutely nothing but yourself. We have enough to

feed a small army. 6 o'clock?"

"I'll be there! Thank you, Profess—"

"Robert!" He chimed in.

"Robert," Ada offered. "Thank you, and I'll see you tonight."

All the way through class and then during the walk home, Ada was going through the teams Robert could have meant but kept coming back to the baseball team. After all, she had seen the coach talking with Robert recently. Oh my gosh. Wouldn't that be something? The butterflies kicked up right when she reached her door. She should wear something nice tonight; that's just what good company does, right?

Ada twirled in front of the mirror, liking how the yellow sundress accentuated her curves and made her skin look tan. She paired it with some strappy sandals and a crocheted crossbody purse. Since the invitation had come at the last minute and there was no time for grocery shopping, she decided to cut up the watermelon she had purchased from the farmers' market on Sunday and bring that with her. By the time she had sliced the sweet, reddish pink fruit and placed it in a nice Tupperware bowl, it was 6:05 pm. She took a deep breath, put her shoulders back, and headed outside to cross the street.

Although the air was still quite warm, the trees lining the walkway to the professor's house provided just the right amount of shade to make it a perfect summer evening. As she neared the end of the path, it occurred to Ada that she had forgotten to ask whether to knock on the front door or go around, but she could hear music in the backyard and thought she'd head in that direction. A tall, wood and iron gate with a welcome sign seemed promising, so Ada flipped up the latch and started to push against the gate. Suddenly, it swung completely open, almost dragging her inside the yard with it. She gained her composure quickly and was met with cheers.

"There's our new centerfielder!" One of the young men shouted.

My instincts were right, thought Ada. *It is the baseball team*. At the same time, she met the coach's gaze. He tipped the bill of his cap slightly as he looked deeply into her eyes.

"So glad you could make it, Ada!" The professor commented, walking toward her. She reluctantly broke eye contact with the coach.

"Thank you so much for the invitation! I know you said not to bring anything, but my mother would have been disappointed with me if I had come empty-handed."

"Ah, watermelon. Perfect for a barbeque!" He took the watermelon from her and sat it on the food table. "Please, come meet my wife," he said, walking toward the back door and gesturing to Ada to follow.

As soon as Ada stepped inside the kitchen, she felt comfortable. The green blue cabinets played off the checkered floors and wood plank ceilings. There was plenty of seating around a large island and a table for seating at least twelve people. Each chair had cozy, thick, quilted pads, and there was a window seat with the same cushions, along with a stack of books in a wicker basket. Ada could make herself at home here easily.

"Susan, this is Ada Cameron, our neighbor across the street I was telling you about this afternoon." Robert gestured to Ada.

"So nice to meet you, Ada! Marilyn would be so pleased to know that such a nice young lady is renting her suite. Welcome! I hope you're hungry!"

"Thank you," Ada said smiling. "I'm so happy to meet you and appreciate the invite. Everything smells wonderful. What can I do to help?"

"Well, since you asked, how about grabbing that pitcher of lemonade from the counter and taking it outside? You'll see a drink table there with other offerings."

"Certainly," Ada smiled and took the pitcher outside.

The guys were all laughing and poking fun at each other as she walked toward the refreshments table. The baseball coach just happened to be right where Ada was headed. *Oh, please don't let me trip or do anything stupid*, she thought.

He looked up to see her coming and offered to take the pitcher.

"Thank you," she said, keeping her eyes on their hands as she passed him the drink.

"That was some catch you made today," he said with a slight smile. "I'm Jason."

"Oh," she laughed sheepishly, "thanks. I'm Ada."

Ada looked straight into his piercing blue eyes and suddenly felt herself become light-headed. She gripped the side of the table with the drinks. Jason reached out his hands to steady her.

"Are you okay?" he asked, eyes wide with concern.

Ada hadn't seen eyes like those since she kissed Troy goodbye for the last time that fateful day. Aside from the similar eye color, the rest of Jason's face didn't look like Troy, but that particular resemblance was enough to startle her.

Feeling ridiculous, Ada tried to recover quickly. "I think I had a bit too much sun today and then not much to eat. I'm sure after some of this wonderful food I'll be fine."

"Hey coach," one of the guys said behind them, "we have an idea who could help with managing our equipment." Jason looked at the guys and then back to Ada.

"Go ahead. I'm fine." She assured him.

"You sure?"

"Absolutely." She smiled softly.

They started talking to him before he had time to say anything further to Ada. She wandered back inside to see if there was anything else she could do to help.

Susan and Ada spent the entire rest of the evening on the outdoor swing and talking about teaching. Susan had just retired from being a 6th grade English language arts teacher for forty years. At some point during that time, she had also taught 4th grade. Ada couldn't imagine being a teacher for that long. Susan agreed that students had changed over time and things were no longer the same. Social media and less parental support were becoming primary reasons that teachers were leaving the profession. She wasn't at all surprised when Ada shared her desire to work in an art gallery.

Although the evening was coming to an end, both were interested in continuing their conversation, so Ada invited Susan over for coffee on the porch the next morning. Ada hadn't even seen Jason leave and felt such disappointment that they weren't able to speak more. He was the most sincere guy she had met since Troy, but Ada wasn't sure why she was getting so ahead

of herself. *I'm leaving to go back home at the end of summer,* she thought. *Time to put my full focus on class, which is the whole reason I came here anyway.*

Ada and Susan ended up having coffee not only the morning after the party, but the following as well, once on Ada's porch and the other at Susan's dining room table. The ladies were fast becoming friends and shared so much in common. Ada wished that she and her mother could have spent time together like this. Susan must have sensed interest between Ada and Jason because she had asked Ada what she thought about him during one of their conversations, but Ada was quick to change the subject. There was no need to carry this thing between her and Jason, if it could even be called that, any further when they didn't live in the same town.

The art course had been worth every cent that Ada had spent; this week they were discussing Realism and Modern Art and were joined by a fascinating guest artist from London. Ada ended up submitting another piece for the silent auction. Her confidence was growing, and it felt good. She had even stayed after and chatted with the artist who was so lovely and seemingly interested in Ada's future plans.

Thursday evening, Ada decided to bake some lemon bread and peach crisp for her and Daisy. She also made sure to get some of their favorite coffee and wine. The second bedroom was set up as an office but did have a cute white rod iron daybed with a comfortable mattress. Marilyn had left clean sheets and a quilt for the bed just in case Ada had visitors.

Ada had everything ready before she went to bed that night and had added a small visitor basket with goodies. She and Daisy loved doing things like that for each other. She almost couldn't go to sleep that night, excitedly thinking about Daisy coming the following afternoon. She revisited some of the experiences this week and decided that the art course had been worth every cent. Ada enjoyed the discussions on Realism and Modern Art and was pleased when a fascinating guest artist from London stopped by. She was so lovely and seemed interested in Ada's future plans, even staying to chat with her well after everyone else had gone. Ada was so inspired that she went back to the bungalow afterwards and finished sketching the picture that had stayed under her bed until this summer. Her confidence was growing, and it felt good. The completion of her intended gift to Troy proved healing. Not sure if she could handle looking at it all the time, Ada submitted the charcoal drawing in class for the silent auction.

Her art professor had announced earlier in the week that he planned to dismiss them early on Friday, as there was a music and art festival coming into town that day. This weekend was going to be a perfect time for Daisy's visit. Ada finally put her head on the pillow and closed her eyes, willing herself to get at least a few hours of sleep.

She awoke the next morning earlier than usual, but she was happy to have even slept as long as she had. Not wanting to mess up her straightened kitchen area, she headed out the door and stopped at the café to grab a muffin and coffee. As she walked up to the café, she saw a familiar figure sitting in the outdoor section. Ada suddenly felt brave.

"Good morning! You're here bright and early, or do you have an early practice?"

Jason took a sip of his coffee and looked up at Ada. "Oh, good morning! No practice until noon, but I'm doing a little mowing first."

"I see. My best friend is coming for the weekend, so I didn't want to mess up the place before she arrived. Just thought I'd grab breakfast here. How do you think your team is going to do this year? I haven't seen them play, just caught them during batting and fielding practice." Ada could hear herself babbling on, and heat began to rise in her cheeks.

"Sounds like you know a thing or two about baseball. Of course, I know you can catch." Ada didn't want to talk about Troy at all, so she opted to mention that her dad was a fan. "They're a good group of athletes. I have four of my most talented players as seniors this year, and I was able to recruit two of the best pitchers from a top high school. I think we'll do well." He didn't seem to want to say anything more.

"That's great," Ada smiled. "Well, I don't want to be late to class. We have to set up our own easel and watercolors today before instruction begins."

"Have a nice weekend with your friend, Ada." He smiled and raised his coffee cup as in a toast.

"Thank you. Enjoy yours as well."

Ada almost detected a sadness about him. He was still such a mystery, and she'd like nothing more than to get to know him better. Under any other circumstances the situation seemed ideal but living a distance away from a romantic partner just didn't make sense for her at this point in her life.

Ada suddenly felt a little sad, too.

Chapter 6

Daisy was already on the front porch swinging when Ada returned from class. As soon as they caught glimpses of each other, they ran, open arms, squealing, giggling and crashing together with a big hug. Nothing had changed since middle school. They were always those young girls when together.

"I think this charming town agrees with you!" Ada laughed. "Why do you say that?"

"You look happier than I've seen you in a while. Is it just the art class, or maybe a new special someone?"

"Oh, there you go playing the matchmaker again." Ada

teased, then stopped suddenly.

She didn't want to make Daisy feel bad about Calin, so she changed the subject quickly. "How was the ferry over? Did you figure it out alright? I know you were worried!"

"Oh yeah, once I found the correct lane." Daisy crossed her eyes and stuck out her tongue, then laughed.

"What do you want to do first?" Ada asked, picking up Daisy's weekender bag and starting off the porch.

"To be honest, I'm absolutely starving!" Daisy said, holding her stomach.

Ada laughed, "I thought you might say that. Let's put your things inside first so you can see my place and get settled in."

"I like it already. The front porch is just as you described, and the street really is like something out of a movie."

They walked around the side of the house, and Ada admired the way the sun shone through the trees, spotlighting the flowers just perfectly. The neighbors had their fountain on, and several colorful birds were fluttering about.

Ada flung the door open. "Welcome!"

"This is adorable, Ada! It's so you. Look at all the rattan and coastal vibes here. And it's bigger than I imagined, and especially the kitchen!"

"I'm able to cook a few things, and the owner, Marilyn, has all the new cookware and appliances. I want for nothing!"

Ada took Daisy down a short hall that housed both bedrooms with the bathroom in between. "It's a daybed, but I tried it out and I think you'll be comfortable," she told Daisy of her sleeping arrangements.

Daisy flopped down on the mattress, spreading her arms out wide. "Most definitely." She sat up and beamed. "I'm just so happy to be here with you. Those two weeks seemed like they'd never pass! Okay, where are we eating?"

"I thought we'd try an Italian restaurant called Pasquale's. I've seen it during my walks. It has outdoor seating and is right on the water."

"Sounds like a winner to me!"

The girls decided to get freshened up and change clothes. When they each simultaneously opened their doors and saw the other's outfit, they broke into laughter. Daisy had on a peach sundress that was belted at the waist and Ada an orange bow-front tube top with matching wide leg pants.

Daisy was the first to be able to regain her composure enough to speak, "So, we purposely matched our outfits in middle school, and here we are continuing to accidentally do it in our twenties! We're hilarious!"

"Great minds think alike," Ada winked at her friend as she threaded her arm through Daisy's and started for the door. From across the street, Robert and Susan were pulling out of the driveway and waved to the girls.

"They seem nice," commented Daisy.

"Super sweet couple. I was at their house for a barbeque earlier this week. He's a professor at the college, and she actually just retired from teaching middle school!" They climbed into Ada's car and took off.

The downtown waterfront on a Friday night was a little busier than Ada had anticipated. She was hoping it wouldn't be a problem getting a table without a reservation. When the girls approached the restaurant, there was somewhat of a line formed outside, and the man behind the desk asked if they had reservations. Ada told him they hadn't made any but would gladly sit outside, so he asked for them to wait a moment while he checked. Appearing a few minutes later, smiling, he took two menus from the basket and asked them to follow him. The outdoor seating was upstairs and offered an incredible view of the water with the marina right in front of them.

Several boats were heading out to sea, lights gleaming and reflecting beautifully on the water. The umbrella-covered tables were adorned with mini lights and candles, and Michael Bublé music was playing in the background. The girls both sighed. It felt like a perfect moment.

The waiter handed them each a smaller menu with the drink selections and said he'd return for their orders.

Daisy looked at Ada, "My thought is that we should go with champagne."

"What are we celebrating?" Ada laughed.

"You!"

"Me?" Ada parroted, surprised.

"Yes, I'm so proud of you! You're finally pursuing your dream of obtaining an art history degree. With the artistic talent you have, the elementary classroom is no place to spend the rest of your life."

"Aww," Ada said tenderly. "I appreciate you always being my number one cheerleader! Okay, champagne it is!"

When the waiter returned, Daisy interrupted Ada asking for two glasses and asked for the entire bottle.

Halfway through her dinner of pasta primavera and Daisy's eggplant parmigiana, Ada really wanted to tell Daisy about Jason.

"Okay, spill," said Daisy, putting her fork down and wiping the corners of her mouth with a napkin. "You know I can always tell when something is on your mind."

"Unbelievable," laughed Ada. "I never could hide anything from you." She took a drink of champagne and leaned back in her chair.

"I recently looked into some crystal blue eyes that made my heart melt." Ada was surprised that just by uttering those words aloud, some tears fell down her face.

Daisy sat up and reached over to hold Ada's hand. "Oh, sweetie. Where did this happen?"

Ada proceeded to tell Daisy about the first time she spotted Jason and his baseball team and then of the barbeque when they stood within inches of one another. "I can't explain what it is," Ada spoke softly, feeling a lump in her throat. "He's not Troy, but those eyes and the whole baseball thing. It has me missing Troy until I can't breathe. I know that I'll never love anyone like I loved him." She reached up and brushed away some tears.

"First, there is absolutely nothing wrong with feeling this way, Ada. You lost the love of your life, and he was a beautiful person. Seeing him in someone else's eyes or missing him when watching baseball—those are completely normal reactions. I think you need to allow yourself to mourn him when things like this come up. Is there any chance that you and Jason might spend more time together . . . like, are you possibly interested in him?" Daisy was extremely gentle in the way she asked and seemed surprised that Ada paused to consider before answering.

"I don't know what to think. I am drawn to him, but I don't know if it's for the right reasons. It wouldn't be fair to Jason if I'm attracted to him because he reminds me of Troy—the blue eyes, watching him coach baseball . . . I mean, he really seems like a nice guy, although I'm not sure that he is interested in me." Ada shrugged her shoulders.

"No way. Daisy shook her head back and forth. Look at you! You're not only beautiful, but talented and the kindest soul out there."

"But Jason seems to have a wall up . . . maybe he's in a relationship?"

"Have you seen him with a girl?"

"No, but I mean . . . it's possible." Ada considered. "I've only seen him a few times." "Well, I wouldn't totally give up on the idea, okay? Just see where the summer takes you. And please know that I'll always be here for you to share things with, happy or sad." Daisy said, feeling a heaviness in her heart for Ada.

"Thank you, my sweet friend." Ada managed to smile as she squeezed her friend's hand. "I don't know what I would do without you."

The waiter walked up to the table, "Ladies, how about some dessert?"

The girls looked at each other, smiled, and nodded yes.

Ada and Daisy walked home arm in arm, reminiscing about the times they'd sneak out of their houses to meet up with Troy and Jackson down at the beach and build a fire. It was innocent enough. They all just loved to be together so much, joking, laughing, and pondering the future. Funny thing was, their sixteen-year-old selves really had felt much older, more like twenty. Sometimes they would take turns naming each other's kids, rolling in the sand laughing at the most ridiculous ones, or they'd pretend bet on who would build a pool or have a boat first. Even though Ada didn't get to make the dreams a reality, it was still fun and comforting revisiting those old memories.

After getting into their comfy pjs, the girls opted to

continue their walk down memory lane and connected the cables from Daisy's laptop to the television to look at photos and watch some old videos. The first video that came up was senior prom. Ada had worn a long, strapless fuchsia sequin gown with a corseted top. She had let her brunette hair fall on loose curls over her tanned shoulders. Troy's classic two-piece black double-breasted tuxedo was slim-fit, and his tousled curls set off those blue eyes. Ada remembered seeing him for the first time at the house when he came to pick her up, her stomach doing flips. Daisy had filmed Troy putting on Ada's corsage and her pinning on his boutonniere. They were so young and in love. Next, there were videos that Daisy's parents had taken of the four of them before they left for dinner. After that there were shots here and there from cell phones at dinner and some at the dance. Troy and Ada were only seen in one photo from the dance, at the beginning.

"That's right!" Daisy said suddenly. "You guys left early. I almost forgot about it because the bathing suits you wear hide it!"

Ada stood up from the couch and raised her sleeping shirt. She only needed to pull down her bikini panties slightly to reveal the tattoo. There it was. The initials A & T within an infinity sign. She and Troy had snuck out early from the dance to get matching tattoos, choosing to get them on their lower abdomens to keep them hidden from their parents. Ada herself even sometimes forgot it was there unless she happened to catch herself in the mirror.

"Aww," said Daisy. "No wonder you and Troy were voted as the most perfect couple. You really were perfect." She put her hands over her heart.

Ada sat back down. "Yeah, I'm glad I have it as a reminder . . . like he's still a part of me."

They stayed up a while longer, looking at old memories until both were too sleepy to keep their eyes open.

The sound of a riding lawnmower and blaring music startled Daisy awake the following morning. She made her way to Ada's room and flopped down on the bed. Ada's eyes were already opened.

"A little early for yard work, isn't it?" Daisy asked with a yawn.

"He's on that thing at least every other day," Ada said of her noisy neighbor, rolling her eyes. "Not Robert. It's a different guy. I think he does it to escape his wife bossing him around. I've heard her out there telling him things that need done on the house."

Daisy rolled over on her back. "Hmm . . . I wonder if that's why Jackson often says he needs to work in the garage when I suggest some things to do?" Daisy teased. "So, what's on the agenda this morning? I don't have to catch the ferry until 4 pm."

"I thought we could get coffee and croissants to take down to the water. There are some nice large pieces of driftwood that make perfect benches. We can watch the sailboats and maybe catch some of the windsurfers. Then, there are a couple of boutiques that open downtown for a few hours."

"Sounds perfect. What are you planning on wearing, or should we see if we end up with the same color palette again?" Daisy giggled.

"I think I'll throw on my sage halter romper with my tennis shoes and maybe a straw hat," Ada thought aloud.

"Cute combo. Guess I'll go in my khaki shorts and white t-shirt. Gotta go wash this face and put on some make up first. I'll be fast!"

It was a beautiful morning for a walk to the beach, and everyone in the neighborhood seemed to be outside doing one thing or another: pruning flowers, washing cars, or reading on the porch. Ada noticed that Robert and Susan didn't appear to be home when she and Daisy passed their house. She wondered if she would see

Jason this weekend. She really wanted Daisy to get a look at him. If nothing else, just to see his eyes. She was happy for Daisy that she could go home to Jackson and continue living the dream that they both had back in high school, but part of her was also envious. Ada's heart ached for Troy.

Looking at the tattoo last night brought back a flood of memories from the night they got them. Even though they agreed about using their initials it was deciding between a heart and infinity symbol that was the hold up. Troy was not crazy about having a heart as his first tattoo, so Ada agreed to the infinity sign. Also, they needed something simple that wouldn't take too long. Both had been excited about doing something in secret and hadn't even told their best friends for several weeks after getting them done. It wasn't until the first day at the beach that the big reveal was made to Daisy and Jackson, who both whistled and gave loud approval. Troy and Ada spent that entire summer before college talking about the future, creating scenarios of what kind of house they would have, like maybe a coastal farmhouse with coastal color schemes, natural elements like driftwood, and old beach cottages. Their first home wasn't quite that, but they kept adding to their wish book for someday.

It was Daisy who broke her train of thought.

"Hey! Watch out, girl! You about stepped in front of that bicyclist."

"Oh my gosh." Ada covered her hands over her mouth, her heart skipping a beat. "Thanks."

"You, okay? You didn't say much on the walk down. Are you thinking about Troy . . . or Jason?"

"Maybe a little of both." Ada said quietly.

Before they had even crossed the street, they could already smell the pastries and coffee brewing at the café. Several people were sitting outside at tables and enjoying the sunshine, and when they got inside, the line wasn't too long, and it moved quickly. Ada saw three students from her class and said a quick hello. One was a nice-looking guy about her age. He sat across the room from Ada and often answered questions the professor asked.

"Umm . . . nice." Daisy whispered to Ada after meeting him.

Ada chuckled quietly. "You're terrible. Come on." Ada motioned Daisy back out of the café.

A few people had found some driftwood seats at the beach but, fortunately, had not taken Ada's favorite spot. A couple of windsurfers were out, along with three sailboats, making for some nice pictures. Daisy took several with her cell phone. The fresh peach croissants were heavenly, and both girls finished every bite. The stickiness had them rinsing their hands in the ocean, which then started a search for unusual shells and rocks. They walked about half a mile up the beach, filling their large coffee cups to the top with collections of both.

"I guess that means it's time for us to turn around," said Daisy. "I like these finds! Home Goods will probably have the perfect wooden display tray for these."

"I agree. Let's get them back to the house and then take the car downtown."

"So, you're suggesting we'll have too much to carry on the way back to be able to walk?" Daisy clapped her hands together and let out a little shriek. Both girls laughed.

Chapter 7

Of the three shops they visited, the girls agreed that Sweet Violet was their favorite.

Aptly named, the glass on the large violet-painted entry door was decorated with iron, and the shop window was adorned with small, violet-shaped lights, spelling out the name of the store. What waited inside was even more spectacular; you were greeted and welcomed at the door with a bright smile and an offer of help at any time. Large pottery vases filled with even more violets framed the racks of beautiful dresses and outfits on display. The boutique was not large by any means, but the two rooms were lined with mirrors, one featuring a large round pink velvet bench that would seat at least twelve people.

A couple of ladies were trying on clothing and asking for approval from others in their party. Savvy shoppers, Daisy and Ada headed to the room that had a clearance rack first. Both girls wore the same size, so they often found clothes not only for themselves, but also for each other. After they had collected a few items over their arms, a young salesgirl offered to take the clothing to a fitting room for them.

The girls moved to the other room of the boutique, which was filled with the latest trends in fall fashion. Although neither of them typically spent a lot of money on high end clothing for school, they each found jackets that they couldn't resist. Ada had picked up a boyfriend blazer in nude and Daisy a tweed fringe jacket in light pink. Coming out of the fitting rooms in their finds, they spun around for the other, and said at the same time, "I have to get this!" They laughed, and the young saleslady watching them smiled.

Ada and Daisy walked out of the boutique talking a mile a minute about all their purchases during the shopping spree. With only an hour and a half before Daisy had to be back on the ferry, they picked up a veggie pizza from a pizzeria next door to Sweet Violet and drove back to Ada's place to sit on the front porch. Ada went inside to bring out a bottle of wine and two glasses.

"What a perfect weekend, my friend! I'd love to do this again; how about I come back in another few weeks?" Daisy took a bite of pizza.

"Really? Jackson wouldn't miss you? Of course, I'd love it!"

Daisy giggled. "Well, I can't say he wouldn't miss me, but he's working with his dad on a new project, so he's pretty busy. It's one that might even launch his own business!"

"Wow! That's exciting. I knew it was Jackson's goal from the start!"

"Yes, he's so happy about it, and I'm really proud of him."

Changing the subject, Daisy said, "I'm hoping you'll still have time to swim in our pool when you get back home, before it gets too cold! I've basically had to spend the time out there by myself this summer, although, I have invited the kids next door to join me several times. They're sweet." Daisy stared ahead, chewing.

"Any thoughts about having your own?" Ada questioned.

"We always talked about it." "I'm not sure. Maybe when the time is right."

"Daisy Adele. This better have nothing to do with my situation. You are like a sister to me, and I can't wait to be an auntie. There is nothing more I want in this world than to see you happy."

Daisy continued to stare ahead for a few moments. When she finally turned to look at Ada, she had tears in her eyes. "I love you, Ada May," Daisy said softly. The girls clasped hands and sat there quietly, enjoying the afternoon sun and the palpable love of their friendship.

"Okay, enough of this sad, sappy stuff," Daisy said, jumping up. "I've got to throw my stuff in a suitcase and be off so I can hurry and come back!"

The girls hugged one last time for what seemed like longer than usual, holding one another tight. It had been a most wonderful weekend. Ada watched Daisy drive up the street and turn the corner, then went back to the front porch to gather things from their lunch. She happened to look up and see Jason taking mail out of the McGuires' mailbox. He waved to her and smiled.

You've got to be kidding me! Ada thought. Daisy missed seeing him by minutes, although she may not have been able to actually meet him because he didn't make any attempts to come over and chat, just took off with the mail tucked under his arm. Ada really wanted to know his story but doubted that she would ever find out.

There was still plenty of evening left, so Ada decided to take her sketch book to a fountain downtown by the water. The sunset looked promising, and she was feeling inspired after her best friend's visit. As she was closing the front gate, Robert and Susan were pulling into the driveway. Ada realized that she had missed introducing Daisy to them as well.

"Hello!" Susan waved to Ada from across the street. "How was the weekend with your friend? I'm so sorry we couldn't meet her!"

Ada smiled and waved back. "Me, too. We had a great time as always! Hope your weekend was nice!"

"Looks like you're headed out?" Susan asked. "Off to make some art?"

"It's such a lovely evening. I thought I'd take a walk and see if I spot anything interesting."

"Do you have any plans for dinner? Would you like to join us later?" Susan invited. "We were going to throw some hamburgers on the grill. Does 7 o'clock work for you?"

"Sounds yummy, and yes, that works just fine! Thanks for the invite. See you then!"

Ada repositioned her satchel across her body and took off down the street. She wondered whether Jason would be there at dinner. She hadn't exactly said anything specific to Susan during their conversations, but she had alluded to finding him interesting. Susan said that Jason had come for the interim baseball coaching position in the spring and that when Robert had met him at the University, they had fast become friends through their shared love of baseball. Ada had learned little else about the mysterious, alluring man.

Ada reached a crosswalk and stopped to wait. She had just begun to cross when she heard a car honking and some people yelling.

"Hey there, artsy girl! Where ya headed?" It was the cute red-headed girl from her class. Whitney, maybe?

"Hi!" Ada smiled and waved. "Over to the park to sketch."

"How about joining us for an evening sail on Lee's boat?" She was stretched across Lee, another member of their class, who was driving, and there were at least three others in the backseat.

"Sounds like fun, but I have dinner plans. Maybe another time?"

"For sure!" said the girl. Lee locked eyes with Ada, tipped his ball cap, and drove off. She wasn't sure if that was flirting or not, but she brushed it off, her mind drifted back to Jason and the hope that she'd see him tonight.

Ada looked up in the sky just in time to see crepuscular rays, the setting sun sitting just above a layer of clouds and creating majestic, emanating shafts of sunlight. She wished she could stop time and draw the spectacular sight, but she knew it would take longer to capture than what the scene lasted.

Fortunately for Ada, she found another desirable subject. A couple sat by the fountain in an intimate pose, holding hands and laughing while their foreheads pressed together. She quickly took her pad and pencil out and began drawing. She briefly worried that she wouldn't have enough time to complete the sketch before her subjects left, but this couple didn't seem to be in a hurry. She was able to outline her drawing to get the correct proportions and overall shape plus even add several of the details before they stood up to leave. Since Ada had another hour before dinner she decided to stay and finish the drawing. This one was a keeper.

After returning home, Ada had enough time to shower and change before dinner. Her hair had become a little tousled from the walk, and she didn't feel like washing it, so she decided a French braid would work with her tropical print tie front romper and strappy sandals. She knocked on the door a few minutes later, and it was opened by none other than Jason.

"Oh, hi." Ada managed to get out, feeling shocked and suddenly shy.

"Hello." Jason stepped back and opened the door wider for her to come inside. "I just stopped by to drop off the mail."

"And we insisted that he stay for dinner!" Susan said as she entered the room. "Perfect timing for both of you. It's ready! Let's eat."

Jason started to protest, but Susan shook her head and took him by the arm, leading him into the dining room.

The grilled hamburgers, along with Susan's homemade potato salad and barbequed baked beans were delicious. Her strawberry rhubarb cobbler with ice cream was probably Ada's new favorite dessert, and Susan promised to send some home with her.

The evening had been full of stories from the early days of Robert and Susan, how they had met as camp counselors in Cape Cod one summer. It was nice to see Jason smiling and laughing. Even his smile reminded her of Troy, although there was still such sadness behind those eyes. Before they knew it, two hours had passed. Ada was the first to pop up and start clearing dishes, followed by Jason. Even though there were protests by both the hosts, there was no stopping the help. Before Jason left, Robert wanted to show him an old baseball photo from the early 80s. As the two men headed to Robert's office, Ada said her goodbyes to all and headed home with a smile on her face.

When Jason and Robert emerged from the room a little bit later talking a mile a minute, Susan interrupted. "You know, Jason, Ada won't be here after summer." Both men stopped talking and looked directly at her.

"Now, Susan. "Don't start with the matchmaking," Robert teasingly scolded his wife. He patted Jason on the back.

"And I'm pretty sure that Ada's boyfriend would object," Jason said flatly.

"Boyfriend? Ada lost her husband in an accident, years ago. She recently went out with someone back home, but it was a disaster. In fact, she was glad to get here just to escape him. He didn't want to leave her alone," said Susan. "Actually, would you mind running this container of cobbler over to Ada on your way out? I forgot to give it to her." Susan handed the Tupperware to Jason as she was speaking.

Jason managed to stammer out a yes, a thank you for dinner, and headed quickly over to Ada's. He knew he had seen a man sitting on the porch earlier today. Ada hadn't even mentioned him at dinner, and Jason thought that was strange.

As Ada walked back to her bungalow, she noticed it was dark. She remembered turning on the outdoor light before she left, as well as the light inside by the door, but they were both off now. Had there been a power surge in the house causing her to lose electricity? It was an older home, but it had been completely remodeled. That should have meant all new electrical work.

Ada put her key in the lock and turned it slowly. She reached inside and switched on the porch light, but it didn't turn on. She felt for the floor lamp inside the door, fumbling to turn that on. Since she had been so busy in this new quaint town, her fear and paranoia had finally alleviated. Until now. Ada's heartbeat filled her ears. Stepping through the entrance into the house, she moved forward slowly to get her bearings in the dark. Suddenly, someone grabbed Ada from behind, covering her mouth. Ada wanted to scream but nothing came out. She reached up to pull the hand away and that's when he whispered in her ear.

"Guess who?" the familiar voice said.

Ada's anger took over, and she whirled away quickly, shoving him away. As she did, she lost her balance, tripping over the corner of the couch and falling backwards, hitting her head on the coffee table. The only light Ada could see was a soft beam filtering through the closed curtains on her bedroom window. Shakily, her head pounding, she dragged herself off of the floor and darted for the bedroom, closing the door behind her. The door didn't have a lock, and leaning against it wasn't enough to keep him from entering the room. He pushed his way in, threw her up on his shoulder, and tossed her onto the bed.

"I knew this is what you were waiting for, Ada. Why did you try and pretend you were something that you weren't? Just admit it."

"What are you talking about, Calin?" Ada said, her voice beginning to fill with panic. "Why are you here? I want you to leave now!"

Ada tried to sit up, but Calin shoved her, forcing her back down on the bed. "Now, now. Don't be so dramatic. Take a breath." He took her face in his hands and kissed her forcefully, just like he had done the first time.

She bit down on his lip hard, drawing blood. He reared back, touching a finger to the bubbling cut, shock and anger darkening his face. She used his shock as her opportunity to escape. Struggling to her feet, she barreled past him, running toward the front door and flinging it open.

Chapter 8

Jason was just getting ready to knock on the door of the bungalow when it flew open, and Ada ran straight into his arms. He stumbled backwards, wrapping his free arm around her waist and dropping the Tupperware from his other hand as he tried bracing for their fall. They both went slamming into the neighbor's privacy fence with a thud.

"What the—?" Jason gasped.

Ada was crying hysterically. Burying her face in Jason's chest, all she could manage to choke out between loud, gasping sobs was, "He's here . . . attacked me . . . ." Jason got up, untangled his limbs from hers, took her by the shoulders, and sat her down at the table next to her front door.

He knelt before her and asked gently, "Is he still in there?"

Ada shook her head yes.

Jason stood up and began to go inside. Ada grabbed his arm, "NO!" she yelled. The next-door neighbor suddenly appeared on the other side of the fence, having been outside taking his trash to the curb when he heard the ruckus.

Jason pointed to Ada, "Can you stay with her a second, please? And call 911." The neighbor nodded, quickly crossing over to Ada and getting out his cellphone.

Jason reached inside the door and fumbled against the wall for a light switch. Finally, his fingers connected with one, and the bungalow flooded with light. He didn't see anyone in the main part of the house, so he headed for the hallway. Never being in the bungalow before, he proceeded with caution. He couldn't be sure of hiding places or entrances from where the intruder might spring.

The first room to the right looked more like an office and had a daybed. Everything looked neat and undisturbed. The bathroom was empty. Making his way to what appeared to be the main bedroom, the bed here appeared disheveled. Slowly and quietly rounding the corner into the room, Jason found a man escaping through the window, one leg already outside. Jason lunged for the man, grabbing him and dragging him back inside. He had the intruder pinned to the floor on his stomach within seconds.

"Please, please, you have to understand, this is all a misunderstanding," Calin pleaded, panic and a whining note rising in his voice. Jason had never wanted to punch someone so much.

Ada sprinted into the room, followed by the neighbor. "I'm sorry, I was trying to keep her outside," the neighbor said breathlessly. "Didn't know what was going on in here, but she was worried about you." Seeing Jason pinning Calin to the floor, the neighbor's eyebrows shot up. "Um, well, looks like ya have things under control here . . ." the neighbor said awkwardly, "the cops just pulled up out front. I'll direct them back here."

"Thanks, man." Jason looked at Ada. "Why don't you go over across the street? I'm sure Susan and Robert are worried."

"Ada? Ada!" Calin yelled. "Tell him to get off me! Tell him that this is all a misunderstanding. He just doesn't understand us!"

"'Doesn't understand us?' Doesn't understand 'us?'" Ada roared at Calin. "There is no us! There is just me and me wanting you to leave me alone! What is wrong with you?!" She was still yelling when the two policemen came into the room.

Calin was put in handcuffs and taken to the patrol car while a female officer took Ada's statement and then Jason's. A second patrol car arrived, and the officers in it ran a background check on Calin. They walked up to Ada, "Do you know this man?" they asked.

"No," she said quickly, then stopped herself. "Well, not really. We met on a dating app and went on one date, but he has refused to leave me alone since, even though I made it clear I was no longer interested."

"What did he say his name was? Calin?" The cop shook his head and looked down at the information from the background check. "Well, turns out this isn't the first time something like this has happened. His real name is Brooks Patterson, and he is wanted in the state of Missouri for three counts of stalking and sexual assault." The cop explained. "He had been fired from his job after the first charge and was out on bond awaiting arraignment for the other two. Guess he fled the state with a fake driver's license and continued his same pattern, making you his new target."

Ada looked down at her hands, "But he had paid for dinner and a rental car, even bought me gifts . . ." Words failed Ada, "How?"

"From what we can tell, the money he had was what he had

earned from his mother's estate after she had passed away from a heart attack," said the officer. "Most likely, she left it to him, trying to help him with his legal troubles." The cop looked at Ada, his face softening. "Either way, it's over now. He won't be able to bother you anymore." Ada wanted to believe him.

Robert and Susan rushed over as soon as the police cars pulled up. They insisted that Ada stay with them for the night. Ada accepted their invitation, but in her heart of hearts, she secretly wished that, instead, Jason would stay with her at the bungalow and sleep in the other bedroom, or better yet, hold her in his arms all night. She scolded herself inwardly. What was she thinking? He hadn't even asked her out, let alone appeared to have any interest in her at all. Pushing thoughts of Jason aside, Ada gathered a few things to take with her over to Susan and Robert's and walked across the street with her friends.

Susan put her in a guest room that felt just as cozy as the rest of the house, complete with cotton sheets, quilted blankets, an iron headboard, and paintings of the sea on two walls. A bookshelf filled with books, baskets holding shells, and other trinkets from the beach sat next to a wicker rocking chair looking out a dormer window. Ada didn't realize until after she had settled under the covers in the soft bed that Susan had left on a lamp on the bookshelf, its soft light emanating through the room. She decided that she was too tired to get up and to turn it off, and finally feeling safe, knowing Calin was gone, and her friends were just a few rooms away, Ada drifted off to sleep

The smell of coffee and other delicious breakfast aromas gently awakened Ada the following morning. She crawled out of the cozy bed and made her way to the bathroom. After washing her face and applying some light make up, she slipped into her black yoga pants and gray ribbed tank top.

Making her way down the stairs, she stopped briefly to look at the family pictures on the wall. Even throughout many years, Robert and Susan hadn't changed that much and still looked so happy together; their son, daughter, and each of their families were quite good-looking. Studying the photos, Ada noticed that each of Susan and Robert's children had two children of their own, so that made an even four grandchildren! Ada knew that Robert and Susan's children both lived in Boston because they were in business together. Susan had mentioned that once Robert retired, they would be moving to be closer to everyone. *How fun*, thought Ada. She doubted that would ever occur to her parents. They currently seemed far too preoccupied gallivanting across the globe.

"Good morning, Ada! I see you've found the stories of our lives!" Robert chuckled. He was carrying a cup of coffee.

"Yes, what a beautiful family! I'm guessing that retirement and moving closer to grandchildren sounds quite appealing?" Ada jogged down the rest of the stairs smiling.

"Ah, indeed! Did you sleep okay? Coffee and breakfast are being served if you would like to follow me."

"I did, thank you," said Ada honestly, "and that sounds glorious." They walked to the kitchen together.

Later that morning, Susan walked over to the bungalow with Ada to help straighten things after the events of last evening. Ada was a little worried that the place would feel less appealing after Calin's intrusion, but she was happily surprised when she walked in, and it still felt just like home. Somehow, with Calin now being completely out of the picture, it allowed her to move on without fear.

"Fortunate for me we don't have classes this morning. Instead, we're all meeting Professor Aglio downtown at his friend's art gallery for a tour tomorrow." Ada said as she smoothed the covers on her bed and put the decorative pillows back in place.

"Ah . . . so glad about that, Ada." said Susan kindly. "You need time to relax today, and we certainly enjoy having you with us. If it's the art studio I'm thinking of then you're in for a real treat! Do you know if the name is Pacific Cove by chance?"

"Why, yes, it is! Are you familiar with it?"

"Actually, I happen to be! The owner, Oscar Ash, and I attended a university back east together! We hadn't run into each other after graduation until twenty years ago when he and his wife moved here. She was hired as a music professor—they're lovely people. Please tell him I said hello and that Robert and I can't wait to see him at the art gala on Saturday!"

"I most certainly will." Ada smiled. She liked Susan so much. She thought her mother would like her, too, if she ever landed back home long enough to get to know someone again. "Thank you, again, for your help and opening your home to me. I appreciate your friendship more than you know."

"We're happy to have yours as well, sweet girl." Susan looked around the once again neat bungalow and sighed, "It is a lovely place, isn't it? Well, anyway, if you'd like to stay another night with us . . ." Susan trailed off, gesturing with her hands.

"Thank you so much, Susan. I have the feeling I'll be okay.

Still, it's a comfort to know that you're right there." She pointed across the street.

After Susan left, Ada curled up on the couch, and before she knew it, she was asleep. Her dreams had her reliving the previous night, thankfully focused more on Jason saving her than anything else. She thought about his strong arms around her and the way that he took down Calin. Waking up, she opened just one eye in hopes that he was there on the couch with her, but it was only the open cushions staring back at her.

The evening was quickly passing, and Ada wanted to get a walk in before eating a bite of dinner, so she got up and went for a leisurely stroll to the park and back. The weather was perfect, sunny and just the right temperature; it made things feel normal. When she returned, Ada made herself a quick salad and grilled cheese sandwich, then turned on the TV. After two episodes of a new drama series and a shower, she headed to bed feeling sleepy. The nap evidently hadn't done much good, but she supposed it was normal to feel drained after such a stressful experience.

The following morning Ada awakened feeling lighthearted and got ready early for her class. She was having fun picking out clothes from the ones that she and Daisy had bought last weekend.

Oh, Daisy, she thought. She would have to call and tell her friend about the most recent drama with Calin. Except, looking at the time, she realized that it would have to be later because she needed to be downtown in half an hour.

Wishing to present a classier look for the studio tour, Ada chose a pastel baby pink suit and T-shirt with matching heels. She quickly ran a straightener through her hair. With the sun she had gotten this summer, very little make-up was needed. So, the mascara she had applied earlier and some added lipstick were enough.

Ada took a quick glance in the mirror and smiled. "Why is Jason not falling at my feet?" she said aloud, giggling. Turning away, she headed out the door, into her car, and, blaring her favorite playlist, she was surprised at how light she felt this morning, given the frightening experience over the weekend. As she pulled up to the stoplight between the University's main campus and athletic complex, Ada saw Jason crossing the street. She considered beeping the horn and waving at him but changed her mind. Then, just like that, almost like he sensed she was there, he turned around and waved to her. Was that a smile? Was he smiling at her? Ada didn't have time to see. The light had turned green, and a honk came from the car behind her.

"Get a life, bud!" Ada shouted. Not that he could hear above the music and the morning traffic, but that didn't matter. It felt like her entire face was smiling and those butterflies in her stomach were at it again. Suddenly, she felt a little bit disappointed. She would have enjoyed getting a chance to speak with Jason today and thank him for what he had done. Maybe she would pick up some type of thank you gift and give it to him after class. Wait, where did he live? She'd have to ask Susan.

Ada found the gallery easily. It happened to be right up the street from the boutique where she and Daisy had shopped. Pacific Cove Art Gallery was a beauty in itself, sitting on the corner and painted a majestic azure blue with creamy white trim decorating the double front doors and framing the many windows of the two-story building. Custom water fountains sat on either side of the doors, creating a grand entrance. Upon entering, the foyer displayed two large pieces of contemporary art, taking up most of the wall space. Ada looked in awe around the large room, its layout open aside from several movable wall room dividers placed in clever configurations. The lighting created a relaxed and inviting atmosphere for visitors and played well off the polished concrete flooring. The light gray, classic brick of the walls kept the artwork as the focus.

Ada wanted to spend more time looking around and studying each piece of artwork, but she could hear voices coming from an area in the back and figured she had better head there to meet up with her class. Several of the students had gathered around an unfamiliar man, whom she assumed was the owner of the gallery. Professor Aglio was also there, engaging in animated conversation with Lee and two other students. At least Ada hadn't been too late. There were seats set up in rows so she guessed that Oscar Ash himself would be speaking to the class at some point. She hoped to introduce herself and mention Susan.

Ada put her satchel and purse down on a chair, then glanced up. In front of her was an intriguing painting and she moved closer to look. There was nothing whimsical or ultra-modern about this piece, as in a few others she had seen on her walk in; this one drew her in because of the simplicity. There was a field of wildflowers surrounded by forests and in the middle sat a young girl slightly smiling and holding a few of the flowers in her hands. Ada stared at it for a while.

"Penny for your thoughts?"

Ada jumped.

"Oh my, I'm so sorry my dear," a male voice said kindly,

with a humorous tone. "I didn't mean to startle you."

Turning around, Ada realized it was Oscar Ash who was speaking to her. He smiled at her warmly.

"Oh, I'm okay," Ada laughed, "Just simply embarrassed," She smiled widely. "I was very mesmerized by this piece."

"I'm so glad, and, really, I would like to hear your thoughts." Ada now felt on the spot, like she should come up with something profound to say. Almost like he could read her mind, Oscar jumped in again, "How rude of me, I'm Oscar Ash, the owner of this gallery . . . and you are?"

Ada relaxed and held out her hand, "I'm Ada Cameron. So nice to meet you. I believe that we have a friend in common."

"Is that right?" he asked, taking her hand and shaking it.

"Yes, Susan McGuire. I'm staying in a house across the street from her and Robert, and we have become good friends. She wanted me to let you know that they're planning on coming to the gala this weekend!"

"Robert and Susan, yes! Wonderful, wonderful! Thank you so much for letting me know, and it is nice to meet you, Ada." He smiled, "Now, please do share with me your impressions of this painting, if you would be so kind."

"Well," Ada hesitated. "I do love wildflowers because they're so . . . resilient. You can find them in the most unexpected place, just like this, right in the middle of a forest.

"Do you see yourself as the young girl?" Oscar asked.

"I guess you could say that . . ." Ada's mind wandered again, and she could feel a lump in her throat begin to form.

"I have a feeling that you just shared something quite personal and meaningful with me, Ada, and that is something that I will always appreciate. I look forward to more conversations with you." He took Ada's hand and patted it, just like her grandfather used to. With that, he turned and headed toward Professor Aglio.

Ada started back to her seat and realized that Whitney and Lee had sat in the chairs next to hers. While he was talking to the guy in front of him, she leaned over and whispered, "Too bad you didn't come sailing with us. What a perfect day! And Lee seemed really disappointed. He mentioned you several times." She smiled and winked at Ada.

"Oh," Ada said, a little taken aback. "I had kinda figured that you two were dating."

She threw her head back, laughing. "Well, that would be weird since he's my first cousin."

Ada laughed nervously, "yes, I guess that would."

114

Thankfully, Professor Aglio began talking then, cutting off any further conversation. Ada could feel her face getting red.

"Alright, folks. Let's get started. I'd like to introduce the owner of Pacific Cove Art Gallery, Oscar Ash."

Chapter 9

Oscar Ash continued to be charming throughout the rest of the afternoon. He talked about his formal education and how he ended up opening an art gallery in the northeast. He spoke about his love of art and discussed with the class some of what they had learned in the courses so far. Since some students had hopes of owning an art gallery someday, Ada included, although she didn't say aloud, he also spoke with great emotion on passion for art, interest in artists, and striking a balance with business. He and the students had just entered a lively conversation about designing spaces when Professor Aglio had to end class, promising to bring them back for another session before the end of the term.

As Ada was gathering her things to leave, Oscar came over to her with a card in his hand. "Ada, I'd like for you to attend the art gala here on Saturday evening, and I have a favor to ask."

"How kind of you, Oscar. I would enjoy that very much! What is the favor?"

"I know that Professor Aglio has asked all of you for submissions during your courses so far for the silent auction we will be having here at the end of the summer. However, I'm also having a special fundraiser for a charity that my wife works with in Reno and am planning on having a silent auction on some select pieces that I have collected this year. I would like to add one of your sketches."

"I'm honored. Which one, may I ask?"

"Of course. It's the sketch of the mountains and the snowboarder in the background. I would have to call it visual harmony, Ada. Your shading and texturing are blended especially well. Just like you couldn't stop looking at the piece today, I was the same with your art."

Of all the pieces she submitted, he had chosen the one that she had gone back to after losing Troy. Perhaps Ada would tell him the story sometime, but not right now. It didn't seem necessary, and she wasn't wanting to discourage him from selling it for charity.

Besides, keeping it only served as a sad reminder.

"I would be happy to donate the piece and am very flattered that you think it merits being alongside the others on Saturday. I'm excited to be in attendance."

"Splendid! Please tell Susan and Richard I look forward to seeing them as well."

The afternoon at Pacific Cove with Oscar Ash turned out to be one of the best days for Ada since arriving in town for the summer. He was a most charming gentleman and seemed like someone that she would happily get to know better.

Even though she was becoming quite familiar with the area and the treasures the local stores had, Ada was having a difficult time coming up with a thank you gift for Jason. What do you give someone who saved you from an attack by another man? Not exactly a romantic reason for gift-giving. On top of that, she didn't even know Jason well at all.

Across from the University were several bookstores. Ada headed there, hoping that maybe something in there would give her an idea. She drove two miles and stopped in front of the largest one. Inside the door was a shopping basket, and Ada took one, feeling hopeful. The first thing she spotted was the rack of hoodies featuring some of the different University team sports. She wondered if an item of clothing was too personal but decided to go for it anyway.

"It's a hoody, not boxers." Ada said to herself. "Good grief." She picked out a University shirt, one in charcoal gray with green lettering. Guessing at his size, although he was built like Troy, she figured he could always exchange it if necessary. Ada moved throughout the store and came to some sports gifts and collectibles for baseball. She picked out a mug that read, "Baseball Coach . . . like a normal coach but cooler."

That made her laugh aloud, and as she did, she thought of Troy. His baseball players always thought he was the coolest. No wonder, though; he'd do crazy dances to motivate them or have them sing songs on the bus even when they lost a game. For a minute, it felt like the old days when she'd shop for Troy's Christmas stocking stuffers . . . but now it was for someone else. She felt a sadness, yet a spark of joy still shown through. Ada so wished she knew how Jason felt about her. It would make things a lot easier.

Right next to the mugs sat a wooden plaque that read: "A Good Coach Can Change A Game. A Great Coach Can Change a

Life." Ada dropped that into her basket, too. *Okay, enough of the cheesy stuff*, she thought to herself. Near the counter, she saw a large container of bubble gum and thought that it would be a perfect addition. There were also some University duffel bags that would be perfect to carry gear to the fields and would hold all of Ada's purchases. She thought about picking up a thank you card but couldn't imagine what to write, so she opted out.

After getting back to the car, Ada gave Susan a call to find out where Jason lived.

Evidently, it was campus housing and within walking distance just like her place, but one street over. Before leaving, Ada made sure the price tags were off, and everything fit into the duffle bag nicely. Jason's place was a duplex, and Susan had told her that he lived on the left side.

Parking in front of the house, Ada checked herself in the mirror, added some color to her lips, and stuck a piece of gum in her mouth. She had only knocked on the door once before he opened it, which made Ada think that he had seen her pull into the driveway.

"Hi, Jason."

"Hi, Ada. What brings you by?" His face was clear of any emotion. *Why can't he just smile*, Ada thought, *was it that difficult?*

"You're really dressed up for class," he said, interrupting

her thoughts.

"Oh," Ada looked down at her outfit and shrugged, almost as if to nonverbally say, "why, this old thing?" She looked back at Jason. "We visited an art gallery downtown today . . . Pacific Cove?"

"Oh yeah, I've seen it."

Why wasn't he inviting her inside?

"What do you have there?" He motioned toward the duffle.

"It's for you," said Ada, passing him the bag.

"Me? Why?"

Ada decided to be bold. "May I come in?"

"Uh . . . sure." Jason held the door for her.

The apartment was mostly bare except for a couch, an end table with a lamp, and a television in the front room, along with a bistro table and two chairs in the eat-in kitchen. A medium-sized painting hung on the wall between the living room and kitchen areas, depicting a sailboat in the water at sunset. Ada was trying not to appear nosy, so she didn't dare let her eyes wander after the door closed behind her.

She held out the duffle to Jason for him to take. "A simple thank you for your gallant behavior Saturday night. You were my knight in shining armor." Oh my gosh, did she just say those words aloud? How stupid. How lame. Ada could feel the heat in her neck begin to rise.

"I don't know about that," Jason stammered out, "but it's very kind of you." He stood admiring the bag rather awkwardly, almost like he didn't want to assume there was anything inside even though he could tell it was a bit heavy.

"Go ahead and look inside," Ada added quickly. "I hope you like everything." This whole idea was beginning to feel like a mistake. Maybe a thank you letter would have been sufficient. There seemed to be such a strangeness between them.

Jason set the duffle on the couch and took out the largest thing first, which happened to be the gum. "Oh, the guys are going to like this in the dugout."

Next, he reached for the plaque. He took his time reading it, then carried it over and placed it on the fireplace mantel. "I like it," he said, standing back and nodding his head. "I hope that's what I'm doing."

Before Ada had time to answer, Jason had retrieved the cup and was reading it too. "Well, I'll enjoy having my morning cup of coffee in this. Lastly, he pulled the shirt out and held it out. Thank you, Ada. This was all unnecessary." He paused, then looked up at her. "I'm so sorry you had to experience what you did, but I'm glad I was there to help."

Those eyes, thought Ada. *I could get lost in those eyes just like I did Troy's.* His personality was also kind like Troy. For just a moment, Ada wished he would scoop her up in his arms, carry her to his bedroom, and make love to her. Knowing that wouldn't possibly happen, she got up and gave him a quick kiss on the cheek. Between the thoughts she was having and the smell of his skin, she began backing toward the door.

"Th—thank you, again, Jason. I'll . . ."

Jason set down the coffee mug and took two large steps toward her, reaching for the door. "Be careful, there. I don't want you to fall."

For a minute, Ada thought perhaps her wish was coming true and he was coming to kiss her, but he was still just playing the knight, rescuing her from stumbling.

"Oh geez, what a klutz . . . thank you. See you around, Jason."

"Bye, Ada."

Once she was back at her place, Ada changed into some

comfy clothes, ate a few bites of cold pasta from the refrigerator, and took a glass of wine out on the front porch. The sun had disappeared behind some clouds and the air had cooled. Ada pulled one of the soft blankets out of the basket and covered her lower half as she sank into one of the wicker lounge chairs. She immediately called her best friend to fill her in on all that had happened over the course of two days.

Daisy answered almost immediately, as she always tended to do. Ada felt such comfort in hearing her friend's voice, almost more so than her own mother's. Daisy was also a better listener, so Ada knew she could share absolutely every detail of what had taken place.

Sometimes people can make it so hard because they want to interrupt and ask questions or make comments when all you want to do is tell the story. Ada's mom cared but would often dispense advice at the same time Ada was talking, as was her way. After Ada had told Daisy about the entire ordeal, she surprised herself by completely breaking down and sobbing. Again, it was almost like Daisy was holding her hand through the phone and being such a comfort. The only comments were quiet ones like, "Aww, sweetie, I'm so sorry," and "I love you, Ada."

Not until Ada's sobs were few and far between did Daisy attempt to make conversation. After a bit, it was Ada who finally brought the topic back around to Calin as she said, "Oh wow, I needed that. Thank you."

"Of course, and when I see you in two weeks, I'll give you a real squeeze! I'm just glad that you have some peace of mind in knowing that Calin won't be bothering you anymore. You can just focus on enjoying your summer and art," she paused for a minute, "and Jason?"

Ada then told Daisy all about her gift-giving fiasco. "I don't think was a fiasco at all!" Daisy said, "I like that you were bold enough to give him a kiss on the cheek. I mean, good grief! It's about time that one of you made a move!" Daisy laughed.

Ada snorted. "I still don't know how he feels. There is a wall there that I don't know how to break down or even if I should try." She sighed. "Anyway, did I tell you that I was invited to a special art show?"

The girls spent the next twenty minutes discussing what Ada should wear and how she should style her hair and do her make-up. By the time they hung up, Ada was feeling even more excited about Saturday. She decided to go inside and try on some of the possible outfits that she and Daisy had come up with for the evening.

Just as she was putting the blanket away, her phone rang. It was both her mom and dad calling. Ada moved inside where she could at least begin putting out clothes for class tomorrow while she talked. The gala try-ons would have to wait, and she'd like to Facetime Daisy for that anyway.

"Hi, Mom and Dad! So, how is it with my world-traveler parents? What? Wait, slow down. I can't hear you very well. What was that, Dad?" Both of her parents were trying to talk at the same time. Evidently, her parents had been on the trip with their new friends in Iceland, where they walked past geothermal areas with bubbling mud pools, explored green landscapes and hiked to glacier and ice caves. On one of their hikes on the way back to Reykjavik, her mother had fallen and ruptured her Achilles tendon. She had to be taken by helicopter to the closest hospital for emergency surgery, so they would be extending their stay until she had clearance to travel.

Ada sensed more exhilaration from her parents than hesitancy or regret. For this she was grateful. They promised to be more careful and keep in touch, only asking about her during the goodbyes. Ada was fine with this as she didn't want to divulge much of anything that had been taking place in her life over the last

126

couple of weeks.

After a steamy shower and blow-drying her hair, Ada laid out white capris and a sage blouse to put on in the morning. If she could manage to get out of bed early enough, maybe she'd have enough time to curl her hair for a change. She took her book off the nightstand table and began to read but noticed that each time she was ready to turn the page she had no idea what she had just read. She kept thinking back on the day and how she could have handled things differently with Jason, from the type of gift to the kiss on the cheek. *Overthinking as usual*, thought Ada. *If I'm too tired to read, then I'm too tired to think.* She turned off the light, rolled over, closed her eyes, and said aloud to the room, "Goodnight."

Chapter 10

Ada was caught in the middle of an intense dream when her alarm went off. She sat up so abruptly that it made her head spin. Ada liked analyzing her dreams as she felt they gave her a glimpse into her present or future self, but this one was a jumbled mess that didn't even make sense, so she decided to leave it alone.

After freshening up and putting some curls in her hair, she decided that she would drive to campus today and get a coffee and homemade croissant from the bakery down by the pier before class. She placed her bakery order online and then made a call to her mom. It was evening there now, so she imagined her parents would be eating dinner or relaxing. When Ada's Mom answered, Ada could hear laughter in the background, so her parents were evidently not alone.

For all the years it had been just her and her parents eating dinner together, they were certainly taking every opportunity to be with other people now. Ada supposed she was happy about that, although sometimes it felt they didn't invest enough time or interest in her life, except to give their opinions on decisions she had made. Just once she would like to hear that they were proud of her or impressed by something she had accomplished.

Once Ada found out her mother was healing well after the surgery, she said a quick goodbye and took one last bite of her breakfast pastry. She pulled into the parking lot ten minutes before class. Several students were walking around campus, and she sat for a moment to watch them. Just like back home, the University contributed an energy to the community that was rich in diversity, the arts, and cuisine. Ada smiled to herself, grabbed her things, and headed inside.

As Ada entered the building, Robert came whistling down the hall. "Good morning, neighbor! How is it with you?"

"Good morning to you as well!" Ada smiled. "I'm doing fine, thank you. Oh! I wanted to let you know that when I had class yesterday at Pacific Cove Art Gallery, I had the pleasure of meeting

Oscar Ash. I let him know that you and Susan would be at the gala on Saturday, and he ended up giving me a personal invitation! Not only that, but he wants to include one of my submissions in the silent auction for his wife's charity work."

"How lovely, Ada! I'm so proud of you!" Robert beamed. She wished her father could have been here to hear this. Maybe he would get a clue!

"Thank you, Robert. That's so kind of you to say. I was very flattered, of course."

"It sounds like you must accompany us on Saturday then."

"I would love to!"

"Excellent! Now, unfortunately, I must be off. Good day, my dear!" Robert continued whistling down the hallway until she couldn't hear it any longer.

Before Professor Aglio began his lecture, he congratulated Ada in front of the entire class for her drawing that Oscar Ash had chosen for the silent auction. There was a round of applause from the students. Ada forced a smile but was rather embarrassed by the attention and grateful that he didn't say anything about her also being formally invited to the gala. Perhaps he hadn't even known.

The professor segued into talking about figure drawing and showing examples from ancient Greece and Rome. Artists were often commissioned to depict religious portraits and scenes of figures during the Renaissance period. Their assignments for the following week were to draw both the female and male forms in the nude. Ada couldn't imagine volunteering for such a job as posing nude but was grateful that some people would since it was a requirement for the course.

During a break for lunch, Ada headed to the food court to get a salad. Several of the students walked alongside her, including Lee, talking about the assignment. Some of the girls were giggling discussing drawing nude models, but Lee was rather serious and looked at Ada.

"I happen to think the human body is beautiful and worth drawing. What are your thoughts, Ada?"

She almost coughed but didn't want to appear phased by his question. "Well, of course drawing is my favorite medium. I've yet to sketch a nude figure but we'll see how it goes." Ada was glad that they had reached the counter so she could place her order and end the conversation.

As they ate, they all sat together and enjoyed getting to know each other better. Ada was pleasantly surprised at how Whitney had traveled the world after her undergraduate degree in art, visiting Barcelona, Paris, London, Cape Town, and Athens. She promised to show Ada her many photo albums of all of them. Ada had only dreamed of going to such places.

Lee had always come across as a lady's man, but Ada found he was quite intelligent and thoughtful. He also had travelled extensively and decided to take some courses in art history because of his work as an architect. Like Ada, he desired to do something beyond the next logical thing. He had worked for a company in urban designs but found himself fascinated with conservation and restoration work.

Ada, Whitney, Lee, and the others talked about joining Lee on his boat for an outing soon. According to Lee, the large craft easily accommodated up to ten people, and the weather had been beautiful this summer. Everyone talked about what they could bring, and it sounded like fun. Ada decided she would for sure go this time.

After talking with Daisy, it was decided that Ada needed to go back to Sweet Violet and get a suitable evening dress for the gala. They hadn't been planning on any fancy events during their last outing, so Ada hadn't even considered looking at the more formal options. She decided to ask Susan to go along just for some female company. It was always nice to have someone else's opinion on selections. It just so happened that Susan knew the manager of Sweet Violet quite well. They had served on the last charity board together.

While the two ladies were catching up, Ada began looking through the racks of evening gowns. She didn't want anything too glittery or over the top but instead something understated and classy. By the time Susan came over to her, Ada had placed four gowns on the portable rack the young associate had provided to her.

"Those all look lovely, Ada," commented Susan.

"I've decided to add two more and then try them on. I'll go with whichever you think looks best!"

"I think you should go with the one that makes you feel happiest."

Ada smiled. She couldn't help but think of what her mother would be saying right now: "Oh Ada, really. You know those aren't really your colors. And those styles . . ." Then she would proceed to take ones off the racks that she preferred.

Susan was right. Ada indeed felt extremely happy with the fourth dress she tried on. It wasn't that spectacular on the hanger, but there was something about it on her frame. The A-line chiffon with a sweetheart neckline fell to the floor perfectly. Not only that, but the champagne rose brought out amber highlights in Ada's brunette hair and made her skin glow. When she stepped from the dressing room, Susan put both of her hands to her mouth and gasped loudly. She stayed like that for what seemed like a full minute and then finally spoke.

"Ada, you look absolutely stunning." Susan's manager friend readily agreed.

"I really like this one," Ada said, turning to look at herself in the floor to ceiling mirrors.

She smiled. "Yes, I want this one."

Ada ended up splurging and getting shoes and a clutch purse to match. At the register the young associate asked Ada how she was going to wear her hair for the occasion.

"I haven't decided just yet," said Ada.

"I think you should wear part of your hair up and let the rest fall," said the associate. "These tear-drop earrings would complete your ensemble beautifully!"

She's good, thought Ada.

Before she could respond, Susan interrupted. "I'm getting these for you!" "Oh no, I can't let you do that!" Ada protested.

"Already done." Susan handed her card to the girl and smiled.

Ada quickly hugged Susan. "I don't know what more to say except thank you!"

"Your beauty will be no competition for any artwork there, my girl," added Susan, as they stepped outside. "Let's go grab some dinner. Robert is working late and I'm starving."

"Sounds perfect!"

The two decided on a newer restaurant that offered authentic Mediterranean dining. Ada chose the Mediterranean pasta and Susan the Baba Ghanoush. They agreed that it was some of the best food they had eaten in a while.

Conversations with Susan always proved to be refreshing. They talked about books, music, teaching, art, and family. Susan had come from a similar background as Ada, so she was familiar with an opinionated mother. Ada was curious why this trait didn't seem to be passed down.

Ada wasn't going to bring up Jason, but she didn't have to since Susan did. "That Jason is the nicest young man, don't you agree?" and she took a sip of her wine.

"I do . . . he's just difficult to get to know."

"Really? What do you mean?" Susan seemed surprised.

Ada recounted several of the scenarios that had played out between her and Jason since she had arrived in town. Susan listened intently. "Hmm. I see. Perhaps Jason has experienced a bad relationship and isn't ready for a new one just yet?"

"I wish it were that simple. For some reason, I feel like there's a lot more to it than that."

The waiter brought their conversation to a halt when he came to check on them. "May I get you anything else? Some dessert?"

"Actually, chimed in Ada, I would love a piece of your baklava to go."

"Make that three pieces," added Susan.

"Of course. I'll be right back with your checks and baklava."

Susan turned back to Ada as the waiter walked away. "Well, I can't wait for Jason to see you in that dress on Saturday!"

"What? Is he going to be there?" Ada almost spit out her last drink of wine.

Susan laughed a little, "Why, yes. Oscar's grandson is on the baseball team."

"Oh, I see." Ada wasn't sure if her stomach was reacting to the news or the food.

After they paid their bills, the waiter handed them their baklava. "Here you go ladies. Thank you and please come back again."

Ada drove them both home and decided to take a shower and put on pjs before diving into the baklava. She stood under the water a little, thinking about Jason and imagining him seeing her at the gala. Would he finally be so drawn to her that he couldn't resist? Good grief! What does a girl have to do anyway? Even if Susan was right and he had experienced a recent breakup, how long does it take to get over it? Usually, guys weren't ones to dwell on emotional issues. She wasn't ready to let this go yet. Playing hard to get was making him even more attractive. Not that he wasn't attractive enough to begin with. He didn't have Troy's movie star good looks, but there was something about his smile, and of course those eyes. He was kind, too.

After the shower, Ada decided it would be best to hang the evening gown from the top of the guest room door so it wouldn't wrinkle at the bottom. She stood back to admire the dress. It was the prettiest one she had ever owned. Ada went out to the living room and logged into Netflix. Between the new season of *Virgin River* and the satisfying crunch of the baklava, she felt rather happy.

Chapter 11

His kiss was so warm and inviting. Ada could hardly feel her legs beneath her as he picked her up and carried her to his bed. He laid her down gently, took off his jacket and tossed it to the side, and then joined her. His lips found the curve of her neck, chest, and—

Ada's body jolted awake. She was perspiring, breathing heavily, and confused as to where she was. That's when the familiar sound of her alarm brought her back to reality.

"Nooo" Ada groaned and flopped back down onto the bed. Why? Why? Why? Why did she have to awaken from this dream?

She couldn't be sure who the man in the dream was but felt in her heart it was Troy or maybe even Jason. Either way, she longed to stay in his arms. How was she to pull herself together and go to Friday class?

Ada made sure the rainwater shower head was a little on the cooler side than what she normally preferred. Something needed to bring her temperature down after that dream. She even needed to wash her hair, so there was no extra time to linger this morning. Thirty minutes later she was ready to go, complete with a cute V-neck belted blue mini dress and sandals. She had French braided her hair and stuck on her fedora. Thank goodness she looked more refreshed than she had earlier. Grabbing her satchel, coffee mug, and a muffin, she was out the door.

It was a good thing she had finished her breakfast before she reached the classroom because as she walked into the art room, the screen was displaying two drawings of nudes, one female and one male. Not that this would have bothered Ada under most circumstances, but the drawings brought back her earlier dream, causing her face and chest to flush hot and her stomach to fill with butterflies. She took a deep breath and moved to her seat.

The rest of the morning was spent listening to lectures on figure drawing and the study of proportion, volume, and how to develop drawing skills to show expression.

The human body is beautiful, Ada thought.

The discussions at lunch were lively; the anticipation alone of drawing live nudes the following week had everyone in chipper moods. No one in the groups had yet to complete a nude sketch except for Lee during his studies at the Art Institute of Chicago. When they asked him about it, he said that the experience was one he couldn't begin to explain and that everyone would have to experience for themselves. At times Ada was afraid they were privy to her dream, and she could feel the heat rise in her face. Nothing that a cold drink couldn't calm down.

Everyone knew that Lee had money. Exactly where that money came from was somewhat a mystery. It seemed like he had been studying and traveling the world since college. He was originally from Los Angeles and did have Hollywood looks. He also drove a sports car, and of course, who could forget the spectacular yacht that he had anchored here for the summer? Even though he had money, he didn't act like it. Lee was considerate and kind. He never left anyone out of the conversation no matter what they looked like or how they presented themselves. Ada did admire that about him. Too many of the guys she knew back home with money only wanted to associate with people who also had money. The only thing she could figure was that he came from wealthy parents. Her parents also had a good amount of money and were traveling the world, but they certainly didn't own their own yacht. She wasn't sure but Lee seemed to be about her age.

While the others were questioning Lee on his time at the institute, he was more inquisitive about Ada and her future plans. At first the others were listening in, which made Ada extremely uncomfortable as she never wanted to talk about herself in front of people she didn't know well. Thank goodness Professor Aglio came through to get a coffee and several congregated around him to discuss the upcoming week, relieving some of the focus. Ada really didn't have much to tell Lee at this point. She was still employed by the school in her town and planning on returning at the start of the year. Still, it was rather enjoyable to share her vision of what she'd like to do with her art studies. Lee was fully supportive and didn't think it was outlandish in the least for her to see herself owning her own gallery. He showered her with compliments on what he had seen of her artwork during class and took notice of both the professor and the owner of the gallery speaking with her about her work. Lee's work was good too, but what bothered Ada was that he gave the impression that he had no appreciation for what teachers do for students. It certainly wasn't at the callous level of Calin but also showed no admiration for what she had given her life to the past few years. She decided that she might have fun going out with Lee and the group but wasn't interested in spending time alone with him, although she was getting the idea that he would like that.

When they got back to class there were no longer nudes on the screen but three quotations having to do with art and the human body:

"The human body is the best picture of the human soul." ~ Ludwig Wittgenstein "The body says what words cannot." ~Martha Graham

"Because the beauty of the human body is that it hasn't a single muscle which doesn't serve its purpose; that there's not a line wasted; that every detail of it fits one idea, the idea of a man and the life of a man." ~ Ayn Rand

The class was divided into smaller groups and asked to discuss their own interpretations of each quote, how they related, how they differed, and how any or all of the quotations might influence their own art and perceptions. Ada thought all three were beautiful but was particularly fond of the second one. She felt that the body could more accurately describe feelings than words could most of the time. The way someone touched you spoke more volumes than what they said. Most agreed with her. She didn't use examples but thought of how Calin had said he cared about her and what his body demonstrated compared to Troy, who could say he loved her with his eyes and not even utter a word. Some of the students were more literal in their thoughts while others were quite philosophical and deep. Ada enjoyed the conversations because they reminded her of the times she and Troy spent discussing topics in depth. With his psychology studies, he enjoyed looking deeply into why people do what they do, much beyond the surface. He also enjoyed reading the great philosophers from Plato and Aristotle to Descartes and Kant. Ada relished the times the two of them spent wrapped up in a blanket together on the beach or driving along in the car having analytical conversations.

The afternoon flew by, and before she knew it, Ada was walking back to the bungalow. She hurried along because she had scheduled an appointment for four o' clock to get her nails done for the gala, and she'd need to drive to the salon. Maybe a pick-up order from the Italian restaurant would be a good choice for this evening.

Reaching the bungalow, she ran in long enough to freshen up a bit and grab a water bottle. As she put the address of the nail salon into her GPS, she realized it was down only two blocks on the opposite side of the street from the restaurant. *Perfect*, thought Ada. *I'll place an order when I'm getting close to being finished.*

It was a cute nail place. A husband and wife owned the salon, and she was greeted by both when she arrived.

"Pick a color," said the nail technician. Ada had already been searching Pinterest for nail ideas and had come across one that would go nicely with her dress. She had decided on a French manicure for her toenails but opted for oval fingernails in champagne with gold accents on the tips. The owner had to laugh at Ada when she could hardly hold still for her pedicure. She had always been so ticklish.

While she was getting her pedicure, her phone rang, her mom's photo popping up on the screen. She answered but was hesitant to stay on the line because she didn't want to appear rude. The technician picked up on the call being from Ada's mother and quickly said with a smile, "Don't worry at all! Talk to your mom."

Ada told her thank you and then proceeded to explain to her mom where she was and why she had been giggling when answering. Of course, her mother wanted to know all about the gala event including who would be there, what type of showing, the owner's name, and on and on. After her mother caught her up on what was happening with them, rehabilitation after her recent surgery, their plans for a quick trip to Rome and then to return home for a while. Ada initially wasn't going to but decided that since she was on speaker phone and knew her dad was listening, that she would share the bit about her work being selected for the silent auction. Her mother's only response was, "Oh, how sweet."

Sweet?! Thought Ada. There is nothing sweet about having your piece chosen by a respected art gallery owner and artist. He didn't choose her work because it was cute, but because he felt her talent was commendable and her piece was beautiful. Her mother could be absolutely infuriating. It was almost like she was afraid that if she said anything too encouraging, Ada might be tempted to leave education. Well, guess what? She was going to! When? Not sure! Going to? Yes, by golly!

On the other hand, her father surprised her, "Ada, I'm not shocked at all that your art was chosen! Do you remember the drawing you gave to me for my birthday when you were ten years old? It was a picture of our backyard, and I was sitting on a chair reading the paper and drinking coffee. You drew the most intricate flowers in the garden surrounded by trees, a birdbath, and our dog, Louis sitting beside me. Might I say you captured him perfectly. You even had writing on the paper I was holding. There was coffee in my cup, and I had a contemplative look on my face. No doubt reading about the current state of things I'm quite certain. Anyway, I'm very pleased for you sweetheart and have no doubts that if it's anywhere as good as the drawing you gave me, it shall bring in a very high bid."

Ada was speechless for a moment. She couldn't remember the last time her father had spoken to her this long or expressed so much. It was moving, and a few tears fell from her eyes. The technician noticed and simply patted her foot gently.

"Thank you, Dad. I really appreciate you saying that."

"Of course, I'm proud of you, too, honey," her mom quickly added. "Thanks for calling," Ada said, then hung up.

Before the last coat of nail polish, Ada called and ordered her carbonara from the restaurant. Her toes would look so cute in the new dress shoes and her fingernails turned out even better than the picture. She gave the nail technician a nice tip for doing such a great job and promised to return.

Ada was feeling so excited about it being Friday and the gala the following day that she also stopped at a convenience store on her way back to the bungalow and picked up some of her favorite Ben and Jerry's ice cream. She had fallen asleep during the last episode of *Virgin River*, so she backed it up a bit and ate dinner in front of the television. The meal was delicious as always, probably because it was authentic Italian food. After finishing the episode, which was a cliffhanger, she got a shower before settling back on the couch with her peanut butter cup ice cream and blanket. Ada always got chilled when eating something cold even in the summer, but that never stopped her.

After the second episode, Ada figured that was enough television and she better get caught up on her reading. She settled into a nice pace and was on the sixth chapter when her cell phone rang. It was Daisy.

"Hey there! What are you up to this Friday night?"

"Hi, my friend! Well, I was doing one of our favorite things to do!"

"Shop? Eat? Watch movies?" Daisy yelled excitedly into the phone.

Ada put her cell on speaker and set it in her lap. "I did eat and watch tv earlier but was actually reading just now."

"Well, you're right. That is one of our favorite things to do, but on a Friday night? I don't remember our doing that!" Daisy laughed.

"I got a pedicure and manicure after class today and figured I'd relax since tomorrow evening is the big gala."

"Ooooh, that's right," Daisy said in an almost eerie way. "You must send pictures before you leave for the ball, Cinderella! I don't want pictures of the pumpkin."

Daisy always made Ada laugh. "You got it! In fact, I can even Facetime you—well, if you're going to be home that is?"

"Sure! Jackson's parents are coming over for dinner, but I can excuse myself to the bedroom. Yay! I know you're going to look incredible!"

"Thank you, Daisy. I can't wait to see you next weekend. It's so much more fun to talk when you're in front of me. You are still coming, right?" Ada asked. Daisy was silent for a minute. Ada's heart almost dropped thinking that Daisy for some reason may not get to come.

"What's that? Oh, absolutely! Sorry, Jackson was saying to tell you hello!"

Ada put her hand to her chest in relief. "Hey, Jackson! Tell him I said thank you for letting you come visit a second time."

"Are you kidding? He doesn't mind giving me up a few days now and then. That just means more golf time with his buddies."

Ada hoped that was true. She would never want to ruin any plans that Jackson and Daisy had made, and these days, with Jackson trying to get his own company off the ground, there wasn't a lot of time for them to spend together. Once again, Ada couldn't help but think that if Troy was still living, the four of them would be swimming in the pool, playing volleyball in the backyard, grilling smash burgers. At least when Jackson was working the three of them could be hanging out. Ada fluctuated between sadness and anger. It was always one or the other. Nothing in her life could ever be right again unless she had Troy back, which was never going to happen. Just how was she ever going to accept the new reality? The hope was always right there beneath the sadness. Lingering just in case. Ada didn't hear the last couple of things Daisy said but jumped right back into the conversation seemingly unnoticed.

The two talked a while longer about things they could do the following weekend and briefly about Jason, although there wasn't much more to add. Daisy was very interested, however, in Ada's recent dream and the upcoming nude drawings. She couldn't even imagine having to study and draw a nude model.

"You wouldn't want me in there. I'd be giggling on the floor." Daisy was laughing hard.

"Oh my gosh, don't I know it!" Ada laughed. "I thought of you when we were told about the assignment but had to block you from my mind in case the professor looked my way."

"So, I'll be waiting for your call tomorrow! By the way, how did you decide to wear your hair?"

"Well, the young associate where I bought the dress suggested that I wear part of it up and let the rest fall over my shoulders."

Daisy breathed in quickly as though in shock. "You haven't worn your hair like that since senior prom, and I thought you looked gorgeous!"

"You know, I hadn't even thought about that when she suggested it." She paused for a moment, once again remembering that night. She shook her head, clearing the memories. "Well, I'll let you go enjoy your more-exciting-than-mine Friday night," Ada teased. "Love you, Daisy."

"Love, you, too, Ada."

What a nice way to end the day, thought Ada. She got up, brushed her teeth, then climbed into bed, closing her eyes and hoping she could pick up the dream where she left off this morning.

Chapter 12

Despite her wishes, Ada's romantic dream did not return. Instead, Ada had been tormented with dream scenarios of her dress not fitting, one of the heels breaking off her shoe, and getting caught in a thunderstorm on her way into the gala. Ada chalked it up to consuming Ben and Jerry's at bedtime. Sugar before bed always gave her weird dreams, and she knew better, but it was so tempting when something ahead of her drew excitement of some kind.

She threw back the covers, changed into some joggers and a t-shirt, and got the coffee ready to run through before heading out for a walk. Maybe a little exercise and fresh air would clear her mind plus get rid of the bloated feeling in her gut. Ada grabbed her AirPods and chose a new summer playlist she had created. They were mostly upbeat songs to keep her moving at a good pace. Not too many people were out and about yet on this early Saturday morning. She figured that Robert and Susan were most likely enjoying their own cups of coffee and conversation on the sunporch out back. The skies were slowly clearing of random clouds and the day looked promising for perfect temperatures.

After walking a couple of blocks, Ada had a sudden urge to start running. She had been a runner in high school and on the track team. Although long distances were not her forte, she always loved the euphoria that accompanied running; it was especially strong on the days when she was by herself and could set her own pace. Ada could think so clearly on those days and was able to map out her entire future in the time it took her to run just two miles. Today was no exception. The same feelings of intense happiness and self-confidence came back. Ada began visualizing what she wanted her life to look like in the future: a husband, children, a career in the artworld, a cozy home with a backyard, maybe a golden retriever. Some might say those were lame thoughts to have if you're creating whatever you could imagine having, but to Ada that was the exact life she had always desired.

I'm going to start manifesting all of it, Ada thought.

She began slowing her running and breathing heavily in through her nose and out her mouth. *Whew!* She had forgotten that although intoxicating, running was also taxing if you haven't been training.

Back at the bungalow, Ada grabbed her water bottle and took it to the front porch to cool down. No need to try to get a shower yet. She'd still be sweating afterwards. Just as she sat down, a young man ran down her road with a golden retriever by his side. Ada sat upright. Had she manifested something that quickly? This was turning out to be a great morning. Hopefully, this evening will prove much the same.

"Hey there, neighbor!" It was Susan walking across the street towards her.

"Good morning!"

"You're up and at it early, and did I see you running?"

Ada laughed. "Well, if that's what you want to call it."

"I certainly do. Good for you!" Susan took a seat on one of the wicker chairs. "Just thought I'd pop over so we can make plans for what time to leave this evening."

"Oh, yes. How early or late is fashionable for an art gala?" Ada smiled and took a drink of water.

"There is a cocktail reception opening before, so we should arrive half an hour before the event. Afterall, we are grand patron ticket holders."

"Oh! Are you sure that I am as well?" Ada asked, very concerned.

"Absolutely, Oscar knows that you will be accompanying us to the event. He is very fond of you. I spoke with him at length yesterday when I stopped by to drop off the charity board information."

"And I am fond of him as well. He is a rather distinguished but warm individual. I found that to be quite contradictory of what I have mostly encountered in the art world."

"Yes, he most certainly is that. Well, let's say we will be in front of your house at 5:15 this evening. No need for you to walk across the road in an evening gown. I can't wait to see you in the dress, Ada. You'll no doubt look beautiful!" She stood up to leave.

"Aww, thank you, Susan. I appreciate you going shopping with me."

"You are welcome. I enjoyed our time together." She smiled

and walked away

Ada decided to eat breakfast and drink some coffee to avoid a caffeine headache later. She didn't need anything to spoil this evening's festivities. After an egg, avocado toast, and a few fresh strawberries, Ada headed to the shower. Her hair was taking priority today with some extra conditioning and she did make certain to exfoliate and moisturize her skin. Looking in the mirror, she wished that the skin on her face and arms had been sun-kissed just a bit more, but a little bronzing oil could make a difference. Ada wanted her make-up applied just right as well. She found it best to let the moisturizer sink in for a couple of hours before putting on foundation, so for now she'd settle for blow-drying her hair.

Ada sat down and opened her laptop. There really wasn't anything else to do at this point except wait. She had two more hours until time to get ready. She checked out Facebook and Instagram to get caught up with friends, family, and other people she followed. Not much was going on. She hesitated, then did a google search for Calin Cooper. Nothing came up at first that had to do with him until she added the words "wanted", "imposter", and "dating website".

Of course, his name really wasn't Calin Cooper. He had changed it to avoid being found for fraud and assault and had managed to be on the run for over a year. He really did have a job at one point in accounting. The trouble seemed to have started when he took things too far with a secretary and was fired. After being hired at another firm, he not only embezzled money but was seeing multiple ladies from dating sites who accused him of sexual assault. Once the warrant was issued, he was on the run. Ada shivered and closed her laptop with a bang.

"Yuck! Yuck! Yuck!" She said aloud.

Ada turned on the television just to take her mind off him once and for all. There was no reason to revisit the unfortunate circumstances again. She reminded herself of her run this morning and her goal to manifest only good things in the future. Since this was July, there was a Hallmark Christmas movie on as part of their Christmas in July movie marathon. Ada was pretty sure she had seen this one. In fact, once the outside setting was shown, she was sure that she had. She and Troy had gone on a trip with Jackson and Daisy one year and accidentally stumbled across the very spot where this movie was filmed. After reading the placard detailing the filming, the girls were so excited that when they got back home, they had to look up the movie and insisted the guys watch it with them. Neither one was as impressed nor excited as the girls were, but they had been good sports about it. That was a special long weekend the four of them had together. The movie was filmed in winter, but they had gone in the summer. Bike riding and hiking took them to waterfalls and scenic lookouts. The Airbnb where they stayed had spectacular views of the mountains and the water. They had stayed up late at night looking up at the stars just like when they were teens back in high school.

The ending of the movie came just about the time Ada's alarm went off for her to start getting ready. She sighed and got off the couch. The first thing would be make-up and then hair. Ada went a little heavier than she usually did but not too much. The bronzer she had picked up at the drugstore was just right.

Thankfully, her magnetic eyelashes didn't give her trouble. She put part of her hair up as she had done so many years ago at the prom. Funny how it didn't really seem that long ago. There were enough curls to fall just right over her shoulders, and the drop earrings could be seen nicely as well. Ada took the evening gown off the hanger and stepped into it carefully. She had forgotten that it had a zipper, and nobody was there to help but she was able to zip it herself. The strappy heels were comfortable and for this Ada was glad. Nothing was worse than standing in painful shoes all evening long. Ada opened the closet door in her bedroom that had a full-length mirror on the back. She stood and took a long look at herself. For a minute, she wished that her mother could be there to see her, and even her dad. Ada figured it had to be normal even at her age to want your parents' approval. She took a slow spin and looked behind her as much as she could to see the back. The champagne color was prettier than she even remembered it at the store.

Picking up her cell phone, she texted Daisy and asked if she could Facetime. Daisy responded instantaneously saying yes, and Ada's cell rang.

"Wow! You had to be on top of your phone," laughed Ada.

"Of course! I was watching the time and figured you should be about ready. Your face looks beautiful, let's see the rest of you."

Ada put the phone down on her nightstand and stood back for Daisy to see. She did a slow spin.

Daisy squealed and clapped. "Girl, you look gorgeous! I knew that you would. Cinderella is going to the ball tonight!"

"Just wish my prince would notice me." Ada said it aloud before she even thought.

"Hey, listen to me. If Jason doesn't get it, he doesn't get it. You must know how much you're worth as a person. Not just on the outside, but especially on the inside. Please just go and have a grand time. Your piece of art is being auctioned off! You are on your way to being in the world of art like you've dreamed!

"Thank you, Daisy. You always make me feel so good about myself. And confident about life. I love you for that."

Ada suddenly heard a whistle. Jackson appeared on the phone. "Look at you! Ada, you're a vision! Have a great time tonight!"

Ada giggled. "Thanks, Jackson. I will!"

Daisy came back on the phone. "Okay, promise you'll call as soon as you're up tomorrow. I want to know every detail!"

"You know I will! Love you, my friend."

"Love you!"

As the call ended, Ada remembered one more thing she had to do. She went over to her dresser and put on some perfume. It was the kind she only wore for special occasions. Come to think of it, she couldn't remember the last time she had worn it. Maybe for Troy?

One last look in the mirror, a big breath, and, lastly, a smile. Closing the closet door, Ada added a few items to her clutch and was ready to go. She had timed things just right, so no rushing around was necessary, which meant she was able to be fully present and enjoy the moment. The lights were turned down low in the living room and kitchen, but the shadows no longer made her feel afraid. Robert and Susan were already waiting for her in the driveway. He was already opening the door to the car for her and motioning her inside.

"You look lovely, my dear. Your carriage awaits."

"You make me feel like a princess. Thank you."

Inside, there was soft jazz music playing and Susan turned around. "You are a princess." Ada smiled and thanked her.

The outside of Pacific Cove had been transformed for the evening. More fountains, plants, and lighting had been brought in to showcase the event. Robert pulled the car right up to the venue and a valet quickly opened the door for the ladies. They were escorted on red carpet to the door by men in tuxedos, then greeted by more cladly dressed gentlemen taking tickets and opening the doors. Inside, the lights were dim, but more lighting had been added, draped around tall plants and strung from the ceilings. Waiters and waitresses in classy black and white pantsuits were offering bubbling champagne in tall, fluted glasses. Ada took one happily, as did both Robert and Susan. They began walking about the gallery and chatting about the paintings that belonged to the special guest artist. Ada had already seen them when she visited with the class but was glad to have another look. Both Robert and Susan were interested in her interpretation of the pieces.

Several people stopped by to speak with Susan and Robert. She could tell that both were well respected in the community. Robert was a well-renowned professor of psychology and author of books relating to traumatic amnesia and therapeutic recovery of memory. Ada had learned this after spending more time with Susan and perusing the many books in their home. Susan, on the other hand, had authored several children's books and of course had given so much of her time to working on charitable events. Ada felt most grateful to know these special people.

"Good evening, friends," a voice came from behind Ada. Turning, she saw it was Oscar Ash. He looked rather debonair in his white tie and dark gray tuxedo. He greeted Susan and Robert and then turned to Ada and bowed as though he was in front of royalty. Ada couldn't help but blush. He took her hand and clasped the other on top. "You are a most beautiful sight. Come, let me show you how we have displayed the silent auction pieces. Yours in particular."

At that, Ada turned to follow Oscar, but as she did, she could feel the weight of eyes following her. Off to her right, she saw him.

Chapter 13

Jason was standing in the entrance to the main part of the room, dressed in a slim-fit, dark navy tuxedo with a white shirt and white tie. Ada's breath caught in her throat. She couldn't take her eyes off of him. He simply put his hand up and waved to her, and she did the same. She wanted to stare longer, but Oscar was beckoning her to follow. She was certain she'd have a chance to talk to Jason later. As she followed after Oscar, she could feel Jason's eyes on her all the way to the back of the room.

There were a multitude of people gathering to view the showcase pieces for the silent auction. Ada spotted her charcoal sketch immediately and was surprised with her emotional reaction to seeing the piece on display. The backs of her eyes pricked with hot tears, and she could feel goosebumps rising all over her body. She wasn't sure where the rush of emotion came from, but she thought it was perhaps because she felt validated as a real artist, or from the reminder of Troy.

A young couple and another gentleman came over and stood in front of her sketch. Oscar looked at her and smiled, leaning in to whisper, "That is when you know."

Still feeling a lump in her throat, Ada simply smiled and nodded.

Some people came to speak with Oscar, so Ada excused herself for a bit hoping to find Jason. She perused the other submissions and recognized two of the artist's names; they were both really well-known. How could she possibly be on the same wall as them? Of course, they were donations given for a good cause.

Ada never gave herself credit for much of anything. A time like this is when she'd like to have Daisy by her side. What if nobody bid on her piece? *How humiliating*, thought Ada. Robert or Susan would probably buy it just to save her from embarrassment.

One of the paintings, entitled "Always," appeared to be of a young mother and daughter sitting on a ridge watching a sunset. The sky was painted with yellow, orange, and purple hues, and the daughter's head was leaning on the mother's shoulder. The painting was minimalistic yet embodied such beauty. Ada would have liked to join them.

She felt a tickle in the back of her brain. Embodied Cognition—she remembered having a conversation with Troy about this very thing. When you stare at a piece of art long enough studying it, you begin to feel as if you are a part of the painting as well. That's one of the many things she missed about her husband. Their discussions. Both appreciated the interests of the other.

The artwork was spaced nicely in the gala, allowing each piece to breathe. The next one Ada looked at was abstract with its vigorous brush strokes and drips of paint. Only bright colors were used, and the title was "Interrupted," which she thought made perfect sense. Next, "Strings Attached" was a charcoal sketch of a violin imposed on musical notations and was quite beautiful. Ada could almost hear the violin concerto by Vivaldi being played.

In the middle of the room there were three sculptures. The first, "See Me," was a metal sculpture of an elephant and extremely well done. Most likely, a torch or chemical had been used to give the copper its warm color. As Ada made her way around the display, she caught a glimpse of another statue. It was of a nearly nude male and female in an embrace. The places where the bodies met covered any sensitive areas, however, the act was still highly suggestive.

This one was called "Amor." Ada blushed and was reminded that next week she would be sitting in front of actual naked bodies, sketching them. This was something that never before crossed her mind as being anything but natural for pursuing an art degree, but lately her mind had been on other things: her past with Troy and her future with . . . well, she wasn't sure at this point. Of course, that didn't keep her from dreaming at night, or even during the day for that matter.

A few people started moving her way, so to keep from feeling awkward, she quickly shuffled herself over to the last sculpture, which happened to be another abstract piece of art constructed of recycled materials. At first glance, it might have seemed to be a jumbled mess, but taking a closer look told a story. Small figures sat on what appeared to be park benches and all around them structures were being built in various stages, as though a town had suffered some ill fate and was trying to reconstruct itself.

"Maybe you could explain that one to me?" asked a quiet

voice from behind her. Ada was relaxed enough by now after her second glass of champagne that it didn't even startle her. She turned around and looked right into those blue eyes.

"Oh, it's you," she giggled slightly. Jason was staring at her intently but not saying a word. "So, I guess you're really wanting me to answer that?"

"Yes." He put his hands behind his back.

"You must look beyond the figure as a whole and study the smaller details. You see this right here? I'm seeing that as a park bench with a person sitting on it. And here's another one on this side of the street."

"You're really seeing streets?" Jason asked inquisitively.

Ada had to laugh. "It's just my interpretation."

"No, please do go on. I find this all fascinating."

In all honesty, Ada was really wishing he meant that he found her fascinating, but who was she kidding? "If you look here and here," Ada pointed several places. "Those appear to be buildings under construction. I'm thinking that there was either some force of nature that caused destruction in their city or town, thus the title, 'Restore.'"

Jason bent over the structure and even walked around it, seeming to study it from all angles. "I can see what you're saying, and I agree."

"Well, it's not like I'm right." Ada laughed, embarrassed. "Again, just my interpretation."

"And your interpretation is spot on, Ada!" They both turned to look at Lee standing beside them now. Ada had no idea that he would be in attendance. She wondered if it had something to do with his or his family's money.

"I happen to know the creator of this fine creation. He is none other than our very own Professor Aglio."

Ada gasped. "Really? He never said a thing about having a piece in the silent auction! How exciting. He's very talented, obviously, so I'm not terribly surprised." Turning to Jason she said, "Pardon me, allow me to introduce you both."

"Jason, this is Lee, who is in my art class. Lee, meet Jason, who is the baseball coach here at the University."

"Make that interim baseball coach, but it's nice to meet you, Lee." Jason stuck his hand out to him.

"Nice to meet you as well, Jason. I always liked baseball." The two shook hands. "Oh, did you play?" Jason asked.

"Not exactly, but I enjoy watching major league baseball."

"Yeah? Who do you root for?"

Lee, seeming to choke slightly on his drink, said, "Uh, the

Packers."

Ada could see that Jason was trying to hold back a smile.

"That's the NFL, but anyway. Nice meeting you. I want to say hello to Robert and Susan."

Ada felt like she had just witnessed a mini high school rivalry. It was almost comical. She was certain that Lee had to feel embarrassed right now, so she came to his rescue.

"Our Professor Aglio is something else, isn't he? I really enjoyed this first course. I'm sure the second will be just as wonderful!"

"Yes, for sure." Lee said sheepishly. He hadn't quite seemed to have recovered.

Fortunately, there was an announcement made for the guests to make their way to the dining area. Ada hadn't toured this part of the building on her last visit. The building seemed to go on and on. It was breathtaking. There were two long tables set with fine linens, table wear, and goblets. The dominant colors of blue and purple were highlighted with the centerpieces of flowers and accented with the greenery of wisteria. Large tapestries on the walls kept the noise level from reverberating in the marble floored room. The only lighting came from candles on the tables and wall sconces. Two sets of double French doors led out to a large private garden area with seating among large pots of flowers. There was lighting on all the trees throughout the garden, as well as the walkways. Ivy and clematis hung over the stone wall in large groups making for complete privacy. Music had been piped in as soon as they arrived and had followed them to their dinner. Ada thought she could see a band setting up outside and remembered Susan mentioning live music.

Lee had followed her the entire way, but he realized before she did that there were place cards with names. He didn't say anything, but just motioned slightly with his hand as if to tell her that he'd see her later.

Robert found Ada before she began to look for her name. "You're with us, so you may follow me."

"Oh good," said Ada, smiling. "I was beginning to feel anxious."

"No need for that," he smiled back.

Susan had already taken her seat. They were all sitting at the same table as Oscar and Professor Aglio. Ada felt quite honored. As they were getting seated, there appeared to be slight confusion with the cards and two couples. After some adjusting, Jason ended up sitting diagonally across from Ada, next to Robert. Ada was sat between Susan and another lady whom she had yet to meet.

After everyone had found their seats and had settled, Oscar stood to say a few words. "My most honored guests, thank you for attending Pacific Cove's Annual Gala Event. We're happy to showcase the work of our esteemed guest artist from New York, Ms. Olivia Dominic. The person next to Ada stood and everyone applauded. Ada was shocked. She couldn't believe that she was sitting next to such an accomplished artist. The class had spent time looking at her work when they were at the gallery recently and Professor Aglio mentioned that she had been a student of his years before when he taught back east. She was an attractive woman, late forties, well dressed without too much flair, as some artists are known to fashion themselves. She thanked him and acknowledged everyone before sitting down. Ada smiled at her.

Oscar continued. "I also want to thank Susan McGuire, board member, charity hostess, fundraiser extraordinaire, and my friend. We've had the most incredible donations this year, which will go to a charity near and dear to my heart, the children's new hospital wing right here in our very own town. I never had children of my own, so these are my children. Art and music are important in the healing process. Your generous dollars tonight will go to fund these very things in the new wing. Thank you once again for your generous support, please enjoy the food, the drinks, the music, and certainly the art."

"Here, here!" the crowd responded.

The music was turned up again and the food began being served, beginning with a most delicious looking mixed greens salad with Roma tomatoes, Julienne cucumbers, toasted pine nuts, fresh herbs, shaved parmesan, and balsamic vinaigrette. It happened to be Ada's favorite combination for a salad. After her second bite she finally had an opportunity to say something to Olivia. Everyone else, including Jason, was talking amongst themselves.

"I so admire your work. Your level of talent is unmatched," said Ada. Olivia turned completely around to face her.

"You are too kind." She smiled. "Thank you. And you are?"

"Ada Cameron. I'm here taking summer courses from Professor Aglio. I'm an elementary teacher in Riverton."

"How wonderful! My mother is a retired schoolteacher. She taught 8th grade math for twenty years and then worked for the federal government for another twenty!"

"So, she ended up having two careers?"

Setting her glass down, she looked again at Ada. "Why, yes, she did. Are you considering a change as well?"

"I've not taught for twenty years, but I would like to pursue a career in the art world. Not just my own personal work but that of being surrounded by other artists and working in such a place as this."

"Then I think that's exactly what you should do! I believe in doing what makes us happy, Ada."

One of the waitresses came at that time to remove the salad plates and another was there to replace them with the main meals. Ada had ordered roasted beef tenderloin, garlic mashed potatoes, and honey glazed carrots. The meal was delicious. Ada realized how hungry she was after being nearly halfway through her meal. She looked up to see Jason looking at her.

Ada blushed. "Am I eating too fast or something? I must admit that I am rather hungry." She wiped the corners of her mouth with her napkin. Nobody else seemed to be paying attention to the two of them.

"Not at all. I just wanted to ask if you have enjoyed the evening so far?"

"Yes, and you?"

"I am. Even though I'm a sports person at heart, I do have an appreciation for the arts." He took a bite of his food.

"I can see that," commented Ada, and she took a bite as well.

Their conversation came to a quick end as the wait staff returned to refill glasses and remove more plates.

Susan leaned over to Ada, "I hope you saved room for dessert. The pastry chef, Claire, is the best! One of her specialties is white chocolate cheesecake."

"You know," said Ada, "Daisy and I have an agreement. No matter how miserable we are, passing on dessert is never an option." They both laughed.

Susan was right. The cheesecake was divine. The crust combined with the caramel sauce on top made it a perfect complement to the dinner, and it wasn't overly sweet. As they ate their dessert, there was more chatter at the table about Olivia and her artwork. She was most gracious when thanking everyone for the many compliments. At one point in front of everyone, she had even gushed about Ada's charcoal sketch, which several had also drawn positive comments. Ada hadn't realized that Olivia had seen her work since she hadn't said anything about it during their conversation earlier. Of course, they really hadn't talked too much, though.

The praise made Ada feel quite good. Too bad Jason was preoccupied with talking to the person on his right. He hadn't heard a thing she said. Oh well. She was beginning to get used to this scenario with the two of them.

Chapter 14

Oscar stood once again and asked all the guests to make their way into the main art gallery for the announcement of door prizes, raffles, and winners of the silent auction. When they reached the gallery, there were chairs set up for everyone this time. Susan made her way up front with Oscar and Ada sat with Robert. Area businesses, groups, and individuals donated the giveaways, and they were all such nice contributions. One older couple won a chef for the night, another a tour of a winery, and Ada even won a cooking class for 2 with the Italian restaurant she frequented. She turned to Robert with a questioning look. She had not entered any of the drawings; how could she have won?

"Susan entered you in everything," he said with a smile. Ada paraded in front of everyone to the front of the room to receive her winning certificate. Who would she take with her? Maybe Daisy?

There were plenty of other prizes, including a golf getaway, personal trainer sessions, spa treatments, and restaurant gift certificates. The community had been most generous, although Susan had already mentioned that it usually was.

Next, Susan and Oscar took turns announcing winners of the silent auction. As they announced, they didn't say who won what piece. They simply read out the names of the winners and asked them to meet with Oscar to pick up their artwork at the conclusion of the evening's events. Jason was one name that they had called. Ada was curious which piece he had bid on. Maybe the recycled sculpture of Professor Aglio's that she had talked to him about earlier?

Susan then gave a small concluding speech, speaking eloquently about the amount raised and how it would benefit the children's wing at the hospital. She thanked all of the attendees and donators, ending with a quote to emphasize the positive impact that charitable giving has not only on the receiver but on the giver as well: "As Jim Rohn said, 'Only by giving are you able to receive more than you already have.'"

After a round of applause, everyone stood, eagerly chatting with one another, and then made their way back through the dining room. The last of the dishes were being collected and Ada could hear some music beginning to play outdoors. She always loved to dance with Troy. Sometimes the four friends would go out to a club for drinks and end up dancing to several songs. Even if there wasn't a dance floor, they'd make their own. Before joining everyone in the garden, Ada wanted to freshen up just in case she did happen to dance with someone later. It appeared there were several ladies with the same idea, so the room was rather busy. After a space in front of the mirror became available, Ada applied a new coat of lipstick and repositioned her hair a bit. *Inhale. Exhale.* She thought to herself as she looked at her reflection. She had a sudden onset of butterflies in her stomach again.

Ada made her way out to the garden. By now, the sky was totally dark except for the scattered stars. She saw Robert and Susan dancing among the handful of other couples. She felt a bit awkward by herself with no date to accompany her, although she also wanted to feel confident enough to not necessarily need someone to lean on. Ada just happened to enjoy companionship a lot. She noticed an empty table and sat down quickly. A waitress came by and offered a glass of wine, then another. After her second one, Ada was feeling a little buzzed. She could see Jason standing by the fountain drinking his own glass of wine. Surely, he had seen her sitting by herself? Why hadn't he even bothered to come over? Ada sighed aloud, although no one could have heard over the music. She stood up a little too quickly and the room began to spin. Determined not to sit back down, she steadied herself with the back of the chair until things began to come into focus. Then, she made her way toward him, not even sure what she was going to say or do. He didn't notice her until she stepped too close to the landscaping and caught her shoe on the corner of a rock. This sent her flying in his direction, which did catch his attention. He set his glass down quickly and caught her just in time.

"That makes twice you've caught me," Ada said looking up at him, her words a little slurred.

"I guess so. Are you okay?"

Ada suddenly felt embarrassed and stood up straight, pushing away from him. "Oh, yes. Silly me. It's quite dark out here, and I wasn't looking down." Ada heard herself ramble. Why did she tend to do this with Jason? "Um, anyway. Would you like to dance?"

"Uh, I . . . uh . . . sure." He led her toward the front of the garden where the band was playing. They had just ended one song and started another. It happened to be "My Funny Valentine." Ada loved that one, although she had never danced to it. As the music swelled, she put her head on his chest and swore she could hear his heart beating faster and faster. Maybe she was having an effect on him. Right when she was feeling comfortable, Jason pushed her away from him and tried to twirl her. It was like he knew she could hear his fast heart rate and didn't want her to. The twirl was not a good idea, though, after two glasses of champagne earlier and three glasses of wine, and Jason seemed to understand immediately. He reached out to steady her and then guided her to a table to sit down. Ada felt angry. Why did he insist on ruining moments for them?

"Sorry, Ada. I should have realized."

"Should have realized what exactly?" Ada asked rather snippily. "That I was drunk? Because that wasn't it, Jason."

"I wasn't insinuating that you were," he said quietly.

A waitress came by to offer more wine. Jason declined but Ada took another glass, pressing it to her lips and taking big sips. This was so unlike her, and she felt like an immature schoolgirl. She so wished Daisy could be here right now.

Jason didn't say a word. He looked to the band and simply said, "Great musicians, don't you think?"

Ada put her glass down a little too hard but managed to say nicely, "Yes, they are."

The two sat in silence for a while and listened to about three more selections. Ada drank the rest of her water instead of the glass of wine. After the more upbeat songs were played, Donny Hathaway's "A Song for You" started. Ada knew it five notes in. It was her and Troy's favorite song. Several artists had done covers over the years, and the guy singing now was quite good.

Ada leaned up so Jason could hear her. "Could we try again?"

Jason turned quickly around. "What's that?"

"Dancing? Could we try it again? I'm feeling better, and I happen to like this song a lot."

Jason appeared hesitant. "Are you sure? You didn't seem to feel well a little while ago?"
He waited for a response, but looking at Ada, he didn't have to wait for one. He stood and offered his hand to her.

They were among three of the only couples dancing. Ada didn't even care. This time she didn't want to get close to Jason and put her head against his shoulder, instead, just swaying along with him. Her hands resting in his were warm.

The singer crooned in the background:

"'Cause we're alone now

And I'm singing this song to you

You taught me precious secrets

Of a true love withholding nothing

You came out in front when I was hiding

Now I'm so much better

And if my words don't come together

Listen to the melody

'Cause my love is in there hiding"

Ada closed her eyes as she listened, and just for a moment, she was in Troy's arms. It was her safe haven, her happy place, her escape from the world.

"I love you in a place

Where there's no space or time

I love you for my life

You're a friend of mine

And when my life is over

Remember when we were together

We were alone

And I was singing this song to you"

The music ended and Ada opened her eyes, looking up into the blue eyes staring back at her. Not Troy's, but Jason's.

Somehow, she was still able to hold onto those same feelings.

Jason led her back over to the table, a little more quickly than Ada thought was necessary.

"I'll be back in a minute," he said. Ada watched him walk inside and figured he was visiting the men's room.

"You two look nice together out there." Ada looked up to see Susan standing there. "Are you having a nice time?"

"Oh, hi! Yes, it was a nice evening. You did such a wonderful job speaking earlier." "Why, thank you, Ada. Coming from you, that means a great deal."

The band started an upbeat song that must have been one Robert liked because he was motioning to Susan on the dance floor.

"Guess my partner is calling me," Susan said in almost a sing-song voice. She began dancing before reaching him. *Those two are such a cute couple*, thought Ada. Where was Jason? He should have been back by now.

Just then, Lee appeared. He had spent most of the night dancing with some of the older ladies who seemed to think he was the most charming man alive. For some reason this seemed to please him a great deal. Maybe he had issues with his mom and was trying to make up for something. Anyway, she wasn't a psychologist and couldn't analyze if she tried.

"Where did your date go?" He said, looking around the room.

Ada looked up, "My date? I didn't come with Jason. We simply shared a couple of dances. Besides, I see that you've been entertaining the ladies all evening." Ada began straightening her dress so as not to look that interested in what she was observing about him.

"You say that as though I was doing it all in jest. I happen to like older women. I think they are most attractive in their knowledge and sophistication. Take your friend, Susan, for example. Wasn't she charming earlier?"

"Of course she was. So, tell me, Lee. Are you close to your mother?" Ada no sooner heard herself ask the question that she regretted it.

"Ha! I knew it. You are trying to diagnose me with some psychological challenges or unhealthy attachment disorder to my mother!" He said, guffawing.

"No, I'm sorry and do apologize," she laughed awkwardly. "I was merely kidding you." She could feel beads of perspiration on her forehead.

Lee looked her in the eyes. "If you must know, my mother and I had a marvelous relationship. I took a great deal after her. She was the bell of the ball, loved everyone she saw, found them all fascinating no matter where they came from or what the background happened to be. She was loving and accepting. She encouraged me to be the same way. 'See the world through colored glasses, Lee,' she'd say. 'It's so much more beautiful that way! Nobody should be the same. How boring it would be!'"

He started looking reflective and sat down in a chair. "She passed away from cancer three years ago, thus, the reason I have yet to land anywhere. My father is a decent enough guy. He loved her a great deal and is lost without her. My sister is happily married to a doctor, and they have twin boys, just turned 8. Cute as buttons.

"My mother is the one who inherited money, although she worked her whole life for it, too. She was a famous author." When Lee mentioned his mom's name Ada could have fallen off her chair. No doubt she had heard of the writer! At least half of the books she owned at home were penned by none other than Lee's mother!

Lee continued to tell her about his family. His father was a retired engineer and spent most of his days playing with the grandchildren who lived nearby. Lee always made sure to spend at least two weeks at home four times a year. His father seemed to understand the need Lee had for staying busy and traveling the world, dabbling in art classes. His mother had always hoped he would become a famous painter but even Lee knew his talents would not take him that far.

Ada was beginning to understand him so much better now, and he was growing on her a bit more than he had in the beginning of their meeting each other. Something about a wealthy man and confidence never seemed to entice her, but this more vulnerable side did.

"How about one dance, Ada?" Lee asked.

"Oh, I don't know Lee. I was thinking of heading home."

"What? Already? No way! Not until you have at least one dance with me!"

"Okay," Ada said laughing. He almost sounded too sweet for her to resist.

Thank goodness the next song was a fast one. Lee led her out to the floor, and he had her smiling the entire time. Maybe Lee wasn't so bad after all, as a friend that is. He even enticed Robert and Susan to get back out on the dance floor. At one point in the song, they switched partners. Robert was quite the dancer himself and swung Ada around to the beat of the music. Thank goodness she was no longer dizzy!

Afterwards, they both were happy to have a seat and grab a drink of water. Lee talked a bit more about the sailboat outing toward the end of the week. Ada kept changing her mind about wanting to go, but Lee had all but insisted. The weather promised to be perfect all week long and it was the best opportunity for everyone's schedules since class was cancelled Friday due to Professor Aglio leaving for a trip.

"What do you even do during a whole day of sailing?" Ada asked.

Lee laughed, "There are lots of things: sipping specialty drinks, anchoring and hiking secluded beaches, catching fish, rocking out to great tunes."

"Okay, everything except for the catching fish part does sound appealing."

"I promise, if you join us, you will not have to touch any fish," he teased.

They would be setting sail Friday morning and return before sunset. Daisy was due at about that time, so it should work out perfectly should she decide to go. Lee was insistent, but Ada wasn't sure yet. It really all depended on what happened to her and Jason. Speaking of, where was he?

Chapter 15

Ada decided to wander around and see if she could find Jason. Most everyone was outside in the gardens by now except for the crew inside cleaning things up from dinner. The tables and chairs had already been put away in storage. Ada still couldn't get over how much room Oscar had here. As she made her way into the gallery, the last of the silent auction items were being picked up by the highest bidders. Someone had already taken her painting. She rounded the corner and almost collided with a waitress who had served her wine earlier.

"Ms. Cameron . . . Ada Cameron?" The waitress asked.

". . . Yes?"

"Hi, I was just coming to give this to you. A gentleman asked that I pass this along. He left a little while ago. I'm sorry that I couldn't bring it out to you sooner. Our catering boss wanted things cleaned up asap." She held out a note, tilting her head to the side and smiling sweetly as a way of apology.

"Oh, that's fine. I certainly understand. Thank you so much." Ada took the note and continued walking. She stopped beneath some light so she could see better and opened the folded paper.

In pen it read, "I'm so sorry I had to leave early Ada. You really did look beautiful tonight. Jason"

What in the world? What guy simply leaves the ball early? The prince never did, and he sure was no prince! Ada felt warmth start in her legs and work its way up her body. It was not the exciting kind of warmth. This was anger, pure anger. How dare he just leave her sitting out in the garden after their dance without so much as a goodbye! No, no way. He wasn't going to do this to her. She took her phone out and texted Susan that she was getting an Uber home and not to worry, that she was simply tired and perhaps had too much wine and would talk to her tomorrow.

Ada did a quick check of Jason's exact address and then opened the Uber app on her cell.

The driver must have been aware of the event and been close by because he arrived within two minutes. After verifying the correct car, Ada was on her way to Jason's apartment.

Ada was counting to twenty and backward to zero repeatedly. Somehow counting to ten wasn't doing anything. She wasn't exactly positive where the strong emotions were coming from, but this connection they seemed to have since her arrival or at least her perception of it . . . well, Ada was determined to get some answers this time. The car pulled up in front of Jason's duplex, so she had to stop counting.

The driver must have sensed that she was upset. "Hoping the rest of your evening is better, ma'am."

Ma'am . . . ugh! thought Ada, but she just said, "Thank you so much," and exited the car Ada almost forgot to grab her purse but remembered at the last minute before completely losing the door.

Heading to Jason's front door, she had to walk carefully in her heels because the parking lot was gravel. After making it to the sidewalk, she took the last two steps up to the door and knocked loudly three times. When there was no immediate answer, Ada repeated her assault on the door. This time the porch light came on and the door opened almost simultaneously.

"Ada?" Jason was standing with his tux pants still on and his white shirt unbuttoned halfway down, showing a sliver of toned chest. The apartment was dark except for the range light over the stove and a light on upstairs in what she assumed was his bedroom.

Ada didn't wait for an invitation. She brushed past him into the living room and stood with her chin held out. She didn't say a word but stood with her hands along her sides. The silence between them was made more intense by the darkness.

"Why?" Ada's voice was shaking at this point. She couldn't believe the tears were starting to fall.

"Ada . . . there are things you don't know about me—"

"Then talk to me! Tell me! Why do you keep them hidden? What could possibly be so bad that you can't share?" She sobbed.

"I just . . . I can't. It's so complicated. I wouldn't even know where to start."

"Please" Ada moved closer and put her hands on his chest. Then, she moved his shirt to the side, freeing up the side of his neck, and began kissing him.

All Jason could do was moan. He took her arms gently and moved them above her head. She didn't stop kissing him. He turned her toward the wall and pressed her against it. Lowering his face to hers, he found her lips and kissed them gently. She opened her mouth for him, and he found her tongue. They moved carelessly around the room, partly because she wanted to continue, and he was trying to stop. They bumped against the couch and fell over on it together. He was on top of her, and she wouldn't let go. They kissed harder and longer. Ada felt the butterflies release from her stomach. She had not felt this way since Troy.

"Take me upstairs," Ada pleaded with him.

This broke his reverie. He quickly got up. In the light filtering through the windows from the street, she could see him rubbing the back of his neck.

"Ada, we can't do this. I'm sorry."

"You know, you keep saying that, but I don't think you are. Otherwise, you'd explain yourself. We're here now. Obviously, we care for each other, and we both want the same thing. What is it? Do you have a wife? A fiancée?"

"God, no, nothing like that."

"Then, what?" Now Ada was standing again. She could see the pained expression on his face. Something terrible must have happened to him, but why couldn't he talk to her?

She tried once more to embrace him, but he stepped aside. This hurt Ada so badly. She looked for her purse, spotting it on the floor. Picking it up, she headed for the door.

"I'll leave then," said Ada. She could barely talk.

"You can't walk home alone at this time of night."

"I'll call another Uber."

"Don't be silly. I'll drive you."

"Oh, so now I'm silly," she scoffed.

"Please, Ada," he sighed. She relented.

Jason buttoned his shirt and grabbed his keys. They went outside and he opened the car door for her. She didn't thank him. On the way back to her bungalow, they sat in silence. It was only a five-minute drive, but the tension made it seem longer. What started out as a promising night had turned sour. The difference between her and Cinderella, though, was that the prince knew where she lived and was dropping her off instead of taking her to the castle to live happily-ever-after.

The car pulled up in front of Ada's bungalow. "Goodnight, Ada," Jason said softly.

"Goodnight," was all Ada managed to say. She didn't even look back as she unlocked her door. He waited until she got inside, and then she heard his car leave. Ada went over to the chair, plopped down, and cried her eyes out. After about half an hour her phone rang; it was Susan.

Ada hesitated to answer but thought she better, or both Susan and Robert would soon be knocking on her door.

She took a minute to clear her throat and try to sound normal as possible. "Hi Susan!"

"Hi Ada. We're finally on our way home and wanted to make sure you made it safely. Sorry, we don't mean to act like your parents, but we care for you so much."

"Aww, thank you. You guys are the best!" Ada tried to act cheerful. "I made it home just fine and getting ready to turn in now. Whew! That was some event. I can't believe how wiped out I feel. You guys are impressive dancers, you sure out did me." She laughed slightly.

"Oh, you know. Just trying to keep up with all of you young folks. Well, get some sleep and we'll talk later. Sweet dreams."

"Goodbye, Susan."

Sweet dreams are unlikely tonight, thought Ada.

Ada removed her shoes and earrings and put her dress on the hanger and in the closet. She didn't really want to see any memories of tonight once she woke up in the morning. Not that the events wouldn't be ever-present in her mind anyway. She jumped into the shower to remove the extra layers of makeup off and the dried tears. Water always felt like it washed away troubles as well, at least part of them. She put on her coziest pajama short set and crawled into bed, pulling the cozy covers on top of her.

Reaching the light, she couldn't help but think how well this morning had started off with her run and how she had timed everything perfectly leading up to the event. Then, Ada started comparing those things with how the evening had ended from the moment she read Jason's note and her ride over to his apartment, their conversation, the kissing. Oh my gosh, that kissing.

Maybe for tonight, instead of mulling over what might have been she'd focus on those fifteen minutes of pure passion. She turned out the light and closed her eyes, smiling.

Chapter 16

Ada climbed out of bed earlier than she had anticipated. She must have had enough glasses of water at the gala, plus she made sure to down another two before bed, so no headache at all this morning. Just sadness.

She made herself some black coffee and toast, then sat down with her laptop. Ada clicked away on her keyboard for about fifteen minutes, making some notes on a small pad of paper. She had also texted two different people. After that, she closed her laptop and went to get dressed. It was another sunny day and Ada was grateful. Today she was going to do something just for her! There were just a couple of people she needed to get a green light from, and then the adventure could begin!

Ada wanted to sit on the front porch while she waited, so she grabbed her purse and keys. Robert and Susan had gotten up super early to antique shop at an annual flea market nearby, so she'd already heard back from Susan. That was one returned text. Next, was the lady responding to her email. Check. Ada began biting the skin around her newly manicured nails when her phone dinged. She almost jumped. This was the last response she was waiting for, and it was good. Check.

Now it was official. Ada was on her way to getting a puppy! She had been wanting one for years, and she and Troy had begun looking, before his accident ended that. Even though she had the run-in with Calin, getting a dog wasn't for security purposes. It was for Ada, for pure companionship and joy.

She felt giddy. Ada had seen a flyer at the University about a dog that needed rehomed but hadn't given it too much thought at the time. For whatever reason, though, she seemed to dream all night long of being in a field surrounded by puppies romping and playing. She was even giggling in her sleep, the cause of her early awakening. Ada took this as a sign.

Ada had wanted to be certain that Marilyn, the owner of the home, was okay with Ada having a dog in the home. Of course, the dog, Maisy was potty-trained already which was a real plus, and she was small. Thankfully, Marilyn was fine with it. Ada also wanted to check and see if Susan would be able to let Maisy out while she was in class. Not only did she agree, but she also said she'd keep her over with them during that time. This was really going to work out great!

The poster at the University had advertised a beautiful eight-month-old Maltese who had been returned due to the owner having an unknown dog allergy. The woman who posted the ad assured Ada that Maisy would be waiting for her when she arrived. It would take approximately half an hour to get there, and Ada was so excited. She couldn't decide whether to stop and purchase things before or after. Probably after because Maisy might already have some things of her own. Ada put directions in her phone and took off.

The music she had played at first was a little too sad and slow. No need to keep being reminded about yesterday. She switched to her upbeat summer workout playlist and was soon bouncing in her seat and singing along. The drive seemed short and quite simple. There were only two roads off the main one. The house sat back against the woods and the driveway was outlined with trees the entire way. She could see some smaller children riding toy cars in the large driveway, so she parked away from them and walked to the side door.

"Are you here for the puppy?" One of the children asked as they rode in circles.

"Yes, as a matter of fact I am. Did I come to the right place?" Ada smiled at the young child.

The little boy laughed and stopped riding. He got out of his toy car and ran toward the door. "I'll get Mommy for you."

"Thank you."

The little girl kept riding her pink Barbie car and looking at Ada. She seemed a bit shyer. "I sure like your Barbie car!" Ada told her. She didn't say anything. Ada then added, "And you are an excellent driver!"

To this, the girl looked at Ada and said, "That's what my Daddy said."

"Hello! I'm sorry I wasn't out to greet you!" An attractive brunette with her hair in a ponytail came carrying the cutest puppy in her arms that Ada had ever seen. The little boy was following behind.

"Are you taking Maisy home with you?" The boy asked, peering at Ada. "I am. Is that okay?"

"Yeah," and he went back to riding his toy car.

Ada turned back to the puppy, "Oh my gosh, she is so sweet!" Ada's voice was pitched higher than she knew it could go.

"She really is the cutest thing and has the best personality." The woman immediately handed the dog to Ada.

Maisy began licking Ada's face and neck and then tucked herself beneath Ada's chin. "I love her already!" Ada beamed.

The woman chuckled. "I'm not surprised, and I believe she feels the same way about you!"

Ada could hardly bring herself to look away from the dog but reached into her pocket for an envelope which she handed to the woman. "Here is the payment for her. Thank you so very much."

"Oh, we're just so happy she gets to go to a good home. I do have a bag of goodies that go with her if you give me a minute."

"Sure!" As she waited, Ada couldn't help but daydream a little. Here she was at a lovely home with two children and holding a dog. She sighed softly.

"Here you go. There is some food, and I jotted down how much she is eating right now. There are a few toys too. Also, I put the veterinarian records in for you as well. She's current."

"I appreciate that," said Ada.

"Bye sweet girl, said the woman, giving the puppy a tousle on the head. "Take care." With that, she turned and started talking to her kids.

Ada got Maisy to settle on the front seat beside her and did a search for the closest pet store. It was only ten minutes down the road, so they didn't have far to go. There was a basic collar and leash in the bag, but Ada wanted something nicer for her new friend. She put Maisy in a shopping cart and then two headed inside. Several people stopped to ooh and aah over her "baby." *So, this must also be what it's like when you have a human baby*, thought Ada.

Ada and Maisy went up and down every aisle for dogs to make sure they didn't miss anything good. Ada was able to get Maisy a soft adjustable pink and white harness with matching leash. They sold the same food that Maisy was eating, so she also decided to go ahead and get another bag. New matching dog bowls, a comfy bed (even though Maisy would be sleeping with her), and lots of toys later, they were ready to check out. Ada put the new harness on the ball of white fur before they got into the car. Maisy was so exhausted by the shopping that she fell asleep before they were out of the parking lot.

This really is exactly what I needed, Ada thought. It wasn't just a distraction, well, maybe a slight one, but also something that she had wanted to do for a while now. The time seemed right. Looking over at Maisy, she was positive.

As Ada was pulling into the driveway, Maisy jumped awake as if to say, "Oh we're home!" As soon as Ada opened the car door, she jumped out and started sniffing around. Ada wanted her to get used to being in a new yard. Maisy immediately squatted.

"Good girl, Maisy," Ada told her.

Two large bags and a puppy were no easy task to get inside. Once Ada managed to get in and get the door shut, she removed the leash, and Maisy began investigating every part of the apartment. Ada laughed at how Maisy kept looking up at her as if to say she approved.

There was a knock at the door. Although curious, Maisy didn't bark. It was Susan, and she had a few containers in her hands.

"Hi neighbor! I thought you could use a little dinner after your big day!"

Ada held the door for her. "You are right about that!"

"Aww, look at this doll baby." Susan put the containers down and sat down on the couch to love on Maisy.

"That seems to be the normal reaction," Ada said while laughing.

"How about you eat and—what is the name?

"Maisy," stated Ada.

"Maisy and I will play. Right, Maisy?" Susan threw a ball for the puppy to retrieve.

The dinner looked delicious, and Ada didn't know what to eat first. Susan had fixed meatloaf, mashed potatoes, green beans, and rolls. As Ada ate, Maisy came into the kitchen to get a drink of water and then curled up in her bed with a toy lion.

Susan joined Ada at the table. "She is just a darling little puppy."

"I know. It seemed so random to do this today, but I've . . . Troy and I were planning on getting a dog. And that dream of mine, like I texted you this morning, couldn't have been more vivid."

"I'm happy for you. Dogs are truly man's and woman's best friends." She smiled. "We had a dog up until a year ago but had to put him down. He was old and sick."

"I'm sorry," Ada said, furrowing her brow and tilting her head to the side.

"Thank you. Even though they are always gone too soon,

I still feel like they're worth having, though. The love they bring to your lives is something else. Who else gets that happy when you come home?" She looked over at Maisy and then back at Ada. "Ada, may I ask you something?"

"Of course," Ada said, taking a bite of her roll.

"Did something happen last night to make you leave the event early? You seemed to be having such a good time until. . . well, later in the evening."

"You know, Susan. I feel close enough to you that I can be totally honest." Ada exhaled. "I have very strong feelings for Jason, and I thought he had them for me, but something is just not right."

Ada spent the next half an hour filling Susan in on the entire evening from the beginning, even from the first moment of she and Jason seeing each other and their discussion on the art piece. She wasn't too specific on the part at Jason's apartment to spare Susan any embarrassment, although Ada figured she probably could have relayed every detail, and Susan would have been perfectly comfortable. There was something about Susan that alleviated all fears. She was a reactor like her mother, and a good listener who never offered to say anything unless prompted. As Ada finished her outline of the evening, Susan reached over and brushed away the single tear that had fallen from Ada's eye. She hadn't planned on shedding any more tears over this, but sharing it with someone was almost cathartic.

They sat in silence for a few minutes. Susan probably wanted to make sure that Ada had said all that she wanted to say.

Finally, Susan spoke. "I'm so very sorry for the pain you have experienced and are experiencing, Ada. I can't begin to imagine losing the love of your life. Just hearing you talk about Troy these past few weeks makes me realize what an incredible person he was. I can see why you see Jason in a similar light. He, too, is kind and caring. I don't pretend to know what kind of experience Jason himself has had to shut you out of his life that way. It's obvious that he has feelings for you as well. What kind of pain did he go through that did not permit him to love again? I don't understand it either. I just know that he is missing out terribly by not allowing himself to be cared for by someone as lovely as you, someone who could possibly understand his pain. Have you even talked to him about Troy?"

"I can't talk to him about much of anything, Susan. He simply closes and refuses. It's maddening. Part of me wants to keep on trying and the other part is too tired of trying. There really is no need since I'm returning home at the end of summer.

"Sometimes people choose to live in their own darkness.

I'm beginning to think that Jason may be one of those people."

"Well, I feel honored that you could share these things with me. I care for you so deeply. Both Robert and I have talked about feeling a connection with you like a daughter."

Ada took Susan's hand this time. "I feel the exact same way. There is no possible way I could ever sufficiently thank the two of you for all you've done. My time here is so much richer because of getting to know you both."

Susan stood shaking off Ada's grip. "Okay, now you're going to make me cry. Enough of this," she laughed.

At that, Maisy got up and began running around. "I think I'll take her on a walk," said Ada. "Thank you for the delicious meal and fabulous company!" She gave Susan a big hug.

"Anytime, my sweet girl! See you later, Maisy."

While Ada rinsed some dishes and put leftovers away, Maisy ate her own dinner, and later the two of them went for a walk. Once back from their walk, they sat together on the porch swing, the day almost over. Ada held Maisy close, giving her kisses on the head. She couldn't have envisioned this day yesterday morning, but that was life, wasn't it? Trying to predict day to day was a joke. There was absolutely no way anyone could know for sure what might happen minute by minute. Sometimes things turned out great and other times they were awful. Ada never liked rollercoasters and for good reason. They were too much like life. It wasn't that she didn't like spontaneity. Sure, the surprise romantic beach picnic or weekend trip, which was great. It was the everyday occurrences that could drive you crazy. Things would be going along super for a few days and then, watch out! Suddenly, life could take a turn for the worst.

Sometimes Ada found herself waiting for something bad to happen during a particularly good run. *Just wait, it's bound to change*, her mind will tell her. That was one trait she didn't like about herself, seeing the glass half empty instead of half full. She was extremely passionate and loving, everyone said so, but she knew in her heart of hearts that a more positive outlook would make her life easier to cope.

"Okay, Maisy. Things are getting way too philosophical out here. How about we call it a night?"

Maisy gave her a big lick on the cheek as if to say, "thought you'd never ask."

Ada laughed. The two companions walked into the house beneath a sky full of stars.

Chapter 17

The entire class arrived early this morning. It was almost comical. Ada made the excuse that she got a new puppy and had to make sure the sitter was squared away. Not that there was much truth in that since Susan was certainly an expert in caring for a dog. A couple of others had reasons as well, but some just flat out said they couldn't wait to get started on the nude drawings and it was all they could think about the entire weekend! Ada had no idea how they could say such things without turning dark red. Sometimes artists were the zaniest people. She tried to laugh it off and act like she totally understood so not to appear too prudish.

Professor Aglio was off to the side talking to a young man

and woman and Ada thought perhaps they were the models. Soon the two disappeared into a side door and he began to speak to the class. The room had been divided in half with easels spaced evenly in a wide circle around the center where each model would be sitting, standing, or lying down. The students' names were already on the easels, so it was easy to find where they would begin. The professor said that since they had three days to sketch, the first day would begin with a warm-up pose where the model will hold a pose for two to five minutes, and you do a quick sketch of them, followed by one for twenty minutes, and then forty minutes. As they drew, Professor Aglio would be walking around making observations and giving feedback. The second and third days would be spent sketching a pose by the male model and a pose by the female model. The Professor was quick to remind everyone that not all become expert drawers of the human body. It would take practice and skill. He simply wanted students to learn and experience this historical part of art, especially with Greeks who placed so much emphasis on the naked body.

The class took their seats and began chatting as the models came back into the room wearing robes. They smiled at the class and even joked a bit to break the ice. Both were probably in their mid-thirties. Ada couldn't imagine being naked in front of a group of strangers. It seemed like a nightmare, especially to sit in the same position for hours at a time when the pay wasn't all that great, so she heard. The female happened to be her first subject and Ada was glad. It would be easier to adjust, she thought. Professor Aglio stood in the middle of the room and announced that each model would choose a pose and hold for two minutes, during which time the students would draw.

This format continued for about an hour. Afterwards, Dr. Aglio thanked the models, pleaded with them to return tomorrow, and everyone laughed and applauded. The models put their robes on, waved, and left the room. Their professor told the class to break for lunch and meet back in an hour. Everyone sighed and started talking to each other as though they hadn't spoken in years.

Ada was so hungry. She had only eaten half a muffin this morning. Most of the students opted for a Reuben or Rachel for lunch since their favorite cook Arnie was there. He made the best sandwiches out of anyone! Those also happened to be Troy's and Ada's number one choices back in college. They also had a favorite cook.

"Good choice, Ada!"

She turned around and it was Lee leaning over her to grab his order. "Oh yeah! They're the best, aren't they?" Ada liked Lee, especially since she had more of his story now. It was more of how you'd like a big brother, but anyway, she hoped he would be okay with that, too.

Since they had been together as a class for several weeks now, and most would be continuing the second course beginning soon, everyone seemed to be quite comfortable with one another. Of course, after looking at naked people in the same room, how could you not bond? But there was little conversation involved around class and more about what everyone's plans were for the July 4 weekend. Some were making a trip home to visit family, while others who lived more of a distance decided to make a fun time of it right there. There would be music groups performing, food trucks, and fireworks. Ada had already set up a time for her and Daisy to take the cooking class from the winning raffle on Saturday. It wasn't like she and Daisy needed a lot to entertain them, they were good at passing the time.

Lee mentioned to Ada once again about the sailing trip on Friday. His cousin, Emma, would be going, as well as another eight, so a total of ten of them would be going. She did think it would be fun but wanted to be certain they'd be home in time for her to meet Daisy. Lee said the boat would be docking before sunset. Ada agreed to meet the gang at 9 am.

Professor Aglio spent the remainder of the afternoon leading a discussion about their experience thus far and answering questions. He put some examples up on the screen to talk about how to resist the urge to erase every line when the model moves, which is understandable, and to try and retain at least some of the history of the pose. Some of the students were poking fun of their many eraser marks and how terrible it looked. The professor again tried to reassure everyone that developing any art technique takes time and practice. Easels and tools were prepared for the following morning, and most were anxious to see if they could improve on their work given another opportunity.

Ada walked home faster than she usually did because she couldn't wait to see Maisy.

Turning the corner, she could already see Susan outside walking her puppy along the sidewalk. It was so much fun to have a reason to go home again. She missed that. Susan saw her coming and waved. She took Maisy over to the front porch.

"How did she do today?" Ada asked and was greeted with lots of puppy kisses and wags of the tail.

"Like an angel. What a fun little thing to have around.

Robert came home for lunch and played with her out in the yard. I think I could probably talk him into getting another dog right now," she said laughing.

"Then, they'd have each other! Well, at least for the rest of the summer." Ada was suddenly a little sad.

"You like it here, don't you?"

"I really do."

"Well," Susan got up to leave. "You just never know. Life is funny that way. I'll see you two in the morning. Bye Maisy Girl."

Maisy wagged her tail.

Ada got herself something to eat and put food in Maisy's bowl. She turned the television on because she didn't feel like doing much of anything and she was coming down off the high from yesterday. Sometimes you were able to be distracted enough to leave your cares behind for a short while. Now, though, the events from Saturday night began to replay over in her mind. Ada wished she could just forget about Jason and move on, but for whatever reason that wasn't happening. Maisy stood at Ada's feet and let out a little yelp.

"You need to potty, girl?" Maisy wagged her tail. Ada gave the puppy a tousle on the top of her head. "What a good girl!"

The two walked out back to the fenced-in yard. Ada hadn't spent much time out here, but Marilyn had it laid out nicely as well. There was a patio covered with chevron patterned stones and outdoor seating around a firepit. Several pink and white rhododendrons outlined most of the perimeter and a crab apple tree that held a mass of small apples already took up one corner. Beneath it was a rope swing with a worn wooden bench, so Ada went over and sat down. She was already thinking this area would make a nice sketch, maybe as a thank you gift to leave for Marilyn.

Ada's phone began ringing in her pocket. She was hoping it was Daisy, but looking at the picture made her stand up quickly. Her Dad hardly ever called. Maybe something happened to her mom?

"Hello, Dad? What's wrong?"

"Well, hello to you, too. Can't a dad call his daughter without something being wrong?" He said, laughing.

Ada laughed with nervousness in her voice. "Sorry, just not used to it being you who calls. So, is everything okay with you guys?"

"Yes, of course. Sorry to alarm you. We were sitting here on our veranda at home and chatting about you, wondering how things are going in the art world?"

Ada wasn't used to her surgeon father being so relaxed and at ease sounding. Retirement was having a positive effect on him. She liked that. "I'm really enjoying my art course, Dad, and will be starting the other one next week! I can't believe the summer is half over! The gala event on Saturday was . . . was exciting." Ada wasn't sure if that was the correct adjective to use. "My piece was sold at the silent auction at a high bid, and the proceeds will go toward a children's wing at the local hospital!"

"Ah! How wonderful, Ada. I'm so pleased to hear that!" She heard her father talking to someone in the background. "Oh, your mother wants to know what you wore of course. Let me put you on speaker."

For the next ten minutes Ada talked about getting the dress with Susan. She sent pictures to her mom, and both of her parents told her how beautiful she looked. There was something in her mother's voice that made Ada think she was a bit disappointed that the two of them hadn't been the ones shopping.

Well, Mom, she thought to herself. *It's not like I stopped you from making a trip here to be with me.*

About that time the neighbor's dog stuck his nose through the fence and Maisy went over to investigate. She started barking and jumping around.

"Is that a puppy I hear?" Her dad asked.

"Yes, as a matter of fact, she's mine. Her name is Maisy." Ada smiled proudly.

"What in the world were you thinking, Ada, getting a puppy during a summer away?" Her mom scolded. "Are you having a crisis of some kind?"

Her mother wasn't too far off from the truth, but there was no way she was getting into that discussion. "Maisy is eight months old and already trained, Mom. You know I had always planned on getting a dog."

"Well, yes, but that was when Troy was . . ." Her mom didn't finish the sentence. Ada thought she could hear her dad say something quietly in the background.

"Why don't you send us a picture of Maisy, so we know what our granddog looks like?" He asked.

"I can do that," Ada said half-heartedly. She knew that her mother loved her, but sometimes she said things before running them through her brain first.

Fifteen minutes later, the three were completely caught up on events, plans, and her mother's recovery progress. Her parents said they had considered visiting Ada but figured she'd be too busy with classwork. That was probably for the best anyway.

After the goodbyes, Ada and Maisy went inside to call it night. The nude sketching would continue tomorrow, and Ada was hoping she'd have one more day to sketch the female form before switching to the other model. She wasn't quite ready to stare at a nude male with Jason on her mind.

Chapter 18

Ada awoke to a little rain pattering on the roof. She was cozy in her bed with Maisy beside her. If only it was the weekend, and she could sleep longer. She tried crawling out of bed carefully hoping the puppy would keep sleeping, but Maisy popped right up and followed her into the bathroom. Ada thought she better go ahead and take the puppy outside before getting herself ready.

Thank goodness it wasn't raining hard because Maisy didn't seem to be a fan of going onto the wet grass. They came back inside, and both ate some breakfast. Ada decided to dress comfortably today and chose a soft baby blue short set with drawstring shorts and a drop shoulder oversized sweatshirt. She filled her water bottle, grabbed her satchel, and slipped on her new

tennis shoes. There was a soft knock at the door. *That is probably*

Susan, Ada thought, and she bent over to pet Maisy and said

goodbye.

Ada internally commended herself on her outfit choice as

she stepped into the classroom.

It was rather cool today. Shouldn't they have made it

warmer for the models? Brr. How she would hate that job on so

many levels. About half the class had already arrived and were

getting their supplies ready. Ada was relieved to see that her group

would have the female nude again. The young model was talking to

a couple of students in the center of their half of the room.

Professor Aglio was on the other side with the male model

and two other students. They began right on time today, most likely

because there was payment involved. He reminded the students of

what had been discussed last week, looked at the clock and asked if

they would refrain from talking. Before removing her robe, the

model climbed onto the table and positioned herself onto her right

side. She rolled around for a bit. Once her robe was on the floor, she

tucked her right leg a little under the left and turned so that her stomach was mostly on the table. She held her torso up with her arms head facing out and her breasts touched the table. It was a quite modest pose.

She smiled and said, "All good."

Everyone nervously laughed and began picking up their pencils to sketch.

Ada could hear the other half of the room begin as well. All was quiet. The professor turned on some classical music in the background which helped with the awkward silence.

Ada started with the basic proportions and the torso, just simple lines. She kept her focus well and established a good rhythm by pushing charcoal around on the paper instead of adding more layers. She didn't rush. By the end of the first hour the light and dark contrasts were beginning to give action to what could have been an otherwise subdued reclining pose. Ada worked with rough bristled brushes and tissues to shade the middle tones. The lighter tones could be created by using a kneaded eraser and lifting them off.

The female model did an incredible job. She had only taken three small breaks the entire time and was able to mimic nearly the same exact positioning, except for the slightest variations. These did not cause any problems for the drawings themselves. After thanking the models, Professor Aglio assured everyone that they would return the following day for one last session. Looking at the models as he said it, they smiled back and shook their heads yes.

"What troopers they are," said one of Ada's classmates to her. "I would seriously hate sitting still for that long."

"I would seriously hate being naked in front of strangers," Ada commented.

The class broke for lunch, and everyone was anxious to talk about their sketches. From what Ada noticed, some were quite good, while others looked like artwork her 2nd graders created. Not all of them were talented in the arts, some were there out of pure love of art. Trish's not only had a flair for clothing but also drawing. Although her sketch was flamboyant and dramatic in contrast to Ada's, nevertheless, it was well done and matched her personality. Lee's was, once again, average. He had the basics down but seemed to lack the trained eye for detail. Ada supposed it was no different than liking music. Some could sing or play an instrument while some couldn't, but that didn't mean you enjoyed music any less.

The remainder of the afternoon flew by as all that they had to do was put the finishing touches on their sketches before leaving. Tomorrow would look very much the same as today except for the simple fact that Ada would be staring at a male body tomorrow and thinking about . . . well, she wasn't quite sure what or who she would be thinking about.

The weather had cleared so there was no need for an umbrella on the walk home. As she walked, Ada saw the baseball team on the field for practice. She spotted Jason out on the pitcher's mound. He didn't see her as she walked by on the opposite side of the street, or at least he didn't appear to see her. Would they ever talk again? Now things were totally awkward between them in a different way.

Maisy was once again happy to see Ada when she got home. Earlier that morning, Susan had invited Ada over for dinner. They were throwing some chicken on the grill and having potato salad and fresh tomatoes from the garden, and Ada was planning to make some chocolate chip cookies to take over. She promised Susan that dinner at six sounded perfect. She turned on some music and began mixing the cookie dough batter. She planned on making extra so that she and Daisy would have some in a couple of days. Oh my gosh, she couldn't wait to see her friend again. It seemed like forever ago since the last time!

Ada put a dozen cookies on a paper plate and covered them with a piece of foil. She had already fed Maisy and taken her outside. Susan had insisted that the puppy accompany her to dinner.

As soon as Ada stepped into the street, she could smell the aroma of chicken being grilled. Her stomach growled. The salad for lunch today was no longer sustaining her.

"Hi guys! I come bearing cookies!" This time Ada opened the back gate and walked right in as though she was at her parents' home.

"Well, you've come to the right place then!" Robert said, grinning. Maisy went running up to Robert, wagging her tail.

"There's that cute puppy of ours!" He said, bending down and petting Maisy energetically. Ada liked the sound "ours" because it was the sound of family, and Robert and Susan were family.

Robert had used a recipe for the chicken that his father always used, some apple cider vinegar, butter, and Lawry's seasoning salt mixed over the stove and then brushed onto the chicken, turning and continuing to do so as it was grilled. Susan's potato salad reminded Ada of her grandmother's with the celery, boiled eggs, and onion with mayo, sugar, and mustard mixture. Everything was so delicious. Robert even surprised Ada by having made some homemade ice cream in the White Mountain crank bucket that she remembered her maternal grandfather using. The best part was that it tasted exactly like it. She could almost have cried. Both went on and on about the cookies, which happened to be her paternal grandmother's recipe.

To Ada, family was everything. Her father was always so busy as a surgeon but made time for her as often as he could. When he did, he was very present and in the moment. Her mother, on the other hand, was busy with social events and friends. She also liked sharing her opinion with everyone, especially Ada. There were circumstances where that had been tolerable but so many times she just wanted her to Mom to plop down on the bed with her and listen, maybe share special memories of when she was the same age or tell her things would be better. Ada felt happy that her dad would be more available now in his retirement. At least they could talk like old times.

Dinner outside had been perfect, and the sun was beginning to set, offering hues of orange and purple. They decided to carry the dinner things into the kitchen so they could enjoy ice cream on the patio and watch the rest of the sunset. Ada was putting away the leftover potato salad in the refrigerator when she caught a glimpse of Robert's study. Two high back navy velour chairs sat facing a large cherry desk. The room was illuminated by two floor lamps. Her eyes immediately saw the auctioned art piece from Saturday sitting on one of the only shelves in the room that didn't contain books. Ada was stunned. She had been certain that Jason was the one who had gone home with Professor Aglio's metal sculpture that they had discussed. Ada knew that Robert and Susan had noticed her pausing to stare into the study, so she quickly spoke up.

"Ah! Now I know who the owner is of this fine piece of abstract art!" Ada turned around, smiling at the two.

Robert was dipping ice cream into bowls and Susan was putting the last few items into the dishwasher. "Yes, Robert is fond of abstract art, and I am a big supporter of reusing what we already have to rebuild. You know, the Scottish build new structures from old stones. I like that."

Robert chuckled.

"Well, I do." Susan said, her smile contradicting her slightly defensive tone.

"I do, too, my love, and that is one of the many traits that makes you so charming." He kissed her on the cheek as he walked by.

"Anyone ready for some homemade ice cream?" Susan and Ada both said yes at the same time.

The three of them sat on the patio for another hour enjoying the last of the sunset. Susan and Ada took their spot on the swing and Maisy sat alongside Robert on the lounger. He had a timer on the strings of lights throughout the backyard, and it was always so cozy. They talked about the art auction, Ada's parents, her art course, and how fast the summer was going. She loved spending time with these two new friends and knew that they would be in her life forever no matter where she lived. This time after thanking them for dinner, she hugged Robert and Susan. Maisy jumped up on them as if to say, "Hey I want in on this, too." They smiled and gave her some attention as well. Ada felt so at home with them, and of course they stood and watched her, and Maisy walk across the street to the door.

Only twice during the last hour with her kind friends did Ada's thoughts drift to the "Restore" sculpture and the question she was ultimately wanting answered. What did Jason purchase if not this piece? She hadn't noticed him looking at any others. She desired to know simply because it might allow her to know him better. He had a wall up, which now he admitted to at least. The summer was already half over, and the question remained as to whether anything would become of their relationship. Could it even be called that?

Ada laid out comfortable clothes for class tomorrow before she took Maisy out one last time. A warm shower and several chapters in a new book had Ada asleep before she even turned out the light.

The clock showed six o' five am when she first opened her eyes. The room appeared lighter than it should have been, which is when she discovered the bedside lamp had stayed on all night. Ada rolled over to see Maisy staring back at her.

"Good morning, sweet girl. Did the light keep you awake? Obviously, it didn't have any effect on me at all!"

Maisy came closer and wagged her tail.

Maybe she'd go ahead and get up even though her alarm would have permitted her to sleep another forty minutes. *No need to lie in bed*, Ada thought. Maybe I'll get there early, and it will help settle my nerves for the last day of sketching, especially given it was the male form.

She had been quite pleased with her work this week. Hopefully, the pose would be another modest one to make the experience as comfortable as possible.

Ada turned on the coffee that was ready to go through the

maker and started for the bathroom, but Maisy had other ideas. She went to the door and barked.

"No make up and clothes first this morning, Maisy?" Ada laughed as Maisy barked again as though answering her.

"Okay, okay." Ada looked down at what she had on. Nobody would pay attention that it was a short and tee shirt sleep set. She picked up the cute bundle and headed to the back gate. After Maisy was finished and they were heading inside, Ada caught a glimpse of movement in the corner of her eye and looked across the street to see Robert opening the front door for Jason. Not wanting either one to see her, she hurried inside. It was barely six-thirty in the morning! That's awfully early for stopping by! What could he possibly be doing?

Ada took her coffee and went to get dressed and apply makeup while contemplating the possibilities the entire time. Were Robert and Susan going out of town again? If so, they hadn't mentioned a word last night. Besides, she still had class today and tomorrow. Surely if Susan wasn't able to watch Maisy, she would have mentioned it. Just then, there was a delicate knock on the door. Ada opened it, anxious to find out some answers.

"Good morning!"

"Why, good morning yourself! Hello there, Miss Maisy." Susan bent to scoop up the dog in her arms.

"She asked to go potty first thing this morning."

"Is that right? Well, I guess we can just head on over to my house then."

Ada was scrambling with how to ask about Jason. "Oh . . . when I was taking her out earlier, I happened to see Jason stopping by early this morning. Are you two heading out of town? I thought maybe I missed your saying something yesterday."

"No, not for another week or so. I'm guessing it has something to do with some project those two have been working on all summer. I have no idea what. It has something to do with a book."

"Really? A book? Jason is writing a book?"
Susan chuckled. "I believe Robert is writing the book, but Jason is somehow contributing? I've not been privy to any of it!" She laughed.

"That is definitely . . . interesting." Ada tried laughing as well, but it didn't really come out as that. Jason had to be the most complicated and mysterious man she had ever met.

Chapter 19

The dainty floral print dress may have been a bit dressy for class, but Ada had a feeling she would run into a certain someone and didn't want to be caught in sloppy clothes today. She opted for strappy sandals and a light-weight cardigan. Part of her hair was pulled back, and she smiled slightly at her reflection when approaching the fine arts building. A couple of younger male students took a few extra steps to open the door for her.

Once inside, she caught up with others from her class. Everyone was chatting about how quickly the first summer term had passed. Ada was all too aware, as she was hoping that she and Jason could have been in a better place at this point. For some reason being distracted by the possibility of seeing him today took away any anxiety about the drawing. She took her seat and began setting up as though she did this every day. The professor wasted no time getting class started and simply reminded them of the time they would have to sketch, break for lunch, and finish details before turning in their final submission. Before the models took their places, he thanked each one and the students applauded. Ada was somewhat relieved but more so impressed with the model's pose. He sat on the table with his left leg bent and right leg straight out. He leaned over his body toward the right and positioned his hands on either side. The entire muscular structure of his back protruded in such a way that it was beautiful. In fact, his entire body was flexed so you could see the muscles along the legs, buttocks, and arms. The only part of his face that showed was somewhat of his profile.

Looking at the model, Ada felt incredibly inspired and was able to sketch quickly. The classical music playing in the background, which she was quite certain was Chopin, almost served like a curtain being pulled on all outside distractions and the rhythm provided an artistic reverence. There was almost no noise in the room today, which also helped. Professor Algio wrote the remaining time on the board behind each model when twenty minutes were left. When time was up, he went to each one and said something quietly. They left the room, and most students continued working. He wrote on the board that lunch was up to the students, final submissions were due by three o' clock, and he would stay in the room if there were any questions.

Ada decided to keep working. She was extremely pleased with the proportions on her drawing. The fine lines and subtle shading brought her art to life. Right then and there she decided that there was indeed life beyond teaching elementary school. Besides being told she had talent, it was more about the pure enjoyment she received from studying and immersing herself in the art world that convinced Ada she was right where she belonged. Surely somehow and at some point in her life it would be possible to make the transition. After another thirty minutes or so, Ada stood up and moved back from her sketch. She looked at it from different perspectives. She glanced up to notice the professor standing next to her. He stood with his arms crossed and one hand under his chin.

Without saying a word, he nodded and smiled slightly before walking on. Ada took that as a positive affirmation that her work was good. After a few more tweaks, she turned in the final piece, gathered her things, and left the room. Some students had left almost immediately, others had gone to lunch and returned, and some were finishing up. By this time, Ada's stomach was growling, so she decided to head across the street to the diner for a late lunch. Then, she wanted to pick up a few things at the store to prepare for tomorrow's outing on Lee's boat with the gang, and to get ready for Daisy's arrival tomorrow evening. This was the big July 4th weekend with the music festival, and it would be so much fun. Ada couldn't wait! It was a great way to end the first summer term. The only thing that would make it better would be if she . . .

Ada was getting close to the baseball field and could see the players gathered at the mound talking. Jason was in the middle giving some instructions. She wanted to get closer but not be too obvious since the diner was in the opposite direction. Maybe she could pretend to be on her phone and sit down on a bench for a while, although she wasn't certain how long she'd last given her level of hunger. Ada pulled the cell out of her purse, and it was already ringing.

"Hi Mom!" Ada kept her eyes on the team while talking to her mom and dad. After twenty minutes of fielding practice, the guys were gathering their things. She was barely listening to anything her parents were saying.

"Ada, are you still there? Can you hear us?"

"Oh! Sorry about that, guys! I—what was that?"

Jason was talking to one of the players while the rest of them headed in different directions. Two of them passed by Ada and said hello.

"Who are you talking to?" Ada's mother questioned. "Oh, just some students."

"You must have made friends quickly over these last few weeks."

"Yes, everyone is super friendly here." Ada saw that Jason was finishing up talking with the last player. "Hey, it has been so nice catching up, but I haven't eaten since breakfast. Class was long today."

Ada knew as soon as she said it. "Oh, Ada, you know that's not good for you. I've always told you . . ." She didn't hear what her mom was saying because she was focusing on what Jason was doing. Fortunately, her dad chimed in and suggested that they hang up and let her go eat.

After the goodbyes, Ada pretended to stay on the line to see where Jason was headed once he closed the gate.

Ada's heart raced. He was headed her way. She stood up, pretended to say goodbye again, slowly put away her phone, and began walking towards him in the direction of the restaurant.

Would he even speak to her? They had ended on strange terms last Saturday when he had dropped her off.

He had been looking down while walking but looked up as he got within a few feet of her. "Hello, Ada. How are you?"

"Hi, Jason. I'm doing well. How about you?" He didn't act like he was going to stop, so Ada intentionally stopped in front of him. "I just finished my first summer term today. I can't believe how fast the summer is going. I only have four more weeks and then will be heading back to the mainland." She purposefully sighed.

He simply slowed but kept walking. "Yeah, summers always go by quickly."

"I'm heading out tomorrow with some classmates on a sailboat and then my best friend is coming again this weekend."

At that he stopped. "Tomorrow evening?"

"Yeah. Lee has a large sailboat that accommodates up to twelve people. It should be a lot of fun! They've been bugging me to go out since I arrived, so I figured I would give it a try."

"Tomorrow morning is supposed to be beautiful, but the evening hours are calling for a possible storm and high waves."

"Lee is an experienced sailor, so I'm sure that he is aware." Ada didn't mean for it to come across sarcastically. It just hit her as strange that he seemed to care now. "Plus, we plan on being back in the afternoon because Daisy is arriving by six o'clock."

"Yeah, well," he started to turn and go but stopped. "Just . . . be careful, okay?"

Ada thought she detected real concern in his voice and on his face. "Thanks, we will." He nodded and pursed his lips as if to say, "I hope so."

"See ya, Ada."

"Bye, Jason. Maybe I'll see you this weekend at the festival and you can finally meet Daisy."

"Sure, maybe."

That was not what Ada had expected today. In fact, she wasn't even certain how to interpret what had just taken place. Before she could contemplate any further, her stomach let out a huge growl, so she quickly made her way to the diner and ordered a spaghetti dinner, which was the evening's special. Loretta, a server she knew, was working and threw in a side salad.

While she waited for things to be prepared, Ada stopped into the market next door and picked up a loaf of French bread, salami, two kinds of cheeses, and some grapes for her contribution for tomorrow's sailing outing. For the weekend, she made sure to get some of her and Daisy's favorite wine, more coffee, the market owner's homemade lemon blueberry muffins, and, of course, some munchies.

Ada dropped everything off at her place and then walked over to retrieve Maisy at Robert's and Susan's. Her little charge was always so happy to see Ada, and Maisy wagged her tail the entire way across the street. Not even once did Ada regret the decision to get her. They were meant to be together for sure. Maisy dug into her food and appeared to be as famished as Ada felt. Instead of eating at the table, Ada took her plate of food to the couch and turned on the television. She looked up her recordings and decided to get caught up on the *Today Show*. The hosts always felt like extended family members.

After the long day in class, the encounter with Jason, and the loaded carb dinner in front of the television, Ada was feeling very sleepy.

"How about a walk, girl?"

Maisy raised her head slightly, but didn't get up, almost as if to say she was too tired as well. Then, as if suddenly realizing what Ada had said, she stood up and got the zoomies. Watching her running from room to room, jumping over things made Ada laugh.

"Okay, Maisy. Let's go!"

The air had cooled down a bit, so Ada put on her sweater from that morning. They strolled down toward the water and could see several boats heading toward shore.

"I'll be out there tomorrow, girl." Ada shivered when she remembered the warning from Jason. "Lee knows what he's doing. Afterall, he's been sailing since the age of fourteen."

After a stroll in the park and stopping to greet some of the neighborhood dogs, they headed back to the bungalow. Ada decided to lay out everything she'd need for tomorrow: bathing suit, cover up, towels, change of clothes, sunscreen, sunglasses, hairbands, and a cooler and bag for food items. No need to wash her hair tonight since it will be sprayed by the sea tomorrow. In fact, she may as well put it in a French braid and not worry about it. Most likely everyone would wear their suits and a cover up there. She may not even need regular clothes but figured she'd take some anyway.

Tonight seemed like a perfect night for a candle bath. That was something she hadn't done in a long time, so Ada set several candles around the bathroom even though it wasn't dark yet. She asked Alexa to play Duke Ellington music sung by various artists from the past, which was a favorite of hers from the time she was in elementary school. Her parents had played it often. The clawfoot

tub reminded Ada of the one at her grandmother's and always

seemed to be made for soaking. She even added some Epsom salts

with lavender that she found in the bathroom closet. It always

worked wonders for calming and relaxing.

Ada closed her eyes and thought about the conversation

with Jason this afternoon. Did he really care what happened to her,

or was he jealous that she was going out with friends on a sailboat?

No, that didn't seem to be Jason's personality. Why then? Why care

but not be able to kiss her, to have a relationship with her, or be able

to explain his past? Also, what in the world was he working on with

Robert? What did a baseball coach and professor of psychology

possibly be collaborating on? Sport psychology? Ada hadn't seen

any books relating to such a topic in Robert's home library. Why

was Susan not even aware? It was such a mystery. Jason was a

mystery. For a moment Ada relived the kiss between them. It was

passionate, wild, and tender all at once. She hadn't believed she

could ever feel that way about anyone since Troy. Without realizing

it, Ada reached up and touched her lips.

"Jason," she whispered. "Who are you? Why won't you let

me know you?"

The bathroom suddenly grew darker and the ambience with

only burning candles provided the perfect backdrop for Sarah Vaughan's "Solitude." Two tears fell down Ada's cheeks as she listened to the song. Only four more weeks to spend here. Four more weeks to try and convince Jason that she could be trusted with whatever secrets he held. She could set him free. She could love him . . . she did love him, even without really knowing him.

Ada stepped out of the tub, dried off, got dressed, and blew out the candles. She went out into the living room to turn off the lamps. Light poured in through the window opposite the door. She went over and pulled back the curtain. There was a beautiful full moon. She had a perfect view between two large pink rhododendrons. The street looked like a wonderland in the light and quite different from the daytime. It reminded Ada of a painting. The town really was lovely and so were the people. She could see herself living here and raising a family. Right now, though, that wasn't looking like much of a possibility. *Oh well,* thought Ada. *You never know.*

She crawled into bed and reached for the book on her nightstand. She barely made it through two chapters before falling soundly asleep with Maisy snuggled against her.

Chapter 20

Hot moist air surrounded her face. The smell wasn't putrid but also was not exactly fresh. Ada reached up to wipe what felt like slobber off her mouth and was jolted out of her dream. She was staring into the most soulful eyes that belonged to the furry creature whose head rested on her chest.

"Well good morning to you, too. Was I talking in my sleep, or are you trying to tell me that you're hungry?"

Maisy stood up at that point and began wagging her tail.

Ada threw on a sweater and took the puppy outside. It was a beautiful morning and showed absolutely no signs of possible bad weather. Had Jason been a little dramatic with his prediction and maybe just hadn't really wanted her to go? She hoped it was for that reason.

She ate a bowl of oatmeal with blueberries and drank coffee. There were two messages on her phone. One was from Lee sending a group text saying he'd plan on meeting everyone at their agreed upon time and place plus a reminder to bring the food and drink items. The second message was from Daisy saying that she was so excited to see her later for their girls' weekend.

Ada took a minute to respond to both before getting dressed in her bathing suit. It was a new one she had ordered online and ended up being so cute. The navy-blue bikini was athletic but had back ties for adjustability and feminine strappy detail. Maybe if Jason could see her strutting around on the sailboat, he wouldn't be able to resist her. Too bad he wasn't going along. The white crocheted coverup that fell to her knees and her Reef Water Vista sandals completed the outfit. She had even picked up the perfect bag for sailing at the downtown boutique; it held the small cooler for food, clothes, towel, and the rest. She took Maisy across the street around 8 and let Susan know that the sailing crew would be back sometime in the afternoon. Susan handed her a gallon bag of macadamia nut chocolate chip cookies. As soon as Ada got in her car, she took one out and had a bite.

"Mm . . . delicious. I knew they would be." She said aloud.

About half of the crew had already arrived at the marina when Ada pulled into the parking lot. Lee threw up his hand and waved to her. All the guys had swim trunks, and some were already shirtless. The girls, except for Jayden and Kristine, had bathing suits and coverups. Jayden had a bikini top and jean shorts, while Kristine had a short set. The guys loaded coolers and helped the gals board the vessel. Painted in large bright blue letters on the side were the words "Santorini, Greece" and beneath in smaller letters, "The Beginning of Us."

Ada thought it was extremely romantic before even asking Lee the meaning behind the writing. Once everyone was aboard, Emma was the first to ask Lee. He explained that when his parents were still in high school on opposite sides of the United States, they were both studying Greek and traveled to Santorini as part of an exchange program for the summer. Both were sixteen at the time and by the end of the seven weeks together had fallen madly in love. They both applied and were accepted to Stanford.

"The rest is history," Lee had said and then laughed.

While the girls oohed and awed Henry and Ben had already gotten into the beer before even setting sail. Henry, Jayden, and Charlotte had all grown up on sailboats, so fortunately Lee had already planned on having good help with the rigging and setting sail. The sun was reflecting off the water and feeling hot already. It didn't take long for them to get far enough from the dock that the people and town looked tiny. Lee piped the music through the speakers and soon they were singing along, and some were attempting to dance. The constant swaying of the boat made it somewhat difficult, and Ada wasn't going to attempt it just to be thrown overboard.

She and Kristine had a nice chat about their impressions of the first summer course. Kristine was a high school art teacher in the Midwest and working on her graduate degree to teach at the college level. The rest of the girls joined them and preferred talking about the male model from the day before. Destiny claimed she had dreamed about him and had awakened this morning, disappointed that they weren't a real couple. She had them all rolling with laughter. Ada hadn't realized how much fun these gals could be. The class had been rather serious throughout the term, and there really hadn't been much time for playing. Of course, Ada had opted out of the last outing, and she did know them better now.

They were all disappointed to find out that Kristine would be returning to Texas after the weekend. Her wedding was the first weekend in August and she still had a lot to do. Ada felt a twinge of jealousy. About that time Noah had yelled over to the girls for them to come up closer to the stern and see a great white he had spotted. They screamed and grabbed to hold on to something for security as the vessel rocked from side to side.

"That's a salmon shark, dude, not a great white."

"Maybe it's a basking shark that's like Noah," added Lee.

"Why's that?"

Henry and Jayden began laughing. "What? Noah looked back and forth between the two."

"I'm just kidding ya."

Jayden held her mouth open wide then she laughed again. "It swims around with its mouth open a lot."

"Oh, real funny guys. Speaking of mouths being open. I'm putting some food in this one."

The rest of them agreed that it was time to break into the coolers. It turned out to be quite the spread of food which included fresh fruit, sliced vegetables, Ada's bread, salami, and cheeses; Hawaiian roll "sammies," popcorn chicken, walking tacos, pasta salad, a variety of cookies and plenty of beer and wine. Ada was hoping she wouldn't get sick after stuffing herself, but everything tasted even better at sea! She forewent any beer and stuck with only one wine cooler and mostly water. The only one looking a little green was Noah. Ada was pretty sure it was because he had started drinking before they even left shore.

Lee turned up the music and they were all singing along. Not everyone had a nice voice, but it didn't matter out here. In fact, Ada felt totally free from stress and worry for the first time in a long while. A glimmer of hope passed by briefly, and Ada tried to hold on to it for longer. She wasn't even sure what the hope entailed. Leaving teaching? Being with Jason? Whatever the reason, she welcomed the feeling.

The expert sailors were once again jumping in to aid Lee as he positioned the sailboat to anchor close to a white sandy beach. There were only a handful of people on this semi-private beach that reminded Ada of a tropical island. Lee had several paddle boards, and both Charlotte and Kristine asked Ada to join them. At least the wind was calm, and they were close to shore and would be able to stand shortly.

"I've always wanted to try . . . not sure how coordinated I'll be." Ada got up from her spot. laughing.

"Great! That will make it more fun," Kristine chimed in behind her. Charlotte got in first since she had attempted it at least once.

"Talk us through it, girl. I'm planning on looking like a pro at this on my honeymoon."

Ada agreed readily with Kristine. "Well, I'm not going on a honeymoon, but I like a good demonstration when learning something new," she laughed.

They both watched Charlotte intensely as she got into the water, climbed on and stayed on her knees while holding to the board on both sides. She looked forward and carefully brought her feet one at a time to where her knees were and stood up, making certain to keep her legs parallel and about hip-width.

Both girls clapped.

"No applause yet, I haven't moved." Charlotte giggled.

"Okay, so next you need to be sure the paddle blade angles forward from the shaft toward the nose of the board." She also demonstrated how to hold the paddle when switching sides. "Another important thing is to always try and keep your balance . . ."

"Easy for you to say since you're the pro!" Kristine teased.

"Hardly a professional. I just took a lesson before going out this past spring with my sister. Anyway, as I was saying, try to keep your balance, but if you fall, do your best to fall into the water and don't try and stay on your board. That will hurt a whole lot more." She rubbed her behind as she said it.

"Come on, Ada. You look ready to tackle this!" Charlotte motioned to her for the next paddleboard.

"Come on Ada, let's not look stupid," Ada muttered to herself. It's what she always said to herself when attempting something new in front of other people.

"You could never look stupid, Ada." It was Troy's voice. He never liked her to say that aloud or even think it.

If you were here with me, I'd be braver, Ada thought. She smiled slightly just thinking of him.

"Come on, Ada. What's the hold up?"

Ada climbed down the few steps with the board, into the water, and was standing within minutes, paddle in hand.

"Woo hoo!" Ada called. She hadn't realized there actually was an audience, probably a good thing. She gave a tiny salute.

"Here goes nothing!" Destiny jumped in and was trying a little too aggressively to get on the board. After the fifth attempt, and some help from both girls, Destiny, Ada, and Kristine were soon paddling around the lagoon and having a terrific time. Music still blared from the sailboat. The guys could still be heard above it. Rose, Emma, and Jayden had decided to swim the short distance to the beach with a small raft holding some towels and other items.

Forty-five minutes later, Ada's legs were starting to ache, and she pointed to the beach. Once at the shore, they offered the sunbathers a turn, but they passed. The boards made nice loungers. Ada was thankful that she already had a good base tan because the noon sun was extremely hot. She had put sunscreen on before leaving this morning but decided another layer might be best. No sense in ruining the weekend with Daisy suffering from an unnecessary sunburn.

The girls spent the next hour covering everything from their youth, relationships, class, and future. Rose also confessed that she had a crush on Henry. Everyone agreed that he was quite a catch. Good-looking, smart, and such a gentleman matched Rose's natural beauty and small-town girl sweetness. Jayden swore she thought Henry had feelings for Rose. At least the possible love match lived within driving distance of each other.

Whistling from the boat came suddenly and the guys were calling them back. "What time is it anyway?" Kristine asked.

Most had left their phones on the boat. Jayden was the only one who had a water watch. "Whew! It's going on two-thirty!"

"I can't believe it! The day went by so fast. How long did it take us to get out here?"

"I think about forty minutes." Emma said.

"My friend, Daisy is due in at four o' clock today, so that should put us back right on time!"

The group gathered up their things and Emma floated the raft back to the boat. They were able to walk most of the way and then shared the boards to hold on to and paddle behind to reach the boat. The guys were there to take their equipment and help them aboard.

"Do you have a potty on this beast, Lee?" Destiny was crossing her legs.

"Sure, it's down below."

"Why didn't you just pee in the water like everyone else?" blurted out Noah, laughing. "Speak for yourself," the girls said at different times and followed Destiny.

"Check this out!" Destiny suddenly forgot she had to go to the bathroom.

The ceiling was lower, of course, but there was an L-shaped navy and white striped couch with a small kitchenette off to the side. The cherry mahogany walls and cabinets made for a rich and luxurious feel. Straight back through a solid door was a large bed with a painting for a headboard. The bathroom included a walk-in shower and contained mostly marble. Ada had never seen anything like it before. By the sounds the other girls were making neither had they.

"This is ridiculously beautiful!" Rose said in her quiet voice.

"Okay, I've gotta go," Destiny said as she ushered everyone out of the bathroom. The rest of them sat down on the bed to wait their turn.

"Did Lee say that his parents left him this boat?" Kristine asked, looking at Ada.

"Yes, although his father is still living. He just isn't interested in doing anything anymore since his wife passed away. It has been a few years, but Lee had to take his time to mourn."

Destiny came out of the bathroom then. "Well, if this is mourning, I'd say it's not too bad."

"Destiny!" Charlotte spoke up and put her finger to her mouth in a shushing gesture.

"I'm just kidding. Next." She motioned toward the bathroom.

"Hey down there, are you girls okay? We're ready to sail!"

"We'll be right up!"

Lee was getting out several large pillows and putting them on the bow of the sailboat. "Have a seat, ladies."

"Thank you, Lee, this looks so cozy," Ada commented.

After they were settled toward the front, Henry brought up the cooler with drinks. He spent a little longer with Rose helping her pick out something, and everyone noticed. When he left, Kristine patted Rose on the arm and smiled. Rose took a drink so she could hide her big smile. Ben brought them some snacks.

"Wow! You guys know how to treat the ladies!" Destiny commented. "Hey, Ben! What do you have for us? On second thought, don't answer that." They all giggled.

"You might be surprised," Destiny, he said and winked playfully.

Lee turned up the music. This time it was some R&B from around their time in school. They all surprised themselves by remembering most of the words, sometimes making fun of each other.

It had been a perfect day. Well, almost. Ada missed having Troy beside her. He'd be gently moving her hair back away from her neck right now and kissing it, then her face, and finally her lips. She suddenly felt embarrassed like someone would pick up on her thoughts, but they were too busy singing. Then, her mind moved to Jason. Would he be the same way if they were alone on this boat right now? Ada closed her eyes and tried to imagine.

Chapter 21

Blue skies had been with them the entire day. Even as they docked the sailboat, the sun's rays were heating up a few places where Ada had missed putting sunscreen. Why had Jason warned her about the weather? It was so random. She had already gathered her things and decided to send the remaining salami and bread with Noah. He had eaten the majority anyway. Everyone had pitched in to help Lee get trash collected, the floors swept, and things wiped down.

"I'll take this crew sailing anytime," he shouted from above as the last sail was secured. There was an eruption of thanks from all and a promise they wouldn't turn an invite down should he offer.

Henry took the large bag of trash to the dumpster at the end of the pier, and Emma followed carrying his duffel bag. She ended up leaving with him instead of riding back to her place with Kristine. Nobody made any comments, but the girls just looked at each other and smiled. Sisterhood was a funny thing. There could be feelings of jealousy and envy, because who amongst them didn't desire true love? At the end of the day, however, they were each other's biggest cheerleaders. Even in this group of new friends, it was understood.

Most of them were planning on attending the 4th of July activities over the weekend, so they said quick goodbyes to return home and get ready. Ada hurried to her car and threw in the slightly wet canvas bag. She took out her cell phone. Three-fifty on the dot. *Perfect timing*, she thought. Daisy was most likely at the bungalow waiting for her.

Hmm, she'd picked up snacks and breakfast things, but what about dinner tonight? To be honest, she was too tired to go back out and figured Daisy wouldn't want to either after the drive. She picked up the phone and called in an order for pizza at the Italian restaurant. They had curbside delivery, so Ada wouldn't even have to get out of her car with windblown hair and a coverup.

She called the number on the parking sign and a young girl

she hadn't seen before brought out her order.

"Hi! Are you Ada?"

"Yes!" Ada was suddenly feeling a little silly not going in to retrieve her own order. "I would have picked it up myself, but I was out sailing with friends all day and didn't look my best!" She laughed awkwardly.

"Lucky you!" She was cute with shoulder length blond hair and a big smile, probably a senior in high school.

Ada handed her a tip and she was very appreciative. Driving off, she heard some whistles and beeps as the young girl went back into the restaurant, but not before waving at the passersby.

Oh, to be that age again, Ada thought.

What a sight it was to pull in and see her best friend and her little furry friend sharing the swing! Daisy put up her hand and waved vigorously back and forth. Once Ada was in the driveway, she picked up Maisy and raced out to embrace Ada in the biggest hug.

"I've missed you more than ever!" She held on to Ada a little longer than she usually did.

Maisy let out a little yip.

"Oh, sorry sweet girl." Daisy bent to give Maisy a kiss.

"Hey, are you crying?" Ada touched Daisy's arm.

"Huh? Oh, nah, just a little tired from driving . . . just so happy to see you." This time she put her arm around Ada and hugged her from the side so as not to smash Maisy in the middle of them. "Susan came over and brought Maisy when she saw me pull up. What a nice lady! I really enjoyed chatting with her, especially about teacher stuff! Boy! She sure loves you!"

"Aww. She and Robert have been so amazing to me. They're like . . . well, like my parents." Ada felt somewhat guilty saying it aloud, but it was true. Her own parents just were never around much. Daisy understood and didn't even comment.

"I have certainly missed my best friend! It's so hard not to have you close by to talk to in person. I'm used to that, you know!" Ada squeezed Daisy's hand. She grabbed her bag and the pizza.

"Yum! Exactly what I was hungry for. How did you know?"

"Because, silly, we're sisters!" They giggled and walked into the house.

Ada poured both a glass of wine, and they sat at the table and devoured every bit of the thin and crispy pepperoni, onion, and green pepper pizza. Both took their turns talking and getting caught up with the most recent news. Daisy reported about the garden that she and Jackson had just planted. They were trying cucumbers, tomatoes, squash, and lettuce. Daisy held up both hands with crossed fingers. She had been wanting to try again after a particularly rainy season two years ago. Ada briefly recalled the tiny garden that she and Troy had that first year. On a whim they had planted some cherry tomato seeds and produced the juiciest delicious cherry tomatoes that both family and neighbors were able to enjoy.

Daisy also had decided to revamp some of her lesson plans and talked excitedly about what creative plans she was going to implement. Ada smiled and acted enthusiastic but couldn't find any part of her the least bit excited about going back for another year of teaching. Her heart was no longer in it. The children were sweet, of course, but just the daily grind was not what brought her joy.

She hadn't realized that she had sighed aloud.

"Hey, you know that I'm always happy to share anything. You don't need to start from the beginning!" Daisy gently slapped her friend's leg and laughed.

"Oh, I know." Ada smiled.

"So, tell me about the first course and, oh, the sailing trip!"

Ada launched into the day's events from the beginning with the beautiful weather, the spread of food, attempting to paddleboard and doing somewhat okay. She found herself giving a quick biography of each classmate, now friend, and had Daisy laughing. She especially found Noah and Destiny hilarious.

Ada felt a feeling of exhilaration being able to share such details about people she had only met a few short weeks ago and hadn't known well at all. Now she was anxious about the prospect of sailing with them again before the end of summer and continuing their friendship for years to come. Daisy and Jackson would enjoy spending time with them as well. Troy would like them . . . would have liked them, too. Once again, her heart dropped a little like it always did when she thought of being alone.

Daisy must have picked up on it because she simply changed the subject in typical Daisy fashion by asking for details on the nude sketch of the male model. Ada had to laugh at that and proceeded to describe in detail the entire week. Daisy just couldn't get over how anyone could possibly be talked into volunteering or even getting a stipend for such a job.

Ada had taken some pictures of her submission knowing that she wouldn't be getting them returned for another week or so.

"Ada, these are incredible! They are works of art!" Daisy

was sitting up straight holding the phone away from her and scrolling through pictures looking back and forth between them and Ada. "I always knew you were talented, but you have a true God-given talent. When you get these returned you need to frame them."

"What?" Ada had taken a sip of her wine and choked a bit. "And display them where?"

"What do you mean? In your home of course! They're beautiful!"

"Well, I really appreciate your saying that."

Daisy handed the phone back to Ada. "Listen, my friend, I know that your dream is not to teach. You don't ever have to pretend with me."

"You really are the best," Ada said as she stopped to hug her friend while taking her things to the sink. "I need to wash the sea water out of my hair and get some comfy clothes on, and then we can curl up and watch some Netflix. Maybe we'll be hungry again by then because I bought lots of munchies!"

"Sounds perfect! You go ahead. I'm going to give Jackson a call. I only texted to say I was here."

An hour later, the two friends were sitting on the couch and looking over the weekend's schedule of events on Ada's laptop. There would be food and drinks from various vendors, magicians, face painting, karaoke, games, two stages with live entertainment, a dance contest, local artisans, wine tasting and mixing your own, the local brewery offering craft beer, and more. The events would be held all day for the next three days. Saturday night at ten o' clock there would be a display of fireworks that they claimed was unlike any other. Ada and Daisy were talking a mile a minute about all the different kinds of foods they wanted to try as well as the entertainment they for sure didn't want to miss.

They were reminded about a similar event back in their hometown several years earlier when the four friends challenged themselves to sample every kind of food and drink, participate in all games if only for a little while, and go hear all entertainment whether they were fans or not. By the end of the weekend two were sick and one had become a country music fan. The girls fell over laughing on the couch, hardly get their words out at times.

"How about I pour us another glass of wine and see how much more we can recall?" Ada started to get up and was still laughing, but Daisy grabbed her hand.

"Hey, hold on to that thought for a minute. There's something I wanted to share with you."

Ada suddenly looked serious and sat down quickly. "Are you okay? Is something wrong?"

"No, no, nothing like that. It's just . . . well, not something I wanted to tell you over the phone. I also don't want to go the entire weekend without talking to you about it."

"Oh my gosh, I can't even imagine. Are you and Jackson moving to the other side of the country? I mean, he always mentioned the possibility of starting his company in New York." Ada sat back on the couch defeated and sighed.

"No, we're not moving." Daisy smiled gently. "I'm . . . I'm pregnant, Ada."

Ada sat up slowly and moved to the edge of the couch and took Daisy's hands in hers. "Pregnant? You're going to have a baby?" She glanced over at Daisy's full wine glass. Then she said it louder as a statement. "You're going to have a baby!"

Ada threw her arms around Daisy and squeezed her tightly. She suddenly pulled away saying, "Oh, I'm squishing the baby! Sorry, little one." She patted Daisy's belly.

"I was afraid to tell you."

"Afraid to tell me? Why?"

"We always talked about being pregnant together. It's so unfair, Ada. You deserve happiness. I really wanted us to do everything at the same time!"

The girls sat together talking for another hour. Ada reassured her best friend that she indeed was thrilled to become an aunt and so happy for both Daisy and Jackson. What happened to Troy didn't mean that Daisy should be punished by not being permitted to experience joy. Ada shared that she believed someday there would be someone for her as well, just as her friend said. Whether or not Ada truly believed what she was saying didn't matter. What mattered was making certain that her friend knew how happy she was for this new life, and she was.

The conversation turned to Troy and then to Jason. Ada filled Daisy in on the latest with Jason even though she hadn't initially planned on doing so. This was proof to her that she was still hopeful for the next four weeks. Maybe something would change, or Jason would change. He would be convinced that Ada was safe to share his past and secrets with. Surely, he wasn't happy either. How could he be living the way he did, not going out and not giving or receiving love? After an hour of heart-wrenching sharing and tears, the two friends hugged.

"Whew! I don't know about you, but I'm exhausted." Daisy

laughed.

"Me, too," Ada sighed. "How about some munchies and ginger ale?"

"I could handle that!" laughed Daisy.

They decided to pick up where they left off last time with *Sweet Magnolias* season three. The girls had to pause the Netflix show for a minute to discuss what had been going on with the main characters Maddie and Cal, as well as Dana Sue. Since the following episode was the last one, they decided to go ahead and watch it, although both were yawning at this point. As all seasons do with their endings, it brought about even more questions. Daisy and Ada decided they would have to binge watch season four over the weekend.

They dragged themselves off to bed with a long goodnight hug and a promise from Aunt Ada that she already loved this little one with all her heart. Daisy seemed relieved and that made Ada a little sad. What kind of person was she to make her friend not want to tell the greatest news of her life? There was no reason she couldn't meet someone and fall in love again, especially at her age.

Climbing into bed, Ada thought about that. Was she in love already? She wasn't certain, but it was not exactly the typical experience when you feel all giddy inside. Jason wasn't sending out the same vibes, so it may be all for nothing. She laid her hand on her belly. What would it feel like to be pregnant? To have a growing being inside of you? One that was created out of love by . . . by? It was not going to be she and Troy now. That dream was over. She began imagining a cute little boy with soft brown hair, blue eyes and long eyelashes. He would play baseball and love his Mama. A little girl? She would follow her Daddy around everywhere and he'd put his baseball cap on her curly head. She fell asleep with those images, and they were sweet.

Chapter 22

For some reason the girls couldn't make up their minds what they wanted to wear for the day, so they chose to stay in pajamas while they had breakfast and coffee, chatting about Daisy's pregnancy and possible baby names as they did.

Daisy was nearly ten weeks along, meaning she had already been pregnant when she and Ada were last together, even if she hadn't realized. Her periods had never been regular since coming off the pill a few years ago, and life had been too busy to think much about tracking dates on a calendar. The thought that she could be pregnant didn't even occur to her until after a couple of weeks of feeling nauseated and fatigued.

It began one morning when Jackson was fixing Daisy eggs,

and the smell had caused her to race to the bathroom and throw up. She ended up on the couch all day sleeping but chalked it up to a virus. It wasn't until two weeks ago, when the symptoms had refused to improve, that she had given in and taken a pregnancy test, just in case. As she sat, counting down the minutes to the test's results, she had begun to finally consider what it would be like if she were pregnant.

She and Jackson hadn't necessarily been trying for kids, but they also hadn't been *not* trying; the idea of having kids had faded into the background after Troy's death. It had always been the plan that Daisy and Ada were going to be pregnant together, and it didn't feel right, Daisy being pregnant while Ada was still struggling to move on from Troy.

The timer that she had set on her phone for the test rang, interrupting her thoughts, and Daisy carefully examined the results. It was positive. She was pregnant! Her thoughts had then returned to Ada. "Oh, Ada," Daisy whispered to herself. There was just no way she could tell Ada over the phone. Telling someone closest to you had to be done in person, and thankfully she had an upcoming trip planned. She was anxious to tell Ada, not only from the worry that Ada would be hurt, but also from her growing excitement about the pregnancy. Truly, aside from Jackson, Ada was the first person she wanted to tell.

From that moment on, Daisy imagined the conversation when she would tell Ada over and over again, picturing good scenarios, bad scenarios, and everything in between. The weight of the secret only grew as her trip to see Ada inched closer, and Daisy was truly surprised that she hadn't blurted it out the moment that she saw Ada. When Daisy did finally work up the nerve to tell her secret, Ada had not been sad, as Daisy had expected, but, instead, thrilled for Daisy and Jackson. Daisy was relieved. It felt like she could finally, fully celebrate, and she was grateful to have such a caring and supportive friend as Ada.

As Daisy and Ada talked, Daisy ran to her room to get a list of names that she and Jackson had made three nights ago, before she had left for her trip. She and Ada then narrowed down the list to the top three for both boys and girls. For boys they had decided on Milo, Noah, and Remi, using Jackson's middle name of Carter. For girls they had chosen Nadalia, Sage, and Rowyn with the middle name being Celeste like Daisy's. As of that moment neither one had a guess or feeling as to which one she was having at the end of January.

By the time the girls were done chatting, it was already going on one in the afternoon, and the decision of what to wear was easier. They wanted to go downtown to all the festivities. The first musical group was performing on stage at two.

Ada and Daisy chose somewhat similar summer dresses because they had ordered them at the same time from Lulu's, but Daisy's was a bit more Bohemian with its multi-print. Ada's was an understated coral floral print and was perfect for her new deep tan. Daisy whistled when Ada came walking out of the bedroom.

"Wow! Look at you, right off the page of a magazine!"

"Oh my gosh, you're too funny, but thanks just the same. You look great as usual!"

"Thanks! Let's go hear some music!" She started dancing on her way to the door. Ada joined her, shimmying along behind.

On the way downtown, they blared the radio and continued the party all the way there. As they sang and danced along, Ada's thoughts began to wander, and she hoped that Jason would make an appearance that evening. Was he even interested in having fun at all? It seemed like he had become even more introverted since she had first met him.

"Hey! Where did my singing partner go?" Daisy shouted above the song.

Ada hadn't even realized that her thoughts had taken over her singing. Without missing a beat, she came right back in on the next verse louder than before.

Downtown had been transformed overnight into a bustling and lively version of large city vibes. The main street had been blocked so that vendors could display their wares, from clothing and jewelry to specialty foods and pottery. The kids' zones were already full of face painting and crafts. The food trucks were parked together, and a large section was roped off containing several picnic tables. The first band to perform was setting up on Stage 1 and doing sound checks.

The girls weren't hungry yet, but the smells were amazing. They had already pointed out at least two food trucks to stop at later. Now seemed a perfect time to check out the sidewalk sales. They reached Saylor's Bookstore with offerings of both old and new books at good prices. Ada picked up a copy of *Wuthering Heights*, which she hadn't read in years but decided probably not the best choice for her to revisit right now given the intensity; she put the book back down. Daisy held up a copy of *Jane Eyre* and reminded Ada of their in-depth study during a college course. Ada decided on a worn copy of *Dr. Zhivago*, a book that she had never read but recalled parts of the movie. It was one of her mother's favorites. Daisy held up a historical romance novel depicting a couple in a passionate embrace. That was her best friend to you. Ada had liked those kinds of books when Troy was alive. They made her very romantic and in the mood. Since his passing she stuck to more serious books that reflected her present emotions.

As they were leaving the bookstore, Robert and Susan walked inside.

"Well, hello there girls! Daisy, how nice to see you again!" Susan said with a big smile. Robert was a few steps behind as he had stopped to read a sign featuring a new author.

He looked up immediately when hearing his wife's greeting. "Hello, indeed! I see you've made your first purchases of the day already!" he said, indicating their bags.

Both girls laughed. "Oh yes! One light-hearted and fun," said Daisy, pointing to herself. "The other dramatic and sad," using her thumb to point to Ada.

Ada gently swatted her hand on Daisy's arm. "Whatever!" They all four laughed.

"Enjoy your day, and I'm sure we'll be running into you again," said Ada.

As they continued walking past the couple, Susan

nonchalantly whispered into Ada's ear, "He's here. Saw him a few minutes ago."

Daisy hadn't even noticed Susan's whisper, so Ada didn't say anything. No need to since she had not a clue what she would say to Jason or if he would want to talk to her. Still, she was hoping to introduce Daisy.

The next couple of stores sold clothing, and the girls were able to pick up a couple of cardigans and jeans. Both chose fedoras, Ada one in blush and Daisy a beige. Given their clothing selections and the bright sunny day, they took off the tags and positioned them on their heads. As they looked in the mirror before leaving the store, the clerk gave them a thumbs up and smiled. He was an older distinguished gentleman with the kindest eyes, and his approval pleased them.

They headed to the car to place their packages and then to the food trucks. The shopping so far had made them hungry. Both were in the mood for tacos and street corn. There was just something about eating out like this that made food taste extra good. Ada hoped that she remembered to put some gum in her purse in case she ran into Jason. Mexican food didn't exactly give you the best breath. Although, she and Troy never cared when they both ate it. Funny how neither paid attention and could make out on the couch soon after without a thought.

Daisy rubbed her stomach and suggested some peppermint tea across the street at Teatime. *Perfect*, Ada thought. They were able to get their drinks in disposable cups, so they continued walking around.

This time they visited vendors set up in the middle of the street. Neither one had anything particular that they were looking for, but they came across some booths with cute Christmas ornaments and jewelry. After looking at some of the personalization available at the Christmas booth, the girls chose the same ornament that said "Best Friends" with two girls sledding. The artist wrote the date and their names on each one.

In the booth next to that, a jewelry designer had the cutest earrings on display and offered to make custom pieces right there as well. What made it extra fun was being able to choose the beads. This time the two decided to match each other and chose big teardrop earrings with pale aqua and pink crystal beads. While waiting to have them made, Daisy chose a rope and leather bracelet for Jackson since his birthday was coming up in August. Ada agreed that she could see him wearing it. They were very happy with how the earrings turned out and gladly accepted the young girl's business cards.

After perusing some beautiful pottery and stopping to watch a few of the children work on crafts, the girls were ready to try something sweet from one of the food trucks and take a walk down by the water. Looking up, Ada spotted a familiar face, and her stomach suddenly did a flip. She didn't mean to, but a little noise escaped from her mouth and caused Daisy to turn quickly toward her.

"Are you okay?" Then she spotted him. He was what she had had expected, about the same build as Troy but curlier hair, as Ada had indicated. He was walking straight toward them but didn't appear to notice the two girls suddenly trying not to look obvious. A couple of the baseball players and their girlfriends approached him, and he stopped to chat.

"Ada?" Daisy became concerned from the look on her face. "That's Jason, isn't it?"

"Y—yes, it is. I have wanted you to meet him, but now I'm not so sure. What we have can't even be labeled as a friendship at this point." Ada stopped and pretended to look through some old albums outside a record store. "In fact, I don't know if there is even a word to describe—"

Daisy interrupted, "Coming this way."

"Hello, Ada."

She turned around and almost knocked over a display of Beatles memorabilia. Trying to play it cool, she secured the stand and looked straight into those crystal blue eyes.

"Hi, Jason. How are you? This is my best friend from back home."

"Daisy, I presume?" Jason had extended his hand and smiled.

"Yes, and I'm guessing that you're Jason? It's so nice to meet you." Daisy was entranced suddenly and started to say, "You look so much like—" but then she regained her composure almost immediately and finished with, "a baseball coach."

Jason gave a little chuckle hearing this and commented back, "I didn't know we had a look."

"Well, the hat kind of gave it away." Daisy pointed and laughed.

"Ah, of course." Jason said and tipped his hand on the hat. "Well, anyway, it was nice meeting you, Daisy. I'm sure the two of you are enjoying the weekend together. The weather is beautiful for the festival."

So that's it, thought Ada. He's reduced to small talk without even appearing like they had spent intimate moments together; he was playing it a little too cool.

Suddenly, Ada felt anger rising in her cheeks and without running it through her brain first, retorted with, "Yes, and yes. Thanks. Oh, Daisy, our favorite music is playing. Let's hurry and catch the second concert. See ya, Jason." Ada didn't wait for either of them to say a word and simply started walking hurriedly toward the sound stage.

"Uh, nice to meet you, Jason," Daisy said as she was running to catch up with Ada. "You, too," he managed to say and raised his hand awkwardly in a wave.

"What in the hell was that?" Daisy asked while threading her arm through Ada's. "You left a trail of cold air back there."

Ada kept up the quick walking and didn't even turn to look at Daisy when she said, "Unbelievable, just unbelievable."

The music became so loud that they couldn't possibly have a conversation. Instead, Ada took Daisy's hand and twirled her around. They joined the rest of the crowd singing and dancing.

The cover band played around ten numbers, and the girls knew almost every word in the songs. The last two were love songs, so Ada decided at that point to seek out a place for dinner. Their favorite Italian restaurant had seating outside, so they decided pasta was a good choice.

The girls went on and on about their selections. Both ended up getting the linguine with pesto and a Caesar salad. The bread came toasted and crisp with olive oil and a little garlic salt. It was delicious. The owner, Alessandro, came out to personally greet them, after they sent word with the server that the food was extraordinary. He brought with him two plates of tiramisu on the house.

Ada was feeling quite at home in the town after only spending a few weeks. The girls discussed colors for the nursery and thought it best to use a neutral color for either a boy or girl. Afterall, Daisy was hoping to have at least one more at some point. She showed some possible cribs and rocker gliders to Ada that she had saved on her phone.

"Maybe we can visit the local Baby Boutique on the other side of town," Ada suggested. "Their storefront always looks so adorable. They appear to sell everything from furniture to clothing." Daisy was looking intently at Ada as though curious how she would know about such a place. Picking up on her best friend's facial expression, she jumped right in with, "I happened to notice it when I stopped to get Maisy's things after picking her up from the breeder."

"That sounds like a great idea! Jackson and I haven't shopped anywhere yet. I think he was hoping we'd take care of that while I'm here. You know he's never been that interested in spending time in stores." Daisy laughed and so did Ada.

"That's right! Well, what are best friends for anyway?"

"Would you like a box for the leftovers?" the server asked. The girls hadn't really left all that much and explained they weren't going home for a while. She took the plates away and left the check, which Ada quickly grabbed.

"I've got it! You drove this entire way to see me, so it's the least I can do."

"Aww, you know I'd drive anywhere to spend time with you! Thanks." Daisy put her glass of water for a toast.

"To best friends."

"To best friends," Ada echoed. The girls clanked their glasses and took the last gulp of their drinks.

They decided to walk down by the pier to watch the sunset. Before doing so they grabbed their sweaters out of the car since it tended to be chillier close to the shore. The two walked in silence to the water's edge and stood looking out. The sun had dropped closer to the horizon and bounced off the water creating arrays that enveloped the entire coastline.

"I smell oranges," Daisy said breaking their silence.

Ada smiled and turned to her friend, "I smell them, too."

The sun warmed their up-tilted faces. Ada put her arm through Daisy's and gently laid her head on her shoulder. The two stood quietly for what seemed like a long time, in their own thoughts, yet tightly bound together like sisters.

Chapter 23

The following morning Ada and Daisy were awoken to the sound of Maisy barking. They had stayed up late into the night talking about their futures, as usual. The girls had always enjoyed planning outings or events, so the months and years ahead of them were often a topic of conversation. It was also interesting to talk about how many times life's changes brought about different scenarios than what was initially imagined. Not that this was unusual in any way, but the two liked the challenges of predicting the future. Daisy was living the closest to the dreams they both had: a husband, career, and children. Ada knew that Daisy was somewhat holding back her excitement about the baby because of what happened with Troy, but Ada wanted her best friend to exude that joy. After taking an inpatient Maisy outside to potty, they decided to take their breakfast out on the front porch. It was a spectacular day with perfect temperature and a bright blue sky. Ada shifted in the wicker swing, brought out a wrapped box, and handed it to Daisy, who sat up and slowly began to smile at her friend.

"What is this? Really? For me? It's not even my birthday." Daisy took the box from Ada with a smile and tilted her head. She slowly opened the box and put her hand to her mouth as soon as she saw what was inside. It was a gold necklace with two tiny baby feet.

"It's beautiful, Ada, oh my goodness."

"The lady last night said for you to bring it back after you have the baby, and she will engrave the name and date."

"Wait, you got this today when we were downtown? The same place where we bought our earrings—when did you do that?"

"Remember when I claimed that I had left something at the store when we were walking around, and I ran back to get it? Well, I quickly purchased it for you."

"My first gift as a new mother," Daisy said through misty eyes, "and from you. This will be my most treasured gift of all time."

"You are so welcome, Daisy. I need you to know that I

truly am happy for you and Jackson. I promise to be the best aunt and that my joy is your joy. Please believe me when I say that."

"I do, my sweet friend, I do." The two shared a hug like they had so many times, but this time they held onto each other a little tighter and a little longer.

"Hi there, girls!"

This sudden statement broke them apart, and they saw Susan across the street waving to them. She was getting her mail.

"Good morning! Would you like to join our breakfast club? We still have muffins!" Ada greeted her.

"I'd love to, but I'm helping Oscar set up an art booth for kids this afternoon. You two should stop by if you're planning on going back downtown."

"We'd love to do that, plus I haven't seen Oscar since the night of the gala," Ada replied.

"Great! See you later then!" Susan took the mail and walked to her car.

"That name sounds familiar, Daisy added. Isn't he the one who owns the art gallery?"

"Yes, it is," said Ada. "I'm glad you'll get to meet him." Ada stood to gather the plates and mugs.

"Speaking of getting to meet someone," interrupted Daisy, "we haven't really talked much about what happened with Jason yesterday at the festival. I feel like you have some unresolved issues with the situation . . . or whatever it could be called."

"My thoughts exactly," replied Ada, a little louder over her shoulder than she had intended. Her friend was right, it was a situation, and one that had continued to cause her confusion and frustration.

After stepping inside, Ada continued, but spoke quieter this time. "Even though I'm so angry and irritated with him, all it would take is for him to pull me into his arms, and I'd be a goner."

"Wow, I didn't realize you felt so strongly towards him. I'm sorry, Ada. That must be so maddening for you to not know what is going on in that head of his. Why can't he just come clean? I can tell he has feelings for you."

"Do you think so? I'm never sure."

"Well, I am."

Another forty minutes went by while the girls discussed possible reasons for Jason to behave the way he did, a past relationship that ended badly, a loss perhaps? It was just unusual for a guy to hold on to things like he did. Maybe it was worse than they could imagine, and he was really hurting inside. Maisy emerged from the bedroom and once again interrupted after seeing the cute Bichon walking up the street with his owner.

"I'll take her for a quick walk," Daisy said. "You might want to adjust your makeup a little. You know, before we go out." She grinned.

"Oh my gosh, are you kidding? Is this an attempt to play matchmaker with some guy on the street or do you think we may run into Jason again?" Ada began rinsing the dishes.

"Hmm. We'll have to see about that." She and Maisy were outside, and Daisy had shut the door before Ada could answer.

Since Daisy had to leave in the morning because she and Jackson had plans for Sunday evening with his folks, the girls discussed how to best plan their last full day together. Both decided that today was a day for updos with their hair, so Daisy French-braided Ada's and she herself wore a messy bun. They selected similar but not matching outfits. Today was warmer than yesterday, so shorts and tops were the look of the day. They opted for tennis shoes this time because the sandals yesterday weren't the best idea for all the walking they ended up doing the day before. There was one more concert they wished to attend, plus visiting Oscar's set up, and some additional food to try. Both left the bungalow feeling energetic and happy to be spending another day together as best friends.

Ada and Daisy spent the rest of the day doing more of what they enjoyed most: eating, shopping, and talking to each other about everything. Neither one mentioned Jason's name nor did he appear anywhere to remind them. There were a few more clothing items bought, as well as specialty coffee blends to try back at the bungalow. They bumped into several of Ada's classmates, including Lee. Daisy thought he was charming and smooth. She wondered why Ada didn't take more of a liking to him, but she wasn't about to question her when it was more than obvious that she had feelings for Jason.

Before they knew it, the sun was setting, and they hurried down to the beach area once again. This time they took along a bottle of Cedrata, a sweet, carbonated drink made with cedar fruit, that they had been given from the Italian gentleman who owned the restaurant. He ordered directly from his hometown in central Italy and the girls had raved about it during Daisy's last trip to visit. After two toasts and glasses, they put the cork back inside the bottle. Maybe a nightcap later was in order, especially given their weekend was about to come to an end. The two best friends hated to part, more than anything. They had been like close sisters for all these years, and to be together felt like the most natural thing in the world.

After showering and getting into some comfortable loungewear, Ada and Daisy sat down to watch another movie and eat some popcorn. It seemed to hit the spot after their second day of Italian pasta. They also split the rest of the sparkling grape juice but sipped it this time in between bites of food. Maisy curled up on the couch between the two girls and had fallen asleep. Daisy caught a glimpse of her best friend smiling slightly at a sweet kiss the couple on the TV had just shared. She put her hand on her baby bump and couldn't help but wish the two had been pregnant together, just like they had always planned. Just then Ada's cell phone rang and made the girls jump.

"Hello?" Ada grabbed her cell phone and answered before seeing who was calling. "Oh, hi, Mom."

Ada was quick to put the call on speaker and inform her mother that Daisy was visiting. She hoped that they could hang up sooner than they usually did, mainly because she wanted every minute with her friend and no interruptions. The three of them talked, and Jean, Ada's mother, was elated to hear about Daisy's pregnancy. Daisy, on the other hand, was feeling rather nervous that something would be said about Ada not being able to be pregnant. Jean was very familiar with the plans that the two of them had made long ago regarding doing everything at the same time. Surprisingly, the conversation was short and sweet with no mention of what Ada should or should not be doing.

"Your Mom sounds good," Daisy commented, smiling at Ada.

"Oh, you know her. As long as she is vacationing most of the time, all is well with the world. At least it keeps her off my back and trying to tell me how I should be living my life. Initially, she didn't see the necessity for my coming here to do two graduate classes. You know, why pursue another degree when you're already busy with teaching? She seems to have slowed down her life notes lately where I'm concerned, and I'm thankful."

"Oh, at least she means well," Daisy said while her head leaned to one side. "She does love you."

"I know. Just wish sometimes she didn't feel like I needed a mentor in my ear constantly. I'm actually pretty good at making my own decisions."

Maisy jumped off the couch and began barking.

"Are you hungry or is it potty time?" Ada asked, as if speaking with a child.

The puppy did a downward dog pose and came up shaking her tail and barking louder. "Okay, okay, how about potty and a treat?"

At this Maisy raced towards the door and then turned to look at Ada while wildly wagging her tail.

"Okay, okay, we're going." Ada laughed.

"She is a sweet dog," said Daisy. "You're both lucky to have each other. It makes me happy to know that you have a companion here."

"Oh gee, some companion." Ada rustled the top of Maisy's head affectionately as they stepped outside.

After Maisy settled down in her doggy bed, the two girls finished watching their movie. Ada was glad they had chosen a romantic comedy this time. She wanted to feel happy before going to sleep tonight and knowing that Daisy would be leaving tomorrow.

The girls hadn't even made it to their own beds the night

before and were awakened by the extra loud commercial on the television.

"Wow! I didn't think I would knock out like that!" Daisy sat up and wriggled out of the twisted blanket.

"I can't believe we slept here all night! I don't think we've done that since the four of us were in Tahoe on vacation," Ada said sitting up and stretching. She noticed Daisy looking at her with a somewhat concerned expression. "What?"

"Oh, nothing . . ."

"Just remembering what it was like when all of us were together? It's okay, Daisy, I think about that all the time. Those are some of my favorite memories, and I treasure them. They were happy times."

"Yes, indeed they were,' said Daisy, reaching over to hold Ada's hand.

"Well, how about some coffee and cinnamon rolls?"

"Umm. Sounds heavenly," Daisy swooned. "How about if I take this cutie out back while you put on the coffee?"

Maisy stood up as though she knew exactly what Daisy was saying and walked over to her harness on the floor.

Daisy laughed, "I'm coming, girl."

They decided to have their rolls and coffee on the front

porch swing. It was a beautiful summer day with plenty of sunshine and bird chatter. She and Daisy had continued their conversation about colors for the baby's room and keeping it gender neutral. They also recapped their conversation with a local furniture craftsman downtown and the crib, dresser, and glider rocker that Daisy had picked out. She ended up getting Jackson on Facetime so he could give his stamp of approval. These pieces would be made exactly how Daisy had envisioned with the country cottage slat crib in white oak. The furniture would be ready about the time Ada finished her summer course, so Jackson and Daisy would make the trip together next time.

After baby talk, they switched to talking about work and working on opening their classrooms for the new year. Ada felt almost sick to her stomach but didn't want to make Daisy feel bad because she really did enjoy most things about teaching. Of course, Ada cared for her students very much but also knew that her heart wasn't in it. Afterall, shouldn't she be doing something that gave her purpose?

Thankfully, her future in art seemed more of a possibility than it ever had, thanks to the courses this summer and the accolades she had received for her own artwork.

Daisy gathered her things and put them in the back of her

car. She squatted down to pet Maisy, who at one point tried to jump in the car with her.

"Hey, you, fuzzy pup, you're not going anywhere, and that includes with Aunt Daisy.

Wow, that sounded so natural and came out easily." Both girls looked at each other and smiled.

"One day, my friend," Daisy said thoughtfully, "one day."

"You never know!" Ada replied as she grabbed her friend and hugged her tightly. "Thank you for driving in again! I don't know what I would have done without your coming to see me this summer!"

"This was so fun for me, too," Daisy said with a big smile.

"Yes, we'll be back before you know it! I love you, sweet friend."

"And I love you, too! Drive safely and text when you get home."

"Will do!" Daisy beeped the horn and waved her arm out the window as she was driving off.

Even Maisy gave a little bark as if to say goodbye.

"Alright, girl, how about a walk? Sound good?" Ada bent down to give Maisy a kiss on the top of the head. *I wonder what the next few weeks will bring*, Ada thought to herself. *I do know one thing; I'm going to make it count.*

Chapter 24

Ada was pleased with her first day of the new semester of classes and decided that the course entitled History of Architecture would prove to be more interesting than she anticipated. She was glad to have Professor Aglio once again since she was familiar with this style of teaching and what to expect. A few of her new friends were in attendance as well. Lee, along with Charlotte, Henry, Rose, and Emma sat near each other. Lee was already planning another sailing trip for them in two weeks. Ada found herself rather excited to go. Besides, what else would she be doing? The group talked excitedly over lunch about what they would do. There was a small island a bit farther south from where they sailed last time. It would require leaving earlier in the morning, so they'd have time to arrive and spend the day. Ada thought briefly about inviting Jason, but quickly changed her mind. The thought of a romantic cruise on a sailboat with Jason made the butterflies in her stomach awaken. *What would he say*, Ada thought to herself. As frustrated as she felt toward him, she couldn't help but picture the two of them together taking a walk on a secluded beach and . . .

"Hey there, so what do you think?" It was Emma directing a question towards Ada.

Ada blinked back to reality. "Sorry, I was daydreaming about the trip. The last one was so much fun."

"Lee mentioned us possibly staying overnight on the boat, or even camping out on the beach. That way we don't need to worry about rushing back."

"Oh! Sure," Ada said. "That makes sense."

"Okay, then that's the plan," added Lee quite pleased with the decision.

"Better get back to class," Henry said, as he stood up and threw away some trash.

The rest of them did the same and talked about who could bring what as they made their way to the second floor.

Susan and Maisy had just returned from a walk when Ada had about made it home. Maisy was excited to see her and pulled away from Susan before she had time to grab tightly to the leash.

"Hey there, sweet girl." Ada bent down on the sidewalk to greet Maisy and hold onto her until she could get a hold of the leash.

"Wow! She is getting strong!" Susan laughed.

They made their way to the porch and Maisy curled up beside Ada on the swing. The two of them talked about Ada's new course and the upcoming sailing trip. Susan thought Ada should ask Jason to join her even though things between the two young people were clear as mud. Ada was thankful that she could talk to Susan easily and not feel awkward to share her feelings for Jason. Also, it was a bonus to have such good friends willing to care for Maisy. Privately, Ada wished that her own parents could be more present in her life. She hadn't thought too much about it until this past year, but having her mom and dad be nearer and more involved like Robert and Susan would be nice. Maybe a phone call later this evening was in order. It had been almost ten days since she had talked to them.

"How about I fix us a salad and pasta for the three of us tomorrow night?"

"That sounds lovely, Ada. Thank you for the invite. What should I bring? How about a little dessert?"

"Oh gosh, I would never be able to repay your and Robert's kindnesses to me since I've been here. You've made me feel like family, and I'm grateful to you both."

"Of course, and we, too, have gained a great deal from your friendship. This has been a very enjoyable summer because of your living across the street!"

Just then Maisy went over and nudged Susan's hand with the tip of her wet nose, as if to say, "Hey, What about me?"

Quick to pick up on the timing, Susan put Maisy's head between her hands and gave her a kiss on the head. "And you have made it even more fun, sweet puppy!"

Maisy wagged her tail vigorously.

"We both thank you for your excellent care of us!" said Ada.

"Quite welcome, and I look forward to sharing dinner tomorrow. How does a strawberry dessert sound? I just bought two containers from the farmer's market."

"Perfect," said Ada with a smile. "See you around 6?"

"You got it! See you later, girls." And with that Susan was across the street and checking mail. Jason was walking down the street at about the same time and yelling hello to Susan. She waited and walked to the front door with him. Before they entered the house, Jason turned to wave at Ada. Surely Susan said something about her sitting on the porch. She couldn't imagine him caring enough to take the initiative himself.

After a forty-five-minute conversation with her father and mother, Ada was asking herself why she waited so late to call. All she wanted to do was to curl up in front of the television and eat a bowl of cereal. The questions kept coming:

"What are your plans for the end of summer? You are going back to your teaching job, right? Do you feel that the University there is providing a good enough graduate degree in art history? Isn't that exciting news about Daisy and Jackson?" Her mom had started to say, "It's too bad—" And Ada knew exactly what she was thinking, but her mom switched the end of that sentence to, "you had to be away this summer instead of with your best friend."

Even her dad jumped in to ask about the sailing trip next weekend. He was always interested in anything that had to do with the water and relaxation. Her mother chimed in about sunscreen. That's when Ada decided that the conversation had reached the end. After promising to be careful and call soon, she plugged her dying cell phone into the charger and went to take a shower. Tomorrow she really was going to find Jason and ask if he wanted to go along next Saturday. This was going to take a little extra hair care and a cute outfit. Those two things always gave her confidence boost.

After getting out of the shower and wrapping her hair in a towel, Ada put on a robe and began looking through her closet to see if anything appealed to her to wear the next day. Maybe something pretty and feminine, like the pale pink mini dress and strappy sandals. She could put part of her hair up and let the rest fall over her shoulders. The tan from the last boating trip and then being out all weekend with Daisy had given her a nice glow. After blow-drying her hair and using the large curling iron for some natural waves, she went out into the kitchen. Ada grabbed a large plastic bowl, a spoon, and half gallon of milk. She put the box of cinnamon toast crunch beneath her arm and walked over to the couch. Maisy ran over as if she was going to share some.

"Aww, sorry girl, I already fed you dinner. This is mine."

Maisy went over to her own bed and laid down, looking defeated.

Ada was on the third episode of a new show and ended up watching two in a row while eating almost three helpings of cereal. She could never do this as a teenager at home because her mom wouldn't even buy cereal. It had to be yogurt, blueberries, or boiled eggs.

All that did was make Ada want the sugared cereal even more, so it was the first purchase she made at the grocery store when moving into her own place. In fact, she always kept her favorites on hand: Captain Crunch, Lucky Charms, and of course Cinnamon Toast Crunch. Only once did her mother open the cabinet to get a glass and make a gasping noise.

"Don't even say it, Mom."

Ada's mother just shook her head.

Her father was too busy in her younger years to notice the strained relationship between Ada and her mother, or if he had, he would have chalked it up to typical teenage drama. In the last few years, she felt that her father's gentle side was what kept their relationship going. He seemed to intervene more when Ada's mother started in with her strong opinions or suggestions. The only problem was that nothing changed with her mom.

She finished the last gulp of sweet cold milk from the bowl and set it aside. Ada rewound to the last part of the episode since her thoughts had removed all focus from what was happening in the show. Maisy jumped up and laid her head on Ada's leg for comfort, or maybe it was to offer comfort.

The following morning Ada was pleased with her outfit and the way she looked. It was just as she had envisioned yesterday. Sometimes she'd change her mind about what she had put out to wear by the time morning arrived. Not this time. She grabbed her bag and passed Susan on the sidewalk coming to get Maisy.

"See you later, pretty girl, have a great day!" Susan gave her a big smile and a wink.

"Thank you," Ada said in return. Had that wink and smile from Susan pertained to her plans for asking Jason to go on the boat next weekend? She couldn't be certain but appreciated the encouragement.

Class went by quickly, probably due to the pictures and discussions of various cathedrals around the globe. Ada had always been fascinated with the ornate and detailed structures. During her junior year in college, she spent time in Germany and France, frequenting several historical cathedrals. She wished the many pictures she had taken during that time were with her. Professor Algio would have appreciated them.

Some of her classmates had decided to go downtown for dinner and invited her, but Ada had some special people coming for dinner. She hadn't seen Jason, so decided to head directly to the baseball fields where she knew he would be with the team. This was the time of the afternoon most practices were held. Ada stopped in the restroom to touch up her makeup and hair.

Ada could see the baseball players out in the field taking throwing practice. It brought back so many memories of the times Troy had his high school team doing the same thing. She loved going with him and watching how he interacted with the teens. He knew the game so well and was a great instructor but was also kind and set a great example of staying positive under any circumstance. They could be down by five runs, or one run and Troy was the same. That was one of the many qualities she loved. Her confidence suddenly subsided, and she felt sad thinking about Troy. About that time, she heard a whistle and looked up to see a wave. It was one of the players.

"Are you the new outfielder?" He was smiling.

Gathering herself together she responded, "You bet! Thought you could use some help," to which they all scoffed and laughed.

Ada found herself continuing to walk closer to where Jason stood by the dugout with a clipboard in hand. He turned and threw up a hand to her with a half-smile. He must have assumed that she was meaning to speak with him because he started to head towards her.

"I guess you made quite an impression at the beginning of the summer with that catch outside the fence."

Ada laughed nervously. "Yeah, I guess so." She didn't feel like idle talk any more so got right to the point. "Lee is taking his sailboat out again next weekend and we're thinking about heading to Bailey's Island for a campout. Well, the guys are staying on the beach while the girls bunk down on the boat. Just thought I'd invite you to go with us. I noticed there weren't any summer games being played over the weekend."

Jason seemed extremely taken aback and almost stammered when trying to answer her. "I . . . uh . . . yeah, that sounds nice, but uh . . . well, uh . . ."

Ada did nothing to help him out and really wanted to know what he was going to say. She moved a bit closer to Jason and sensed it was making him nervous.

"Thanks for the invite, but, well, Robert and I planned on spending the entire weekend wrapping up the project we've been working on. I wasn't able to this weekend because of the local tournament."

"Oh, I see. What exactly have you two been working on? Susan doesn't even seem to know."

Jason laughed nervously, "Oh, just a book about

cognition and—"

"Is this a baseball book?" Ada asked inquisitively.

"I guess you could say that!" Jason agreed quickly. "Thanks so much for asking me, and your friends seem super nice. I just better stick with the plan for a working weekend."

For some reason, Ada wasn't upset with his answer. At least it wasn't some lame excuse, and she was very aware that he and Robert had been working on a book of sorts. If he hadn't been doing that, well, maybe he would have agreed to go.

"Okay, sure! I understand." Ada smiled sincerely and Jason appeared appreciative. "Have a good practice. Second one to the left there needs to get his hand back closer to his ear when he's throwing."

Ada wasn't sure if she had said something wrong or what, but Jason looked at her with a look that she hadn't seen from him before. The silence was almost awkward.

Jason turned toward the player and then looked back at Ada. "You're right. I'm going to need to talk to him about that. Thanks."

They said goodbye to each other, and Ada walked home with a bounce in her step. Maybe things were looking up finally. It felt good.

Ada cooked a delicious Italian dinner with linguine and a pasta sauce from scratch. She had learned how to make pasta correctly when her family had hosted an Italian exchange student when she was a senior in high school. Ada had also made a salad with leafy greens, cucumber, shredded carrots, and tomatoes, tossed with a vinaigrette. The three of them had a wonderful discussion about all their travels. Robert and Susan had been to Italy and Greece the year before. They thought that Ada's meal was reminiscent of their dinner in Tuscany. Ada felt it was a huge compliment, but she gave most of the credit to the cooking class she and Daisy had taken.

Susan took the lid off her Tupperware holder. It contained three dessert bowls that contained a cream cheese mixture with strawberries on top. Every bite was delicious and paired well with coffee.

"I did ask Jason to go along on the sailing trip next weekend," Ada said aloud suddenly.

Susan was feeding herself a bit of dessert with the fork in her mouth which she promptly removed. "Really? So?"

"I think he may have considered going, but unfortunately has plans with this guy right here." Ada motioned her fork towards the direction of Robert.

"You don't say?" Robert said and took a bite of food, leaving a bit of cream cheese on the corners of his mouth.

"Oh gee, honey, let me get that for you." Robert licked it off before she had time to get a napkin. "You silly goose! So, what are you and Jason working on? You've never shared that with me."

"From what I ascertained it's about baseball . . . and cognition," said Ada.

"Hmm. In fact, it does contain those very topics. Sorry, my dear, to keep Jason from doing something enjoyable. We've just been trying to wrap things up before the end of summer."

"No problem, Robert, I understand." Ada smiled and took another bite.

After a little more conversation revolving around the food, great friendships, and her art class, Robert and Susan helped Ada with the dishes and made their way back home. Both gave her a hug and bent to give Maisy some love as well.

When the door closed behind them Ada felt a sudden sadness. How could she go home at the end of summer and not have these two people living across from her anymore?

Chapter 25

Another week had flown by, and Ada had only seen Jason from afar, usually on the baseball field. She was down to three weeks left for her course, and any kind of relationship with him looked hopeless. There was nothing else to do except move forward. Fortunately, Oscar Ash had called her in the middle of the week and asked Ada to stop by the gallery on Saturday. She was curious as to what he wanted to discuss with her. Today was Friday, so she decided to dress casually and put on a baby blue romper with white tennis shoes, along with a ponytail since last night was hair night but she gave herself a pass.

Susan had come over a little earlier than normal to get Maisy because she had someone stopping by to discuss another charity event. Ada felt like walking to campus this morning and taking in some fresh air. The streets were still quiet except for a couple of joggers and a family sitting outside on the driveway while their children played with riding toys. She couldn't make out what they were saying to each other, but the wife was laughing and leaning into her husband. *What a perfect scenario,* thought Ada. This was how she saw her future, or at least wished. She shifted her backpack to the other side and the couple looked up and waved to her with smiling faces. Ada smiled back at them as she put her hand up and gestured.

The music coming out of her AirPods happened to be a melancholy song from back in the day with the four best friends. Even though it brought a tear to her eye, she didn't skip to the next selection. Sometimes Ada allowed herself to hurt and be sad. It was healing.

Today's class focused on the architecture of cathedrals in Europe. Most contained a narthex at the entrance, along with three aisles. Central was the nave, a transept or chancel area gave the church its cross shape and contained an open choir. At the far end was an altar.

Professor Aglio showed several on the large screen, and most of the students were full of questions. Ada had written down three cathedrals that she hoped to visit someday. Her favorite subject this week had been the study of castles. She had been fascinated by these from the books she had read as a child. After being reminded by Lee about their sailing trip next weekend and saying goodbye to classmates until Monday, Ada left the building to walk home by way of the baseball field side. The guys were there as usual, and Jason was yelling some things out to the players as they practiced. She remembered when Troy had down this very thing with his high school team. Ada felt the same butterflies now as she had back then.

"Why are you continuing to torture yourself," she questioned in a whisper. Obviously, nothing is going to change, especially since Jason wasn't going along on the outing next weekend. That really was the only window of time for something possibly serious to happen between the two.

Ada stopped by the corner market and picked up some pasta and pesto sauce. She grabbed some of her favorite praline ice cream, too, and hurried home to get it in the freezer. Susan still had Maisy at her house with company because Ada could hear them out back and caught a glimpse of Maisy chasing a ball.

She met the program director for the new discovery center opening downtown. A middle-aged lady, who was most enthusiastic about adding a place for children, shook Ada's hand ferociously and was all too happy to talk about the plans. Sensing Ada was anxious to get home, Susan cleverly interjected with an excuse to show her some pictures inside, and Ada mouthed a thank you to her when the lady wasn't looking.

Ada kicked off her shoes first thing when she got home and changed into soft cotton shorts and a well-worn Bob Marley t-shirt. Grabbing an orange and napkin, she plopped down on the papasan to call her parents. They mainly called her, so she thought it was time to reach out herself. Neither of them answered their cell phones, but her father called back immediately.

Ada's mother was getting a manicure, and he had been picking up a few items at the store. She enjoyed talking only to her father this time. Since he was no longer practicing as a general surgeon, he appeared more relaxed and eager to hear about his daughter's life. He was fascinated when Ada talked about the cathedrals and their architecture. He had been to several places when traveling Europe between graduation and the start of medical school. Ada assured him that she would call again later in the weekend to speak to her mom.

The small egg salad sandwich she had for lunch hadn't staved off hunger, so Ada got the pot of water on for her linguine pasta. She added rock salt as was taught to her by the foreign exchange student they had when she was in high school. Valentina had them quickly adjusted to eating pasta at least three days a week. Ada learned that any sauce was stirred into the pasta instead of being added to the top as she was accustomed to doing when her mother cooked. It was so much better that way. Ada had cooked only a half pound of pasta but was so hungry that she ended up eating all but a small container's-worth that she put in the refrigerator. Afterwards, she and Maisy went on a walk before the carbs from the pasta made her too sleepy to do anything. She put her AirPods in and about fifteen minutes later her cell rang. It was Daisy.

"Hi there, whatcha doin?" Daisy asked.

"Well, hi yourself. I happen to be taking a walk with Maisy and listening to music, although I'd rather hear your voice any day! How are you feeling?"

"I'm doing just great! The nausea has finally stopped, and I can eat most things, except for spicy foods and coffee."

"Oh gosh, so no more fajita nachos or cappuccinos?" Ada laughed.

"Yuck!" Daisy made a gagging sound. "I hope that will change once I have the baby! Talk about no fun!"

Talking to Daisy always gave Ada a boost of energy. She was so upbeat and laughed easily. Ada talked to her about class, Maisy, the upcoming sailing trip, and of course, Jason. Leave it Daisy to not be discouraged despite having only three weeks left in town. To her, time didn't matter. If something was meant to be then circumstances would see to it and make dreams a reality.

Ada wanted to be sure that the baby shower she was planning for her best friend was spectacular. She needed to talk to Susan and get some ideas. Daisy deserved the best.

After finishing their conversation, Ada jumped in the shower and washed her hair. She had enough pep to even do a rosemary oil and comb massage, plus hair mask. Ada blew her hair dry and used the large curling iron to smooth fly-aways and obtain some nice curls. Usually, the following day there wasn't much she needed to do to it. She and Maisy made their last trip outside for the night. She gave Maisy a dog treat and then settled herself on the couch with a bowl of ice cream to continue binge-watching a series.

Ada ended up falling asleep at some point because she awakened to a lick on the cheek. She sat up and took the remote to stop streaming and made a mental note to go back three episodes

311

since she missed seeing them. Still half asleep, Ada brushed her teeth and then crawled into bed.

Her alarm went off at 8 am, and Ada felt ready to get up. She took Maisy outside to potty and then put some coffee on while she went to get dressed. Surely Oscar wasn't inviting her to anything where she would require dressing up, but just in case she opted for a coral jumpsuit and wedge sandals. The color against her skin was Ada's favorite because she always appeared more tan than her skin was. Her hair turned out great with just enough curls to soften her face. A boiled egg, yogurt, and blueberries for breakfast settled well following her heavier foods the evening before. After she took the last sip of her coffee and brushed her teeth, Ada headed out the door to her car.

For a Saturday morning, the streets were quiet. She and Oscar had decided on meeting at 10, but it wouldn't hurt to arrive a few minutes early. This she had learned from her mother, who was a stickler for time. Ada was able to pull into a parking place right in front of the gallery. The only other car parked was a black Audi, which she was pretty sure belonged to Oscar. The front door was locked, and she didn't see anyone inside the main part, so she knocked. Ada looked up and down the street and noticed several storefronts were opening and setting out sale items.

"Good morning, my dear Ada!" Oscar almost made her jump.

"Good morning to you!" Ada smiled at him.

He held the door for her, and she made her way inside. Things were back to their original places since the gala.

"Right this way," Oscar gestured with his hand for her to go ahead of him. "We'll go to my office." Classical music was playing softly from speakers and the office was full of shelves of art books and paintings. "Please have a seat, and what may I get you to drink? Have you already had coffee?" Oscar appeared to have nervous energy this morning, and Ada couldn't even begin to imagine what they would discuss.

"Yes, I have, but thank you."

"Very well then, I may as well get right to the point." This made Ada sit up in her chair.

Instead of sitting at his desk across from her, Oscar sat in the adjacent chair. "Thank you so much for coming in to speak with me today. No doubt you are curious regarding my request." He spoke the words as more of a statement than a question, so Ada didn't answer but smiled slightly.

"Ada, when we first met a few weeks ago, and you shared with me your desire to move away from teaching and own an art gallery someday, how serious were you?"

She was taken aback a little but answered without hesitation. "Yes, absolutely. In fact, after taking courses this summer, I'm even more certain. It's just a matter of when someday."

"What if I told you that your wish could come true sooner than later?"

Ada tilted her head to the side and followed with, "What do you mean?"

"I'm saying that I've never met anyone more passionate about the art world than you. Oh, yes, people come in and out raving about art, but you my dear, you take it to heart. I see the look in your eyes when you examine paintings or sculptures, and you also have quite a gift."

"Why, thank you, Oscar. That means a great deal to me coming from you."

Oscar took her hand in his and patted it gently. "I'm moving to New York City to help open a new gallery with an old friend, and I would like you to run the business in my stead. This place is important to me, so I'd like to see it continue being open."

He slid a piece of paper across to Ada. It had a dollar sign followed by a number, and she looked up at Oscar and back down at the paper before saying, "Seriously? This appears to have another digit at the end. I'm not used to that as a teacher."

"Oh yes, it's a serious offer, Ada. You need to be well compensated for the time spent acquiring art, organizing and running showings, and selling pieces. It's a lot of work but well worth the effort with the returned amount of pleasure derived. I've been meaning to hire an assistant, so you won't have to be solely responsible for all the nitty gritty. You'll have plenty of time for vacation, travel, and . . . perhaps other things?"

When Ada didn't answer, Oscar realized he may have hit a nerve, and finished with, "like opportunities to meet many people from around the globe."

Ada was quite certain that he had intended to say a husband or family. That was okay because he would have been correct.

"If you decide to accept my offer, we can talk about the details at that time. For now, I wanted you to at least know some important information regarding your salary and an assistant."

Ada's mind raced with thoughts about her job teaching to picturing herself living a dream, and of what this might mean staying in the same town as Jason. She took her other hand and

315

placed it atop Oscar's.

"I'm beyond flattered and appreciative of Oscar. I can't believe that with all the people you know that I would be the one you ask."

"Listen, I really meant what I said about you, and I know that there are many things to consider. It is not my intent to pressure you at all, but I'm leaving at the end of the month and need an answer soon. Please don't feel like you owe me a decision this week. I want you to take time and think it over. Just promise me you'll indeed think it over for a week before making a decision."

At this point Ada really couldn't think of an answer and would require time to process what just happened. She wanted to call Daisy first thing. Her parents would not be good ones to help decide. Well, maybe her dad, but her mother would have too much to say.

"I will indeed think it over, Oscar, and once again I value our friendship and your trust in me. I promise to give you an answer by next weekend to say if that is acceptable."

"It is, indeed," Oscar stood, smiling.

Ada took a while getting back into her car and pressing the ignition button. What had just happened? Was this real, or was she dreaming? Ada pinched herself to make sure, and then yelped.

Ouch! Okay, it's real. She raced home to call Daisy. Also, she'd want to speak with Robert and Susan to see what they thought. Both were like surrogate parents to her, and she trusted them implicitly.

Chapter 26

Daisy was speechless for a minute. "Wow, Ada, your dream is coming true! I can't believe it!"

"I know! Isn't this crazy? It's all happening so fast, and my head is spinning," Ada said slowly.

"What are you going to do? I mean, of course you have a week, but . . ." Daisy's voice trailed off.

"Aww, I know. It would mean that we wouldn't be teaching across the hall from each other anymore or be able to make it to each other's homes within ten minutes."

"That's true, Ada, but an opportunity like this doesn't come along every day. It's just hard to wrap my brain around." Daisy caught herself and added, "but obviously this is the same for you on an entirely different level. Have you talked to your parents?"

Ada laughed, "No way, I had to call my best friend first. I knew that you'd help me think things through."

"Of course, whatever you need, I'm here."

The two friends talked for another half an hour, listing the pros and cons. Daisy had placed Jason at the top, but Ada assured her that he couldn't be the main consideration for her decision. After all, he basically didn't seem to want much to do with her. If he had really wanted to be with her, the sailing trip was a perfect answer. It's not like Robert wouldn't have understood. As far as her teaching job back home was concerned, there were a couple of new teachers in temporary positions who would be more than happy to apply for the position.

Although Ada deeply cared for her students, she knew that as far as the job itself was concerned, it was easy to leave. Her vision board in her apartment reminded her of what she really wanted, to be surrounded by art and work in a gallery. Now, the entire board had landed in her lap! What was she to do? Was she crazy for thinking twice about it, and not immediately phoning Oscar to say she was all in?

Daisy suggested that her friend do her best to sleep on it

for one night. Usually, a new day allows for better decision-making. Ada wasn't convinced that she'd be getting a lot of sleep but did agree that she needed more time to think and even discuss with Robert and Susan. As soon as she and Daisy got off the phone, Ada crossed the street and knocked on the door.

Robert answered. "Why, hello there, neighbor. Come in." Ada stepped inside and Susan appeared in the doorway of the kitchen.

"You're just in time to have some homemade pizza."

"It smells amazing!" Ada said, sniffing the air.

"Wait until you taste it!" said Robert. "She has been perfecting this dish for ten years! I keep telling her that it can't possibly taste any better, but she surprises me!"

Robert walked out to get the mail, so Ada followed Susan into the kitchen as the oven timer was going off. She took her oven mitts out of the drawer and then carefully brought out the pizza stone with the bubbling cheese.

She sat it on the wire rack on the island and turned to Ada. "I haven't asked, what brought you over? You probably needed something, and neither of us even bothered to ask you!"

"Are you kidding? I'm thrilled to get to eat your delicious pizza! But yes, you're right. I did come over with ulterior motives."

"Do tell," Susan said looking" up at her with a half grin. "Something good, I hope?"

"Yes," commented Ada.

They all sat down at the table, and Robert brought out a bottle of Corvina from northern Italy. "This is the best wine to pair with Susan's Margherita Pizza," he said. "You want something that is ripe and fruity red."

Halfway through her second piece of pizza, Susan turned to Ada and said, "So tell us why you came. We distracted you with the pizza!"

"I'd call that a great distraction! It's delicious, Susan. Thank you for inviting me! And, yes, you're right." Ada stopped to wipe her mouth and laid down her napkin. "I do want to talk to you both about a life-altering decision I need to make within a week's time!"

"That sounds serious," interjected Robert, as he took a sip of wine. "Please share with us, you know that we care about you like family."

"I do know that, Robert. You both have been beyond kind to me, and I'm grateful that I have the two of you in my life. I love my parents, but they . . . well, mostly my mother wants to do all the talking and not much listening." Ada didn't wait for a response because she didn't want to put either of them on the spot. "So, I had a meeting with Oscar Wells this morning downtown."

Susan took a sip of her wine, and then sat back like Robert without saying a word. Ada launched into the entire conversation she had earlier with Oscar. Both Susan and Robert listened intently and nodded occasionally. When she had voiced all her reasons for taking the position or not taking the position, the excitement seemed to outweigh the apprehension. Ada noticed that herself. Funny how speaking things aloud does a world of good when you're trying to decide.

Robert and Susan looked at each other, and it was Susan who spoke first. "Ada, when you and I first visited that evening right out there on the swing, you shared with me how teaching wasn't really your passion and how you longed to work in the art world, specifically in a gallery. I'd call that kismet because here you sit merely six weeks later with this news." She reached across the table and patted Ada's arm. "I realize it must be a bit of a shock, though."

"I know that Oscar must have the utmost respect for you and confidence in your abilities to make that offer after having only known you for such a short time," said Robert "Of course, we're both certain you'd make him proud. He would be fortunate to have you. Not to mention how wonderful it would be to keep you here in town." He looked over at his wife.

"That's for certain." Susan smiled. "We would want you to feel confident making the decision and support you either way."

"Of course," Robert chimed in.

"Oh, thank you both so much." She got up and gave each of them a hug. "I do have a great deal to think about. I guess that I'll do what I did as a young girl, make a list of pros and cons."

"Can't go wrong with that process." Robert smiled.

Ada was so excited about the new opportunity that she had trouble falling asleep that night. Even the next episode of her favorite series didn't keep her mind from wandering. Once again, she found herself having to rewind several times when her mind drifted off thinking what it would be like to give up her teaching job and move here permanently. Maisy sensed Ada's restlessness and nudged her on the hand.

"I know, girl, I'm a little on edge. How about you and I go for a jog around the block?" Maisy wagged her tail and raced to the door.

The evening air was getting cooler and was just what Ada needed. She breathed the crispness in heavily and blew out, trying her best to clear the clutter in her brain. As soon as they returned, Ada drew a warm bath for herself and put a pen & notebook on the stand beside her.

After half an hour of soaking and pondering, she came up with more pros than cons to accept the offer. Ironically, staying for Jason appeared on both sides. Since they essentially canceled each other, she scratched it. Maybe she would sleep on it before adding any other thoughts.

Her hair had gotten wet around her face and neck. The curls wouldn't hold after that, so a messy bun it would be tomorrow.

Again, the week was flying by. This week in class there were oral presentations being given Wednesday through Friday. Ada had chosen to present on the castle that inspired Disney's Sleeping Beauty. Neuschwanstein, a Bavarian castle, was commissioned by King Ludwig II of Bavaria and built in the 19th century. She had a few more things to add to her slide show and would be ready to present them on Thursday.

Ahh, Sleeping Beauty. What she would give to be kissed and awakened by her prince. Even at a young age Ada had thought it rather romantic, though most of her friends thought she was silly, that love truly conquers all. For a while she had lived a fairytale life with Troy. He was everything one expected from a prince: brave, strong, gallant, handsome, she could go on. Although Jason appeared to possess some of these attributes, he was too much of a mystery to know for certain. Ada remembered the way he had kissed her at his apartment, in control but gently. She liked that. A sigh unexpectedly escaped from her lips and brought her out of the reverie.

"Time for bed, Maisy. I've got to quiet my brain and get some sleep."

Maisy raced ahead of her to the bedroom and turned around to bark at Ada as if to hurry her along. They were both asleep within a few minutes of getting in bed.

Most of the presentations in class were interesting, and Ada added a few more places to visit on her bucket list. She decided to stay after class to connect her laptop to the projector and do a test run before she was to present the next day. Only Rose was left when Ada looked around the room once she gathered her materials.

"Are you working on your presentation, too?"

"Well, I think it's basically finished, but I wanted to see how well a picture shows up on the screen. I was hoping the colors would appear more vivid in here than on my phone." She laughed slightly when saying it.

"Oh, sure, I hope so! Go ahead because I have some things to organize first."

Once she had the classroom to herself, Ada inserted the thumb drive into the laptop and soon had the wall filled with beautiful pictures. Ada reviewed her notes:

Nuschwanstein Castle was a blend of various architectural styles including Gothic, Romanesque, and Byzantine which resulted in an impressive structure. What Ada liked most were the towers and turrets soaring high into the clouds which made the castle seem like it was indeed right out of a Disney movie. The craftsmanship inside the castle was impressive as well with the stained-glass and detailed carvings from wood. There were three stages to the construction, which began in 1869 in which the foundation was laid, along with the bottom floors. The second stage saw the castle coming together with the second floor, turrets, and windows. During the third stage is when the chandeliers were installed, and furnishings were brought into the massive place. Stages of Construction of Neuschwanstein Castle weren't finished after King Ludwig passed away.

Ada stood back to admire a beautiful overhead shot of the castle. What would it have been like to live there? She would like to have found out, although she wasn't crazy about the clothing, way too restrictive for her liking. She preferred more comfort.

"I think I'm ready for tomorrow," she said aloud, not sure if anyone was listening. They weren't. The afternoon was usually the quietest time on campus. Ada thought she might stop by the diner and pick up a breakfast meal for dinner since they served breakfast all day. She remembered doing that a few times while growing up back home. Funny how eggs, sausage, and pancakes tasted even better in the evening. Her mother's favorite meal of the day happened to be breakfast, so she thought nothing about having it for dinner instead, and that suited Ada just fine.

She gathered her backpack and headed out the exit doors which were being held open for by a man, for her, she assumed. It was Jason, and she was not expecting to see him inside.

"No practice today?"

Jason let the door close and turned to Ada. "Yes, but I came to grab bag of ice. One of the guys took a pretty hard hit on the shin from a fast pitch."

"Ouch! Hope it's nothing serious."

"You and me both."

There was awkward silence after the short conversation, and she turned to go. "Say, Ada, I was wanting to check with you about the sailing trip on Saturday."

At this, Ada's stomach began doing flips and she blurted it out before realizing: "Oh, did you decide to go?" By now she was smiling and there was no way to contain her excitement about the possibility of Jason going along.

"Uh, n—no. I wanted to let you know that there is a possible storm expected to come up the coast and hit on Saturday night."

Ada stood stunned. That's what he wanted to tell her? Now the blood began to rise in her face, and instead of feeling sad, she felt rage.

"I didn't know you graduated with a degree in meteorology. Too bad you weren't able to get a better education, your prediction last time was off by a mile." She said it before thinking and her tone and volume caused Jason to take a step back.

"Wow, sorry to have upset you. I was merely expressing concern about your going, er, the group going. The waves can be intense and it's difficult to manage a large craft."

"Lee happens to be an expert, and we have three others going who grew up on boats. We'll be fine. Thanks for your concern." Ada turned to go.

"Ada . . . did I do something to make you angry with me?"

She started feeling a little guilty and turned towards Jason, setting her backpack down. "It's just that . . . well, I thought we . . . I mean. . ."

"What?"

"Seriously, you have no clue at all? I thought we were developing a friendship at the beginning of my stay, and . . . the kiss we shared?" Once again, Ada hadn't meant to be so forward.

"Ada, I told you that there were things you didn't know about me, and I—"

She cut him off. "Well, you know what, Jason? That's fine. I don't have the time or energy to figure you out. And I'm accepting a job offer to stay and run the gallery for Oscar."

Jason appeared in shock.

Ada continued, "You heard right. You'll have to get used to seeing me around because this will be my home, too. It is what

I've dreamed about doing for years. I'm thrilled about it, absolutely thrilled. Don't worry, I won't be asking you to join me on any more outings. You're free to wallow around in self-pity and waste your life not loving anyone!"

Ada snatched up her backpack, turned, and stormed off toward the bungalow. Jason stood watching her, or at least Ada thought she could feel his eyes at the back of her head.

What had she just done?

Chapter 27

Ada's heart raced all the way back to the bungalow. She saw Susan on the front porch and felt like running with arms open and collapsing into her. On second thought, Ada was rather ashamed of the way she reacted to Jason and was too embarrassed to share the exchange with Susan.

"Calm down and put a smile on your face," Ada told herself.

Maisy's tail wagged and she lunged toward her as Susan was saying, "I know girl, she's almost here! Oh my gosh, this puppy loves you so much!"

"Aww, and I love her."

Ada sat down on the steps and let Maisy jump on her lap and lick her face. It was lowering her heart rate, which was a good thing.

"How are the presentations coming along? Are you ready for tomorrow?" Susan asked her as she stood and straightened the cushions on the swing.

"Good! I've really enjoyed learning about the architecture of certain cathedrals and castles, although most were built well before my so-called Sleeping Beauty castle."

"Oh well, the class will enjoy hearing from you because you're so interested in it! Plus, didn't you mention that during college you were there?"

"Yes, and it was beautiful."

"They'll like knowing you were at the castle. In fact, I remember at the time there was filming going on for some local advertisement. Several younger people were in costume reminiscent of the time-period for the princess. It was magical."

Maisy began barking at a neighbor jogging with her golden retriever. She so wanted to make a new friend. The girl waved and smiled at them.

"Come on, Maisy, let's go inside. I've got to put the

finishing touches on my presentation. Susan gave me a few ideas."

"Oh, well glad I could be of service. See you two later."

"Thanks again, Susan, see you later."

Ada was happy to get inside, kick off her shoes, and flop down on the couch. Before she could even think about her class, she had to process what had taken place a short time ago. It seemed like a whirlwind.

In one way she felt perfectly justified with her response. After all, Jason had for sure liked her at some point because that kiss was intense. She couldn't figure out what had happened between then and now. It was like he had completely put up a wall where any likelihood of a relationship, or even a friendship for that matter, could exist. On the other hand, Ada was humiliated with her behavior. She would rather have handled it with a response that said, "I'm just so sad because I thought we had something." Or why not put the ball in his court so he would have to respond to the question? As usual, her emotions got the better of her.

"It is what it is," she said sighing. "There is nothing I can do about it now. Although one thing is for certain, and that is I'm staying." The first thing she wanted to do was to call Oscar with the news, and secondly, she wanted to reach out to Marilyn about the bungalow to find out there was a possibility for her to stay on and rent the bungalow long-term. Afterall, the rental was separated by heavy wooden pocket doors into the owner's quarters. Maybe Marilyn wouldn't mind having little company.

Ada took out her phone to call Oscar. He was thrilled to hear the news and said the coming weekend would be so much more enjoyable just to know that Ada was staying. He couldn't wait for the two of them to get together and chat about everything. He wanted Ada's thoughts on the coming year and what she might do differently to encourage more people to visit the art gallery. One suggestion Oscar made was for Ada to showcase some of her work out front, although she was hesitant to do so. She promised to think about it. They hung up on plans for a meeting the following week.

Next, Ada went to the kitchen to retrieve Marilyn's number on the refrigerator. The two of them conversed for almost forty minutes. Marilyn wanted an update on how Ada's classes were going and her opinion of the town. She also shared the news that her daughter was expecting a baby and wanted her to live closer. *This is crazy how things are working out*, thought Ada. When she mentioned the reason for calling, Marilyn jumped right in to say that Ada should just buy the house. It was all so overwhelming to Ada but made perfect sense. She loved the bungalow, and especially living across from Robert and Susan. Marilyn was going to consult with her realtor friend in town and send Ada information.

After two exciting conversations back-to-back, Ada had more energy than she knew what to do with, so she ended up warming up leftovers and sitting down in front of the couch to eat. She was dying to call Daisy, run across the street and talk with her friends, plus she really should call her parents. *Maybe after her presentation tomorrow*, thought Ada.

"I've had enough excitement for one day, right girl?" She patted the couch so Maisy would join her and proceeded to bury her head in Maisy's soft fur. After a while, Maisy got up and ran to her food bowl, wagging her tail.

"Oh gee! How could I forget to feed you? I was too caught up in myself!" Besides feeding Maisy, she also gave her a lick of peanut butter in a spoon.

After a shower and washing her hair, Ada laid out clothes for the following morning. She wanted to dress a little nicer since more eyes would be on her in the front of the class, and she was pleased with her choices. She stood back from the bed admiring them. Ada had chosen a pair of cream-colored linen pants with a white silk blouse and belt. Her wedge sandals matched the belt, and she chose a gold necklace and tear-drop earrings to complete the ensemble. Maybe she'd wear part of her hair up. Ada made a few changes to her presentation notes and then packed things for the morning. She practically fell into bed but had trouble falling asleep as her thoughts centered around how things had played out with Jason today. *Who knows*, Ada thought. *He's friends with Robert and Susan, so we'll have to talk again at some point.*

The following morning Ada woke herself talking out loud in her sleep and saying Troy's name. A tear had escaped, and she reached up to brush it away. He would have been so happy for her knowing that she was getting a chance to change careers. Troy had known about Ada's dream of working in the art world and had been a great encourager. In fact, he was the one to suggest a graduate degree in art.

"Thank you, Babe," Ada said quietly. "I feel you are here with me."

"Wow! Great outfit!" Susan called as Ada walked out of the bungalow. "You look like you're dressed for success, or should I say working at an art gallery?" Susan winked at her.

"I was planning on running over to talk to you guys this evening. I've taken the job and already called Oscar last night! And guess what else?" Ada didn't even give Susan a chance to ask but simply blurted out, "I'm buying Marilyn's house!" For some reason, saying it aloud made her heart almost leap out for her chest. Was she doing this to spite Jason or because it was the best decision? *Of course I'm making the right decision*, Ada thought to herself.

Susan hurried over to hug Ada. "I'm so happy for you and for us! This is very big news all around! Well, I know that you must go give your presentation, but how about coming over for dinner tonight so we can talk all about it?"

"I'd love to!"

"Good luck, although I don't think you need it!" Susan smiled.

"Thank you!" Ada threw a kiss to Susan as she got into her car. Today she had planned on driving since she was dressed up. How could she possibly get through this eventful day? Yesterday proved that sometimes when you're feeling so horrible, the day can turn around and give you a different outcome altogether!

Ada was the third student to present. Everyone was intrigued that she had been to Neuschwanstein Castle, especially the girls. Ada's slideshow turned out well, and the professor complimented her on the organization of her presentation. She was the only one so far who had been asked questions about some of the architecture. It had to be the teacher in her that prompted that, and it tickled her. There had only been one person left to present, and it happened to be Trish, the first person she had met at the beginning of the summer. Everyone agreed to stay longer to hear her and not have to attend class the following day. Although she stayed to herself and was a bit eccentric, Ada thought that Anita did an excellent job. The professor said a few words and then dismissed the class until Monday.

What luck, Ada thought. *Now I'll have time to get ready for the excursion this weekend.* Those who were going decided to grab a quick coffee and plan what everyone was bringing. Lee had a tent on the boat and Ben said that he could borrow one from his uncle who lived close by, plus a couple more sleeping bags for the guys. Lee told the girls to be sure and bring their own pillows and an extra blanket since it could get cool at night.

Ada was going to contribute bagels, cream cheese, oranges, and grapes for breakfast on Sunday morning. Others were bringing hotdogs to roast on the fire, buns, condiments, chips, drinks, and other snacks. With twelve going, they'd have plenty of food. The group decided to meet at 8:00 am with the boat crew volunteering to go aboard at 7:30 am to get the sails ready. Ada was excited to go this time! She would have lots to talk about with her new friends.

As Ada pulled into her driveway, she noticed in her rear-view mirror Jason making his way up to the porch across the street. Robert opened the door to let him inside. There was no way Ada was going to go over for dinner tonight if Jason was there. She'd have to text Susan and let her know. Just then, Susan walked across the street with Maisy.

"So, I just noticed . . ." Ada started to say with her head to the side.

"No worries, my dear, he's not staying for dinner. I figured you'd be concerned about that when I saw you both out here at the same time. I know that things haven't been that great between the two of you, and I don't want to put you on the spot. Just know you can always talk to me about anything."

"I do know that and appreciate you so much."

After changing into shorts and a t-shirt, Ada began fixing a dessert to take across the street. She had bought some fresh strawberries at a stand the day before after seeing a recipe online. Some cream cheese, sugar, and cherry juice mixed went inside a dessert cup rolled in butter and sugar was baked in the oven for ten minutes. You then topped it off with cut up strawberries. Thank goodness Marilyn had every size of container possible. Ada closed the lid and stuck them in the refrigerator after which she scraped the cream cheese mixture onto her spoon and enjoyed every bite.

Susan had fixed a salad and homemade lasagna. They drank red wine and sat at the table for two hours talking about the last several weeks but mostly about her purchasing the home and settling in as the owner by the end of summer. They were both quite certain that Marilyn would be fair in her pricing because her late husband had owned an investment company and left her quite comfortable. Besides, she would be so happy to see her home go to Ada.

The only topic that didn't come up was Jason. Ada always had the feeling that Robert avoided any conversation revolving around him. She didn't understand why he wasn't sharing anything about the work on his recent book involving Jason. Susan appeared to be in the dark as well and seemed to accept it without question. Ada wasn't about to question Robert on such personal matters. Before she left, Susan had once again made some goodies and put them in a picnic basket for Ada.

"Oh, you didn't have to do that again, Susan. How

sweet of you! Everyone will be thrilled as your cookies were a hit last time!" She gave Susan a hug.

"You're most welcome. I added a few extra things this time since you're planning on staying over a night."

"Please be careful, Ada," said Robert. "The water can get choppy out there and storms can happen unexpectantly." He patted her arm, and the look of concern was sincere.

"You sound like someone else I know." Ada said before thinking about it.

"Oh, I do? Your father, I'm guessing."

With a half-hearted chuckle, Ada responded with, "Of course." She waved back at the couple who waited until she was at her side door across the street.

Ada cared for them so deeply. She couldn't help but wonder if Jason had already told Robert about the sailboat outing on Saturday and expressed his concerns. Ada was quite certain that she would never know.

Chapter 28

Friday was a total blur. She ended up talking to her parents for an hour and Daisy for two hours! Other than that, Ada hadn't accomplished much of anything else besides packing for Saturday. Two swimsuits, coverup, leggings, shorts, tee shirts, and deck shoes. That was it besides some toiletries. She had taken food and toys over for Maisy last night. In fact, Susan had insisted that she stay over to save Ada time in the morning. Thank goodness, because she was moving in slow motion. The endless discussions of the last two days had made her exhausted.

Her parents were stunned by the news, especially her

mother.

"Ada, darling, don't you think you're being a little rash in your decision? Afterall, it just came up. Why didn't you take more time to think about and consider everything?"

"What's there to consider, Mother? That I've wanted a career in art forever? That I wasn't very happy with my teaching job? Maybe I need to move away from the town that holds so many memories of Troy?" She was in tears after saying the last one.

"Oh, my goodness, I didn't mean to make you cry, Ada. I was just trying to—"

Ada cut her mother off between sniffling. "Trying to interfere with my deciding what is best for me? Don't you want me to be happy?"

"Of course I do, darling."

Ada's father interrupted both of them. "Okay, I think we're just trying to process the sudden news, but know that we are happy for you and proud, Ada. God knows that living your life doing something you don't enjoy would be misery for everyone."

"Are you saying you'd rather have not been a surgeon?" she asked her husband.

"Not at all, I'm saying that you should follow your heart. If I had listened to my own father, he would have had me in business with him. It only took one summer of working there with him to know that I wanted nothing to do with stocks and bonds."

Ada was speechless. Had her father just used the words "follow your heart" and expressed his pride and happiness for her?

"Thank you, Dad. It means a lot to hear you say those words."

Ada's mom spoke up. "I've always been proud of you, Ada, even if I haven't said so. I'm sorry that I took after my own mother instead of being my own person. She made me miserable, and I know now that I am doing the same thing to my only child."

This made Ada tear up again. "I love you both so much."

"And we love you," they both echoed.

The conversation with her parents had been cathartic. Tiring, but healing. Daisy, on the other hand, was ecstatic as a best friend would be hearing such news. She guessed that Ada would take the job and said she would have smacked her if not. They talked about plans and making the distance between them work. There was no way that either of them would give up seeing each other often, and Ada expressed how she wanted her niece or nephew to know her well.

"I plan on spoiling your little one, just so you know."

Daisy laughed, "There would be no stopping you!"

The only tinge of sadness that Ada had throughout the conversation with her best friend was not getting to see her every day like when they taught across the hall from one another. If only Troy had lived . . . it was the third time crying that day, but Daisy reassured her with promises of good things to come in her future.

"Your day will come, my sweet friend, and the rest of your dreams of a husband and family will come true. Keep the faith."

Ada finished putting things into her car but had to run back for her cell phone. She had left it on the counter because her hands were too full. "Food, water bottles, clothing, toiletries, and phone," she whispered to herself. "Here we go." Pulling in beside her was Charlotte.

"Hey, girl! Are you ready for our next adventure?"

Ada giggled, "An adventure? That sounds involved. I was hoping to get a tan, listen to some good music, and snack all day."

"For sure!"

Henry and Jayden were helping Lee get ready to set sail. It was a beautiful morning, albeit a few passing clouds. The winds were stronger than normal, which Lee said would make it faster to get to the island. The guys had piled their sleeping bags and tents in the captain's quarters, so the girls went ahead and made themselves at home below.

Besides the separate bedroom, the benches and table were made into a bed, and the couch was spacious. Lee had already pulled those out and set them up for the girls, along with the sheets and blankets he did have. They were glad he mentioned bringing their own pillows and extra blankets. After getting everything set up, the girls joined the guys on the top deck. They were already moving away from the dock and Lee hit the horn of the boat indicating their departure. As soon as they were safely away from shore Lee turned up the music and Jayden and Kristine performed the newest dance trend. They yelled at Ada to join them, but she had not had much time this summer to stay up to date on those. That's something she and Daisy, along with the other teachers, had done when going out for their girls' night once a week.

Ben came around with a choice of drinks that had been on ice. Ada surprised herself by choosing an IPA, which she usually never did. *This is a new start for me*, she thought to herself. May as well change my drinks, too. They toasted to a weekend of sailing.

A little later Ada and Rose pushed around a cart loaded with various sandwiches and chips. They decided to go around the circle and share their most favorite and least favorite day in class so far this summer. Two of them chose the nude sketches as their least favorite while three landed on those as their absolute favorites. Everyone got a big laugh out of that.

The next conversation was all about Ada and her decision to stay and run the art gallery. They were blown away by the offer that Oscar had made but most said they weren't the least surprised since Ada was the most talented student in the class. She quickly disagreed but thanked them all the same. They also thought it cool that she was purchasing the bungalow located in the perfect part of the town—halfway between the University and the water. She wouldn't be walking to work, however, as it was at least a ten-minute drive, plus she would be dressed up and wearing heels. It was funny how nobody ever questioned if she had been married or dating someone. Maybe Lee had said something to spare Ada from being sad.

She liked talking about Troy and their relationship, their hopes and dreams. The other strange thing was that not one person had asked about Jason, although Lee was the only one who had attended the gala when the two of them had danced together. She had confided in Lee that night about Troy, but maybe he didn't want to assume anything serious had happened between her and

Jason.

Lee organized a game of cornhole for them, and they took their sides. Ada always loved playing at home with the gang. She got pretty good at it. Lucky for her, she still had skills and sunk the first two with ease. Whistles and claps erupted from both sides of the playing area, and Ada was glad that she had sunglasses on as her face was turning red. She wasn't used to having so much of the attention directed at her. They were a great group of people, and she would certainly miss them at the end of the summer. Only two lived in town and the rest were at least two hours or more away, with Emma living the farthest in Virginia. Ada was quite sure that they would all remain friends and hopefully come back to the town for reunions occasionally.

Lee and Henry took turns guiding the sailboat and playing the game until finally around 4 o'clock in the afternoon they arrived at their destination. Since there was not a place to dock the boat, it would have to be anchored away from shore, and they would use the large dinghy to reach land with the supplies. The men also had to take sleeping gear and tents to set up for the night. The small craft was motorized and got them to shore quicky. Lee and Ben hopped out to pull the boat up on the sand. Everyone took a load when they stepped out onto the shore. They decided to set up camp a few yards from the water up on a little sand bank where even high tide wouldn't reach them.

Someone had built a fire recently and there were still a few pieces of kindling to help start a fire. Several of the friends gathered more pieces of wood, trying to get the driest pieces they could find. Soon the fire was crackling and providing heat, which was a good thing as the sun had settled behind some clouds and the breeze was slightly cool. Several chairs surrounded the fire pit, while a large blanket made room for the rest to sit. Ada started getting the food set up, and Rose helped her. They placed their hotdogs on the sticks that Lee had brought with him. Some liked their hot dogs barely warm while others went for the charred taste.

Kristine had made potato salad, and it reminded Ada of her grandmother's recipe with mustard and mayonnaise. Some pickles and pasta salad rounded out the evening meal, and everyone was moaning about having eaten too much. That was until Ada brought out Susan's chocolate chip cookies and brownies. Suddenly, their appetites found room for a few more bites. Ben had made coffee on the fire, and it was delicious. He called it cowboy coffee. It was too strong for some of them, but Ada loved it. She had to laugh when thinking about how her mother-in-law always made sure to have coffee when they were over for dinner, but you could see through it.

It was the thought that counted, decided Ada.

Jayden had an idea to play truth or dare. They all laughed, but then soon realized that she was dead serious.

"We haven't played that since our teenage years. What the hell are we going to dare each other to do?" Lee broke out in a big laugh.

"You'd be surprised," said Jayden winking.

"Oh, do tell."

"Not unless I accept to tell the truth. I might prefer the dare." They all laughed.

Several rounds later with two or three drinks in them, things were getting hilarious. Ben had ended up daring Emma to run into the woods and find proof of an animal. She surprised everyone when she came out with a dried-up toad and flung it towards Ben. He started chasing her around and they all laughed once he caught up with her and carried her to the water and dunked her.

Up until now Ada had easy ones like, "what teacher did you have a crush on in high school," or "what was the worst thing you did in college?" The first answer was Mr. Haynes, who she had in her sophomore year for math. He was closer to their age, as he had graduated only two years prior from college. His approach made them love math, especially with the songs he would sing like,

"Too late to apologize" from One Republic when someone would forget their homework and try to explain. The worst thing Ada did while in college was to steal a letter T from a sign on the main road while jogging with friends. They would run to Dunkin Donuts for two cream-filled foods and then jog back to campus. On a dare she took the T to put up in her room. Nobody asked her to explain anything about it, which made her think that Lee indeed had told them not to talk about Troy. The dares had gotten more and more ridiculous, so Ada decided that no matter what she would tell the truth. The last one was asked by Charlotte, and it was, "Who did you last kiss?"

Without thinking, Ada almost answered Troy, but then suddenly realized that it would be a lie. She had kissed Jason just recently. If she said it aloud then Lee would know, but wouldn't he already have been suspicious of that anyway? So, she took a deep breath and uttered, "A guy named Jason . . . but it meant nothing." Even saying that made her feel sick to her stomach because that was absolutely a lie. She hadn't felt that way about anyone since Troy.

Lee just looked at her, but being the good friend, he simply started whipping his fist into the air, saying "Whoop whoop" and winked at Ada. The rest of them laughed.

"Okay! We better get the girls back on the boat before it gets any darker. They cleaned up the food items and got into the boat with Lee and Ben who took them back. The others stayed behind to set up the tents. The water was a little choppier than it had been when they first arrived. It was probably just the night winds. There were plenty of lights on the sailboat, and Lee assured them that the door locked securely to the downstairs cabin. They would have everything they needed until morning. Thank goodness the girls had an actual bathroom. She would hate having to go in the woods like the guys.

It felt like a slumber party from her youth with the girls in pajamas. They all ended up sitting on the king bed initially and decided to drink limoncello shots. The girls had to know if Emma had feelings for Ben. It looked obvious from what they saw. She had to admit that at the last outing she noticed him but wasn't sure if he had a girlfriend. During the first day back for the second course something came up and she found out that they had broken up before summer.

That would make two couples formed from the classes. First, Henry and Rose and now possibly Ben and Emma. The rest shared what relationships they were in or wanted to be in. Thank

goodness all Ada commented was that she was waiting for Mr.

Right. Everyone agreed wholeheartedly on that. It wasn't until after

one o'clock in the morning that the last of the girls went to bed.

Jayden and Rose had gone back to the other room and had fallen

asleep a while before. Ada had volunteered to take the couch and

decided to head to bed. The alcohol she had consumed today

caught up with her and she fell asleep as soon as her head hit the

pillow.

Chapter 29

Ada was awoken by a feeling of nausea, probably from too much alcohol the day before. It had been more than she was used to drinking.

The rest of the gals were still asleep. She stumbled on her way to the bathroom and felt like throwing up. After standing over the toilet for ten minutes she decided that maybe getting some crackers into her stomach would take care of it. Brushing her teeth helped some, and Ada changed into a pair of baby blue shorts and a cropped white tee shirt. She put things into her overnight bag and folded the blankets that Lee had set out. They hadn't made too much of a mess last night, but Ada took a few minutes to straighten what she could without waking anyone.

Leaving her things in the lower cabin, she climbed the stairs to the deck and looked around. It was about 7:30 in the morning, but instead of a blazing orange and yellow sunrise the sky appeared almost black. She looked toward the shore and could see the tents but no one outside of them. Ada guessed that the guys had done the same as the girls and celebrated with a few too many shots.

A few rumbles of thunder startled her, and she gasped. She had better call Lee and have him assess the situation. She went back down to grab her phone and noticed that a couple more of the girls were now awake. She didn't want to scare anyone but figured it would be best for them to get up and dressed. She mentioned it to Jayden who was closest to the couch and then headed immediately back upstairs to the top deck. Maybe she'd get the best reception up there. About the time her phone started ringing, Lee stepped out of the tent stretching and answered the phone.

"Morning, sunshine!"

"Uh . . . not so much today."

"Really? Why not? You didn't sleep well on the boat?"

"I slept fine . . . it's just the sky that has me worried."

She could see Lee looking in every direction and then he responded with, "Nah, we'll be fine, that's way off to the north, but

I'll go ahead and get the guys awake so we can board."

Ada didn't say anything and just stared at the sky.

"It's going to be fine, Ada. Why don't you get out the bagels and cream cheese you brought? Everyone will be ready to have something on their stomachs before we set sail home."

"Uh, okay. Just, well, just hurry," she responded. "Will do."

They hung up, and Ada wasn't feeling any more convinced that things would be okay. Emma and Kristine came upstairs to join her.

"Yikes! That sky looks mad!" Kristine was pulling her hair back into a ponytail.

"Yeah, I thought so, too. Lee said it was too far north to be overly concerned, but he's getting the guys and heading this way. He thought maybe everyone would want some breakfast before we take off."

"Sounds good to me," Jayden said. "That was one of too many shots of Limoncello last night!"

"That makes the two of us," Ada added.

"Make that the three," Charlotte said reaching the top of the deck stairs.

The girls went about forming an assembly line on the outdoor table with the bagels, cream cheeses, and jams that Ada brought. They set out some cups and juice, while Rose made a pot of coffee. They could hear the guys approaching and one of them yelled to come down and grab the rope when they threw it. Ada was down the steps before anyone else moved away from the food. She caught the rope as Lee flung it over and tied it to the dock as she had watched them do several times.

"Good job, mate!" Lee shouted, seeming to sound chipper and without a care in the world.

Ben jumped out and began setting the coolers on board, along with the tents and gear. They secured the dinghy to the sailboat and came aboard.

"Do I smell coffee?" Ben questioned.

"Come on up. We have everything ready so you can eat right away."

"What's the rush," Lee asked. "You in a hurry?"

Ada pointed to the sky and made a scared face.

"Ah . . . we'll be back to the dock before that catches us. It's farther away than you think."

"I hope so," Ada added and then ascended the deck steps.

Her stomach was churning, and she couldn't tell if it was from nerves or the drinking the night before. Either way, she took about three bites and figured that would have to do. Coffee or juice didn't sound appealing, so she drank what she could of a water bottle and thought she'd let that settle.

She wished that Lee would move with more urgency, but he truly did not seem concerned. Ada began thinking about what Jason had said concerning the waves being rough at times and a storm coming on quickly. She hoped that with Lee's sailing experience he would know better and surely not put any of them in danger.

An hour later the sails were up, and they were heading back. Thunder rumbled in the distance again and a flash of light made a couple of the girls scream.

"Okay, okay. We're going to be fine," Lee said. "The wind is working in our direction today and we'll make better time than yesterday. You can always go below and lie down, or better than that how about I play some music to get your mind off things?" He tuned into a radio station instead of using his cell phone to stream music.

After several songs playing and just when they were all beginning to calm them a bit, an announcer interrupted the music with a weather alert. "Small craft advisories are issued for the entire stretch of coast. Sustained winds of 48 knots expected. You are advised to head to shore as quickly as possible," said the radio.

"Well, that's just great, thanks for scaring everyone, dude." Lee said with a half grin on his face. He tried to appear calm steering the craft but couldn't hide the fact that he was struggling a bit.

"Just a little more effort is all that's needed." He turned up the radio when another song began playing. Emma and Rose said they'd feel better down in the cabin. The guys stuck close to Lee in case he needed assistance. Nothing was going to make Ada feel better except to reach shore.

The thunder and lightning seemed to be chasing them, and the sky was almost all black. A few raindrops began falling and once again the announcer came on the radio: "All crafts are advised to head to shore and heed the warning which has changed to winds possibly reaching 63 knots and waves up to 8 feet high. Please notify the coast guard if you are in trouble or need assistance to reach land safely."

At that, tears welled up in Ada's eyes and she covered her mouth to stifle a cry. Jason had been right. Lee glanced at Ada with an expression that said he was sorry and then motioned for her to go below. She had almost reached the bottom of the stairs when the boat tilted suddenly to one side and threw her towards the table. Her forehead hit the corner, and she fell to the floor.

359

Emma rushed over and knelt beside her. "Oh my gosh, Ada! Let me see your head." Ada used her arms to sit up slowly and felt the room spinning. She laid back down. "You're bleeding. Someone get me a towel."

Jayden grabbed a clean beach towel nearby and sat down on the other side of Ada. They both attempted to make her comfortable by positioning her head and shoulders slightly raised with a pillow. Neither one could tell how serious the wound was because of the bleeding. After several minutes of applying firm pressure, Emma took the towel away to assess the damage. Ada had a gash above her right eyebrow. Jayden found a butterfly bandage in the first aid kit. While Emma attempted to push the skin together, she secured it over the wound. They gave Ada sips of water, and all sat on the floor until she seemed more stable. They got her to sit up slowly at first and then stand. Jayden wanted to move her to the bed as quickly as possible before they were thrown again.

Ada didn't argue with anyone about lying down. She was feeling even more nauseous than before, so they also got an empty bucket for her. Her skin felt clammy, and she didn't want covered with any blankets.

Just then, Henry came running down the steps to check on the girls.

"Everyone okay? We had a sail come loose and it caused us to change direction too fast." He stepped inside the bedroom area and saw Ada lying there with a blood-soaked towel. "Damn! Ada, I'm so sorry."

Looking at Rose with concern he mouthed "Is she okay?"

Rose shook her head yes while at the same time shrugging her shoulders slightly as if to say, "I hope so but not sure."

"The weather report for this weekend was all good. Nothing showed on the radar until tomorrow morning. The high winds got it here sooner, I guess. All of you stay down below and position yourselves where you can grab onto something quickly, but nothing metal. We're trying to keep things steady as possible, but it's no small task."

Rose ran over to give him a hug and whispered something in his ear. He kissed her on the top of the head and went upstairs.

Kristine put her arm around Rose. "He'll be okay. Henry seems to know what he's doing more than anyone else!"

Everyone stayed in the back room with Ada. Emma and Kristine joined her on either side while Jayden and Rose sat on the small couch and Charlotte sat on a floor pillow. Nobody said anything for what seemed like the longest time until Rose broke the silence asking, "Does anyone feel like eating a bite of fruit and crackers? We probably need something in our stomachs with all this rocking."

They all responded by shaking their heads up and down. Ada didn't feel like speaking but she did want crackers, so she raised her hand.

Rose brought a bowl of strawberries and bananas, along with two packages of Ritz crackers. She went back to get some water bottles and passed those out to everyone. They continued to sit in silence, and all ate at least a few bites and drank some water. They could hear the guys all shouting at one another up on deck, and it was comforting but at the same time frightening. Ada wasn't sure how it was possible to stay aboard when you're being tossed around in the water so ferociously. She was anxious for all the guys and knew that the girls were feeling the same.

"I've got to pee!" It was Kristine, and they all giggled. Leave it to her to get them to laugh a little under the circumstances. After she came out of the small bathroom, each one took her turn. Ada tried sitting up because she had to go as well. It took two of them to get her there and back. Ada hated being so helpless. Usually, she was the one taking care of everyone. It was the teacher in her. On the other hand, this time she was the one who needed help.

Another hour passed with little to no discussion. There wasn't anything to talk about during this time, except to say they hoped the guys would be okay and they couldn't wait to get back to shore. The thunder and lightning kept getting louder and louder, which had to mean they were going in the direction of the storm, or it had completely caught up to them.

There were two hard rocks on either side and shortly after water began pouring down the stairs like a waterfall. Charlotte was first to witness it and gasped loudly. The three girls joined the others on the bed as the water flowed back into the cabin. Ada was scared to death and her life flashed before her eyes. She thought of Troy, then Daisy, then Jason. Why hadn't she believed him? Why had she been so mean and not realized he cared . . . at least for her safety. What she would give to go back and make the decision again.

Lee came running down the stairs in his deck boots and rain gear. He looked exhausted. "It's okay ladies. Hopefully, that won't happen again, but that's good . . . just stay on the bed and out of the water. I don't want anyone to get—" He stopped there and realized it didn't need to be said. Of course, if lightning were to hit the boat they could be electrocuted. The entire bed was solid wood and a natural ground. He nodded gently and smiled slightly through pursed lips.

Poor Lee, Ada thought. *He feels entirely responsible for our situation. That's unfair. After all, he checked the weather report, and we all made the decision to come along.*

Another two hours had passed without much more water entering the cabin. The girls tried to sleep, but about the time they relaxed long enough, another hard rock to the side would cause them to grab a hold of each other and the sides of the bed or headboard.

Henry came back down to tell them that their only option was to ground the boat on the small island they were sailing beside. The beach had a sandy shoreline and would be perfect for grounding. He wanted them to brace themselves in approximately ten minutes. The storm made it too dangerous to keep going.

They didn't say a word to Henry. He looked lovingly at Rose before ascending the stairs. A single tear fell down her cheek, but she kept quiet. Ada understood better than anyone about the fear of losing someone. She had felt the same thing when Troy left that day to go snowboarding down the desolate mountain by helicopter.

After five minutes they made attempts to anchor themselves in the bed with blankets tucked in all around them and each took hold of the headboard attached to the wall. They each had put pillows in front of them to act as a sort of air bag. Ada was sitting up by now and was gripping so hard that her knuckles turned white.

Suddenly, the guys were all yelling at once, and then it happened. It was like someone had slammed on the brakes of a car. The girls were thrown forward into their pillows and desperate cries were heard as Ada's fingers slipped from the wooden slat, and she was thrown onto the cabin floor in a foot of water.

Chapter 30

The boat had come to a stop. There was more yelling from up above, growing louder as the guys suddenly appeared.

"Is everyone okay?"

Ada looked up into Lee's concerned face. He was completely drenched and worn out. Henry went to Rose's side as she was trying to stand. He picked her up in his arms and carried her up the stairs. Ben assisted Emma and Kristine to their feet while Lee lifted Ada out of the water. Charlotte and Jayden assisted one another.

Once the crew had all assembled on the deck, Henry began

gathering as many supplies as possible to set out of the boat. The heavy rain and winds made it difficult to see as Lee and Ben lifted the girls out one by one and told them to take cover closer to the group of hemlocks.

Everyone worked together to get the two tents set up and tied to the trees. The girls took one and the guys the other after their bags of clothes, albeit a little wet, were delivered to their tent by Henry. The look in Rose's eyes pleaded with him when he handed her a bag, but she didn't say anything.

"There are a couple of dry beach towels in this garbage bag if you all want to get into some of your drier things. Hopefully, this storm will subside, and we can build a fire if we're able to locate some dry enough wood."

Rose zipped the tent shut when he left.

"That was so scary." It was Emma speaking the first words since entering the shelter. "I'm so glad we made it to safety. I just hope we'll be rescued soon."

"Me too," Ada offered in a hushed tone.

"How's your head, Ada? Did you get any other injuries?"

Ada put her hand to her forehead and felt the dried blood. "No, I don't think so. Probably just battered and bruised like the rest of you from being thrown around inside the cabin."

Once they had all exchanged their wet clothes for something drier, the rain had slowed down and there was no more lightning or thunder.

"I wonder what time it is?" Rose asked. "My phone is somewhere on the boat."

The others echoed in agreement. Jayden was the only one to have it in her pocket, but it wasn't coming on. It either had no charge or had sustained water damage.

"Hey in there, we have a fire going if you gals would like to come out and get warmed up." It was Henry.

Rose unzipped the tent quickly and stepped out to embrace him. She was crying at this point. "I was so scared that you were going to fall overboard," she managed to say.

"No way would I leave you." He kissed her gently on the mouth and led her to a spot by the fire.

Ada's heart ached a little. *That's something Troy would have said*, she thought to herself as she exited the tent.

Lee had spread out some blankets that managed to stay dry inside a storage bin on deck. As night fell, the warmth of the fire felt good. They passed around leftovers from earlier in the day and commented on how delicious everything tasted after their frightening adventure.

"I managed to get a few SOS calls to the coastguard," said Lee, "so I'm hoping they heard my approximate location and plans of running the boat ashore. It's possible we may need to spend the night, but at least we have enough supplies."

One by one, they went to the edge of the woods to relieve themselves. Fortunately, there were some large rocks blocking views, and Lee had told them that the leaves from the Rhododendrons nearby were okay to use as toilet paper.

After a round of coffee made on top of the fire, they began talking about the day. Lee apologized repeatedly for what had happened. He didn't even care that damage had been done to his boat. All he cared about was the safety of his new friends. They all assured him how grateful they were to be alive, and thanked him, Ben, and Henry for saving them. Ada wasn't going to say a word about Jason warning her about a potential storm. What good would it do now anyway?

A motor purred in the distance, and Ada could see lights peeking through the darkness.

Then, there were shouts of "Anyone out there?" from a bullhorn.

"Yes! They did hear our distress calls!" Lee started

yelling and waving his hands. Henry turned on a flashlight and waved it around. There appeared to be at least three boats in the water. All at once lights appeared inside of the vessels, and Ada could see it was the Coastguard. Small skiffs were deployed and sent toward shore. The girls grabbed their bags and headed toward the rescuers.

That's when Ada heard her own name being called by a familiar voice coming from the dark.

"Ada! Ada!"

She turned to see Jason running toward her on the beach. Her heart started racing and the butterflies in her stomach almost made her nauseous.

"Jason? What . . . what are you doing here?" Ada stood up too fast and thought she was going to get sick. He then noticed her head where his flashlight was shining.

"Oh my gosh, you're hurt!" It was at that moment Jason picked her up gently into his arms.

She laid her head on his shoulder and didn't even bother asking where he was taking her. It wasn't in the direction of the other boats.

"You have her, Jason?" Lee yelled over.

"Got her!" Jason shouted off to the side. He waded into the

water with her, holding her above the waves and then set her gently inside a boat. It carried them to a larger craft. Ada didn't even ask.

Once Jason had the dinghy fastened, he took her below. It wasn't fancy like Lee's, but rather homey. The Scottish plaid quilt and dark navy sheets made it masculine against the knotty pine walls. He had her sit down on the sofa and covered her with a fleece blanket.

"You stay here where it's warm. I'll get us back to the dock. It should take around an hour or less since the storm is over."

"If you need anything, help yourself." He motioned around the cabin.

Ada's head was spinning by this time. She was overwhelmed with exhaustion, excitement, and relief. What had just happened? Did her knight in shining armor come to rescue her? Had he changed his mind about her, or was he doing this out of duty? *It must mean something*, Ada thought, *or he wouldn't have come looking for me and just let the Coastguard do their job.*

Those questions swirled around and around her head. She curled up on the couch and fell asleep.

When she awakened and focused her eyes, she could see flames and sat bolt upright. She then realized it was a fireplace and the only light in the room. Where was she? Ada rubbed her eyes and looked around. Reassured that she was still on the boat Jason had helped her onto, she put her head back down on the pillow. There was not much movement except for gentle rocking. Ada thought she heard Jason upstairs talking to someone. Was he planning on taking her back home to the bungalow? It had to be late, and she just wanted to lie in her own bed with Maisy curled up beside her.

"Ah, you're awake. How's the head?" Jason came over and inspected her forehead. He had also brought a ginger ale and a slice of Italian bread. "Feel like eating something? I thought you should have some Tylenol, but you need some food first."

Ada began sitting up again.

"Easy," Jason's voice was firm yet kind.

Ada gladly took the bread and drink because she desperately wanted something to stop her head from hurting.

"Maybe we had better take you to the hospital to make sure that you don't have a concussion."

"No, I'm okay. I'd really like to get a warm shower and wash off the salt water."

"There is a bathroom right in there with clean towels," he said pointing across the room, and then quickly added, "but I can take you home if you'd rather."

"Is this your boat?"

"Yes, it is. Not the luxury offered on Lee's sailboat, but it's cozy enough."

"My husband and I enjoyed—" she started to say but stopped. "I would like to get a shower here if you don't mind?"

"Not at all. Help yourself." Jason reached out a hand to help steady her when she stood.

She walked to the door and turned around. "Why did you come for me?"

"I . . . we were worried about all of you. I saw the storm approaching and called the Coastguard to let them know about the excursion since I had an idea where you were going."

"Right. But you only brought me aboard?"

"Yeah, well Robert and Susan made me promise to bring you home safely. Uh, towels are in a closet behind the door."

Ada didn't say anything more. She closed the door behind her and kicked off her shoes. It hurt to bend over and take off the socks and pants. The orange glow from the tiny lamp was just enough light for her to see. No need to turn on the ceiling one. She grabbed hold of her shirt and tried pulling it over her head but struggled. Ada's entire body hurt, most likely from tensing up so often over the last several hours, not to mention the couple of falls she experienced. She leaned over and attempted to remove it that way. No luck. This was ridiculous. Ada reached into the shower to turn on the water, stepped inside and closed the glass door. She started sobbing and wasn't aware that it was loud enough to be heard by Jason in the other room.

"Are you okay in there?" He was knocking gently.

Ada couldn't answer because her sobs became louder as she slid to the floor, letting the water pour over her head.

Jason opened the door slightly. "Ada?"

She gave up trying to stifle her crying with hands over her mouth.

Before she realized what was happening, Jason opened the shower door and stepped in with her. He didn't have shoes on but was still dressed in his shorts and t-shirt. He reached down and gently pulled her up and into his own arms, not letting go. She placed her head on his chest and continued letting the tears mix with the warm water.

Jason was hesitant at first, but then stood with one arm around her waist and the other hand on the side of her head. They stood for several minutes.

"I couldn't get my top off. It hurts to lift my arms." She looked up at Jason so helplessly while the tears continued to fall.

Without saying a word, he began gently pulling the shirt up over her head and tossed it over the shower door. She stood there in her bra and panties and reached for the shampoo bottle. Jason took it himself and put some in his hand then proceeded to wash her hair.

Ada let him finish washing and rinsing her hair without so much as a sound. He pushed the hair back away from her face, and she once again looked into those blue eyes. Reaching her hands down to her sides, she slipped her panties down over her hips and pushed them to the corner with her toes. Next, she unfastened her bra and let it fall and stood before him. The light was barely enough to illuminate either of them but enough that their eyes were speaking volumes.

Ada stood with her hands down at her side. This time she wouldn't be the first one to make a move. Jason reached out and placed a finger under her chin lifting it up toward him. He bent down and kissed her softly on the mouth. Ada felt herself almost give way to falling. This time her head was spinning but for reasons other than her injuries.

He stepped back, removed his clothing, and tossed them in the corner with hers. In another instant he had them both covered in soapy water and began rubbing her shoulders, back, and stomach. The warmth of the water fell over them, and their kisses became longer and more intense. By now their bodies were washed clean, and Jason opened the shower door.

In one move, he picked up Ada and made his way to the bed, kissing her as he laid her down and straddled her without any of his weight resting on her. He began at her forehead and proceeded to kiss every inch of Ada's body all the way to her feet until she was breathing heavily. She reached for him and felt his need for her as she wrapped her legs around his lower half begging him to become part of her. Their lovemaking lasted hours with only moments of rest. It was as though they couldn't get enough of each other. Neither of them said a word and only sounds of pleasure escaped their lips. Exhausted, they both gave in to sleep around three o'clock in the morning.

When Ada awakened, she was smiling and lying on Jason's chest. Both of his arms were around her, and she hadn't felt this safe and happy for a long time. Why had it taken something so dramatic to finally bring them together?

Thank goodness she decided to stay and take over for Oscar at the gallery. This would allow them more time to talk and get to know one another.

There was so much Ada didn't know about Jason but wanted to learn. Her parents would approve, and she knew that Daisy would be over the moon at what had taken place. Obviously, those feelings would come after the relief that she had survived a storm at sea.

She allowed herself to think about the future with him and what it would be like. Would he propose this year? Would they live in the bungalow together after getting married? The house would be perfect for raising a couple of children. It was close to the beach for family picnics and close to the University where their father worked. The joy was enough to stir the butterflies in her tummy, and she wanted more of him. Ada took her time getting out of bed so as not to disturb him while he was still sleeping. She needed to pee.

There was morning sun streaming in through a crack in the curtains when she came out of the bathroom. It created enough light that she was able to look through her bag, hoping for some clean dry clothes to put on later. The only thing left was a pair of running shorts. Maybe Jason would have a shirt she could wear. She opened a small closet door beside the bed and reached for a long-sleeved button-down white shirt. She used to love wearing Troy's shirts occasionally, and he always thought she looked sexy. The sleeve caught on something, and she moved other clothing aside to retrieve it. At the back of the closet sat her painting from the gala. He had purchased it, and her heart skipped a beat.

Before she climbed back into bed, she stood for a moment to watch Jason sleeping peacefully with what appeared to be a slight smile. Had she brought him as much pleasure as he had to her? The sheet was pulled slightly to one side, and Ada could see the beginning of a tattoo. She wondered for a moment if his had as much meaning behind it as her own.

Sighing slightly, she quietly joined him and nestled herself in the crook of his raised arm. Ada traced her fingers over Jason's chest and began kissing it, making her way down his body. He stirred slightly, and she hoped he would awaken soon. She began sliding off the sheet as she continued kissing him and stopped abruptly and sucked in her breath so fast that her head began to swim. No, it couldn't possibly be.

She sat up in bed quickly and covered her mouth with a pillow so she wouldn't scream. Maybe her mind was playing tricks on her . . . but there it was, off to the side several inches below his belly button. A tattoo. Ada recognized it immediately because she had one just like it that said "A & T" inside the infinity sign. She was too stunned to yell or cry or speak and put the pillow aside then. She jumped out of bed and grabbed the pair of shorts and his shirt that she had laid out just moments ago. Ada nearly fell over stepping into the shorts and knocked over an empty bottle on the table.

Jason sat up quickly and noticed her hurrying. "What's wrong?"

She climbed the stairs as fast as she could.

"Ada? Ada! What?" Then he looked down and understood what she had seen. "Dammit!"

Chapter 31

He knew deep down that she didn't want him to go on the trip. Ada was an adventurer but not when it came to extreme sports. An avid snowboarder, Troy had always wanted to try the helicopter drop off for an exciting trip down a mountain without loads of other people getting in his way. The call came at the last minute when there was a cancellation. A guy's wife had gone into labor, so they had an extra seat for him.

Even though he knew that she didn't want him to go, he also knew that Ada enjoyed seeing her husband so happy doing what he enjoyed. It was one of the many traits Troy loved about her. He didn't want to worry Ada but tried to convince her that everything would be okay.

The day had started out fine. He had arrived early at the heliport and met with the other guys, including the pilot. Once the snowboards were loaded and Troy signed some paperwork, they climbed up and buckled themselves inside. They were all around the same age and the entire time heading up to the mountain they were talking a mile a minute. It wasn't until the ride got a little rough that they stopped to look out the helicopter windows. The pilot spoke through their headsets and told them that he was trying to find a place to land, but a storm had come up over the other side and was producing heavy blizzard conditions. They could all hear the concern in his voice and looked at each other.

For the next several minutes, the men were quiet and watched as the pilot did his best to steady the chopper. The high winds were pulling them in one direction and the whiteout conditions made it impossible to see in any direction.

The pilot spoke again, "Sorry for this, but we can't—" He was interrupted by a large tree limb that slammed its way through the side of the helicopter and punctured him in the side. He slumped over. It was a sickening sight, and one of the guys yelled, "No!"

Everything happened so quickly, and they began spinning out of control while the blades cut into the tall Sitka tree. A hard, loud bang was heard as they landed on something solid. Troy looked out the window in time to see a cliff face and figured they were on an edge. He thought maybe that would stop them, but no sooner had he had the thought that the helicopter turned on its side and began tumbling over and over.

Once the broken machine reached the bottom of the canyon, it exploded. At this point everyone who hadn't already passed out was screaming and yelling in pain as their clothing caught fire. They struggled to loosen the seatbelts. Troy could see the youngest of the group next to him and tried pulling him away from the flames and toward the door which had already fallen off during their descent.

Then another explosion occurred, this one even louder than the last. It thrust Troy out of the helicopter seat, setting him on fire, and throwing him on a bed of icy snow. He reached his hands up to shield his face and the flames from the gloves burned him so severely that he screamed out. He struggled to roll over in the deep snow, but it was no use. He could feel the toboggan on his head burn away along with his hair. The flames from his coat were licking his face. Troy's adrenalin was in full force by now and he had no choice except to turn and bury his face in the snow. He couldn't breathe but knew that he had to douse out the flames.

When Troy pulled his face away from the wall of snow, he could see pieces of his skin left behind. Nauseated from the sight, he began throwing up. His body was shaking and going into shock. He looked up to see the helicopter several yards from him, still in flames. There was no way any of the guys could have survived. Troy crawled on his hands and knees to put as much distance as he could from the crash and then felt himself slipping away.

When he awakened, the sun was setting behind the mountain, and he could hear voices somewhere. Troy tried focusing his eyes, but everything was blurry. His head hurt terribly, and his body felt like he was being stung by a mound of fire ants. Shouting for help was no good because his voice was gone when he tried to speak. Troy was determined to stand, but it took several tries while bracing himself against a rock. Where was he? What had happened? He was thirsty, so thirsty.

"Got to get help. Got to find help," he said to himself. His head felt like it would explode, and he cried out in pain with every step until he made it to the end of a group of pine trees. There was a cabin in the distance without smoke coming from the chimney, so most likely it was empty. Troy needed someone to be there. The trek took him over two hours, and he couldn't feel his toes by the time he reached the cabin. In fact, he couldn't feel his face either. It was a strange sensation. He reached up to touch it, but quickly brought his hands down in case more skin would fall off.

The cabin door wasn't locked, and Troy walked straight inside, scanning for signs of a human. Through his blurred vision it looked to be empty except for a bed in the corner and two chairs in front of a fireplace. *Fire*, he thought. As much as he needed warmth, building one was out of the question. He took off as many clothes as he could manage and laid down on the bed then pulled the covers over him. He was cold and shaking so hard he thought the bed would collapse.

A beautiful girl was running towards him with her arms out. She was smiling and holding wildflowers with one hand. He tried to run toward her, but his legs wouldn't move. She turned and began running in another direction.

Come back. Please, come back.

"There, there. You're safe now. I made some soup, and you must eat."

Troy reached up to touch his face, and realized it was

covered completely with something except for his eyes, nose, and mouth. He became frightened and sat straight up. The warmth from the fireplace was emanating, and his body welcomed it.

An older woman with white hair and a soft face was smiling at him. "You're okay. I'm taking care of you. Take a few bites of this soup, won't you? You must regain some strength."

Troy opened his mouth like a little bird and swallowed the broth that tasted like what his mother made when he was sick as a little boy. He gladly accepted several more bites then asked for water.

"Yes, yes, you must hydrate as well." She held the glass of water to his lips so he could drink. "What happened to you? Where did you come from?"

"I . . . I don't know. I don't remember. I—"

"There now, don't get yourself upset. We'll figure it out. I was able to use some coconut oil and gauze on your facial burns. The rest of you seems okay, other than a gash on your head. We need to get you to a hospital. I put out a call, and Tom should be here soon."

"Tom?"

"Yes, my husband. I'm Millie, by the way. This is our cabin, and we come here several times a year. Just got in late last night and I found you. He wasn't driving up until today, needed to get our cattle taken care of until our cowhand arrived. We were planning on doing some work inside the cabin."

The door opened and in walked Tom. "Why, hello, there." Tom walked over to where Troy was lying. "Let's see if we can get you off this mountain and to the hospital. I'm afraid my wife has done all she can do for ya."

They both helped Troy sit up and put a coat on him. It was short but warm. His boots were still wet, so she had put three pairs of socks on his feet first. It was a painful walk to the truck, but he made it. Millie patted him gently on the leg once he was inside.

"You take care . . . I didn't even ask your name."

"Uh, I'm . . . uh . . ."

"Now, now. No need to think so hard. You'll remember it soon enough." With that she closed the truck door.

He couldn't think of his name? Who was the girl in his dream? Panic set in, and Tom seemed to pick up on it.

"We've got good doctors in town, and they'll help you along."

The hospital, as it turned out, was smaller than Troy thought one should be. It was only one floor with two small wings on either side of the entrance. A young nurse came out with a wheelchair for Troy, and she and Tom helped him to sit down.

After two different doctors assessed Troy's injuries, it was suggested that he be life- flighted an hour away.

"The kind of help you need is more than what we could offer here. You'll be in good hands."

Troy was wheeled out on a gurney toward a helicopter. "No, no helicopter," he managed to say.

The two EMTs didn't seem to hear him over the noise, and lifted him up and strapped him in. He already had an IV in his arm, and the bag was placed on a hook above his head. The other technician put a blood pressure cuff around his other arm and began taking readings.

Neither spoke but patted him on the shoulder from time to time. The ride didn't take long, and Troy had fallen asleep after being given pain medication through his IV.

When he awakened, there were several doctors and nurses standing around him. The sounds of beeping were rhythmic and almost hypnotic. One of them noticed he had opened his eyes and went over to greet him. They introduced themselves and proceeded to ask a string of questions. They explained that he had sustained a major concussion, an isolated fracture to the tibia, as well as third degree burns to his face. Troy wasn't able to respond with a name or an explanation as to what had happened. Panic set in and he could feel his breathing become rapid. A smaller in statue doctor with kind eyes came closer to Troy and took his hand to place in his own.

"I'm guessing that you are in your late twenties, young man. I'm Doctor Langley. What an ordeal to have gone through, and you must be confused and frightened. You most likely are suffering from amnesia due to the severe blow to your head. Hopefully as the swelling resolves, you will regain your memory. We were able to set the bone without surgery and you'll have a cast for a while. Regarding the burns to your face, we have some options."

Another doctor brought over a stool for him to sit and be more at eye level with Troy. "We're able to do some skin grafts, but due to the severity and extent of your burns, there is too much area to cover." He glanced up at his colleagues standing around and back to Troy. "Have you heard of allotransplantation?"

"Someone else's skin on mine?" Troy spoke softly.

"Exactly, but there's a little more to it than that. It is reconstructive surgery by using someone else's face over another's." He felt Troy grip his hand.

"I know. I know it sounds incredibly like science fiction because it has only been performed a few times. There is a good amount of skepticism surrounding the medical procedure for various reasons . . . ethical, technical, the risk of infection, the psychological impact on the recipient, etc. We have lots to consider, however, the decision must be yours."

"So, I wouldn't look like myself any longer?"

"You already—" a fourth-year medical student spoke up before one of the attendings pushed him aside.

"We have a donor, who just lost his life today in a motorcycle accident. He sustained internal injuries which led to his death. The family is coming to terms with their son's wish to donate his organs, including the face. After a lengthy discussion as a family, they granted permission.

"You meet the match requirements including blood and tissue type, similar age and facial structure, skin color, and similar age. You also have enough healthy skin on the rest of your body that we can perform skin grafts should the transplant prove to be unsuccessful. I don't want to rush you, but time is of the essence. The success rate rapidly declines the longer you wait. I'm sorry this life-altering decision must be made so quickly. I wish there was someone we could call for you."

"I have no idea." Troy closed his eyes for a moment and the physicians looked at each other. All walked out of the room except for Dr. Langley. When Troy opened his eyes again, he turned his head toward the doctor. "With the transplant, I'll look like someone else?"

"Correct."

"Without the transplant, I'll be disfigured?"

"Correct."

Without much hesitation, once again closed his eyes as he answered, "Do the transplant."

During the two weeks in the hospital, Troy struggled to regain his memory. His dreams seemed to hold the only answers, but nothing ever made sense. It was a hodgepodge of scenarios that didn't provide any clarity for what his life had been like before the accident, nor did he recall anything about that either.

Detectives from the local police station had come to question him on a few occasions when the nurses permitted it. They had also done searches for missing people without any luck. The helicopter crash would have made sense but some DNA from the ashes of all six individuals had been identified and they were assumed dead. There was no possibility of anyone surviving the explosion.

Even though the bandages had been removed earlier, Troy didn't wish to see himself until most of the swelling was gone. His surgeon, Dr. Langley, had his hand resting on the top of Troy's shoulder and Nurse Sarah was standing on the opposite side the day he decided to look at himself. She was holding a mirror and asked if he was ready to look. He nodded, took a breath, and stared into the mirror.

Troy felt the same as when he passed a person on the street; there was no sense of identity, nothing familiar except for his blue eyes. His nose was sharper than the one he was born with, and he was uncertain about his mouth because of the swelling. It was strange. On one hand he felt like screaming and crying, but on the other he was thankful that his face wouldn't be disfigured for the rest of his life.

His thoughts turned to gratitude for the donor who lost his life, his face, and to the grieving family who had to make a most gut-wrenching decision. They had only asked that when Troy was ready, they could see him just once. He felt it was the least he could do for them.

A few minutes had passed with only Troy's thoughts. The

doctor and nurse stood silently until finally, the surgeon spoke.

"There will still be swelling for several more weeks, and of course your scars will heal over time. You have done beautifully in the recovery process and ahead of the timeline with your breathing, swallowing, and speech. We'd like you to focus more time on recovering your memory and there are several specialists here to assist." He nodded to the nurse to take the mirror away.

Troy was eventually transferred from the transplant unit to rehabilitation for continued work with physical therapists and psychologists. Since he had no known family or a place to go, the hospital insisted that he stay, especially kind Doctor Langley who treated him more like a grandson than a patient.

Chapter 32

A year passed, and Troy's leg had healed completely. The scars on his face had also disappeared for the most part, and he was fairly used to looking at himself in the mirror. His memories had come back in dreams or when he was reminded of something from listening to a particular song or watching television.

Dr. Langley and his wife had him move into their spacious home where he had his own wing, along with continued physical therapists and psychologists visiting him on a weekly basis. They had given him the name Jason since he was still unable to recall who he was or where he was from. So, he had belonged to another family entirely, yet these two very kind people were the only ones he knew. He began questioning the future and what was to become of him. Living here for the rest of his life was not an option.

Frustration set in shortly after the anniversary of his accident. Dr. Langley, or Samuel, as Jason called him now, sensed this and reached out to a friend of his on the west coast who had spent part of his career researching and treating individuals trying to recover memories. In fact, he made a trip to see Jason personally. Dr. Robert McGuire was every bit as patient and kind as Samuel, and Jason immediately felt comfortable. After spending time together for an entire weekend talking and testing, he invited Jason to move to his town so they could continue the work, and he was set up in a small apartment close to campus.

Most of Jason's memories had come back within six months except they were out of order. He and Robert focused on creating a timeline of events. The most difficult memory was that of Ada and wondering how she was doing and what she had endured. Troy had felt a sense of guilt for what had happened because she hadn't wanted him to go on the trip. Had she met someone else? Maybe she changed towns or states? He had so many questions regarding Ada, and Robert had assured him that they would get those answered eventually.

One memory that had emerged was that of baseball,

playing and coaching. Robert suggested that he take the interim

position at the college in the coming summer. Doing something

familiar would be good for Troy and help restore his memory bank.

He agreed to coach the baseball team and do lawncare for the

summer on campus but wanted to keep the name Jason for the time

being. He was most happy that he could afford to pay the apartment

rent and purchase groceries. Perhaps he would make a trip back

home to Riverton to see if he could find out about Ada.

The first day of practice with the team in April happened to

land on the two-year anniversary of his accident. It was surreal to

think how much his life was altered in two years. He wasn't sure if

he'd be able to start over without Ada, but there was absolutely no

way he would put her through more trauma than what she had

endured. He didn't look the same either. She may feel nothing

towards him besides hurt and confusion. All he wanted to know

was that she was okay.

The young college players provided Jason with purpose

again. The skills he had acquired as a former player and coach were

restored quickly. Muscle memory was an amazing thing. The guys

liked Jason's style of coaching and preferred his positive approach over that of their outgoing trainer. He had left the school for a job in broadcasting, and Jason was grateful for the opportunity. It strengthened his determination to be the best version of this new self, and he started working out at the gym.

Robert's help was incredible, and with each passing day Jason remembered even the most insignificant things, like repairing a leaky faucet in the home he shared with Ada. Life would be incredibly difficult without the love of his life, but that was just it. He cared about her enough to set her free so that she could find love again.

Robert asked Jason if he would want to collaborate on a book with him about memory loss from injury or traumatic events and assured him that he would remain anonymous. Jason agreed as he felt an obligation to give back at least in part what Dr. McGuire had given him. The two began meeting weekly and spent a few weeks designing an outline for the book. Robert had also encouraged Jason to pick up where he had left off with his counseling degree. There was no reason why they couldn't at some point have the hours transferred from the online university.

Toward the end of the month, Jason discussed going home with Robert. Even though the good doctor thought that he should be honest with Ada about what had happened, Jason assured him that his decision was final. She would never know.

So it was that he traveled by train back to Riverton on a Saturday morning. His hands were sweaty the entire way, and his heart raced with thoughts of seeing her. There was no reason to disguise himself since his face was that of another man's. Even his own parents wouldn't recognize him, but they no longer lived in the house where he grew up and had moved farther south. His mother had become frail after her bout with cancer. Troy longed to see his parents and decided that was one trip he would make soon. The last thing he wanted to do was shock them, so needing to be assured of their health would come first.

The train pulled into the station and Jason looked at familiar surroundings. He only had a few hours before the trip back. First off, he grabbed a sandwich from one of his and Ada's favorite restaurants and had an Uber drop him off two blocks from his neighborhood.

The day was sunny and warm. People were out walking, and some were working in their lawns. He and Ada had enjoyed living here and had so many plans, including children. When Jason turned the corner and caught the first glimpse of his home, there was a family outside with three children: a girl and two younger boys. The father was washing their car, and the mother was chasing them around the yard as they laughed. Did Ada sell their home? Maybe it was too much for her to keep it, both cost wise and memory's sake. His heart sank and guilt set in. Seeing the picture before him of the life they wanted together made him surer than ever that Ada could never find out he was still alive.

He walked the entire way back to the center of town and was ready to cross the street to the station when he spotted her. Jason's breath caught in his throat, and he nearly wanted to call out to her. That's when he saw a man rest his hand on the small of her back and escort her inside a restaurant. It was one that he and Ada never ate at because she wasn't a fan of seafood. Nevertheless, it was obvious that she had moved on. Jason's emotions got the better of him, and he decided to hurry to the train before he changed his mind and went inside the restaurant to scoop her up in his arms.

The train ride back left him in a somber mood. It would be some time before the sadness of not being with Ada wasn't the main thing on his mind. She was able to go on, but could he? There really wasn't a choice, especially now that she had someone new in her life. Jason tried to be happy for her.

The following month after contacting the retirement home where his folks lived and being told that they were doing very well, Jason made another trip to see them. Their initial shock soon gave way to cries and hugs. He held onto them for what seemed like hours. The entire weekend was spent telling them all that had happened over the last two years. They assured him that they understood and loved him no matter what he looked like. At one point his mother even took Jason's head in her hands and kissed his face several times saying, "My son, my son."

His plan was to move them closer to him once he was more established in the town and knew that his job would be permanent. They parted on happy terms knowing that they'd be together again soon.

Life was going along rather smoothly. His and Robert's work on the book was proving to be cathartic for Jason. The baseball team was looking even better for next year. He had been able to scout three more top players who helped replace the outgoing seniors. The summer camp would all but assure them a spot in the playoffs next spring after some tournament plays in the fall.

Jason liked the chance to focus his thoughts on coaching strategies while mowing the campus. Landscaping had been something he enjoyed doing back home. His father had taught him well about how to keep the blade higher on a mower in order that the grass become thicker.

All was well until one day at practice he thought he saw someone who looked like Ada. She was sitting on a bench across the street looking toward the baseball field. It was about that time that a foul ball was hit high in the air and began its descent right over the trees where she was sitting. Before Jason had a chance to say something, one of the other players yelled over. Without any hesitation, the young lady got up off the bench, walked a few feet while looking up and caught the ball. The team erupted in applause and whistles while a player ran over to retrieve it from her. That's when he knew for sure. It really was Ada.

What was she doing here? How was it possible that she ended up in the same place as him? The answers to those questions would come sooner than later when she joined him and the team at Robert's and Susan's house for a cookout. His entire body was shaking when she entered through the gate in the back of the yard.

She was even more beautiful than he had remembered. The sundress she was wearing accentuated her curves, and Jason blushed thinking about their lovemaking and how afterwards she would snuggle into him then reach up to touch his face. This was going to be the most difficult encounter he could imagine.

Chapter 33

Jason had warned her about the predicted weather, once again, before the sailing trip.

Ada had invited him, but he had turned her down. So, she was extremely cool with him this time and didn't hold back when responding to him. He really was worried about her, and he had lived here long enough to know that a storm could brew quickly at sea, especially the direction they were going. The thing was, Ada had no idea how much he longed to go with her as her husband, Troy. The unexpected summer with her had brought back feelings of remorse that he had been selfish enough to go on an extreme trip, especially knowing how she felt deep down.

Who knows where they would be in life right now and what happiness they could have found? The picture of them swinging children at the park popped into his head. Of course, Jackson and Daisy would most likely have had kids around the same age, and they would be living their dream. The face in the mirror each morning reminded him over and over why it could never be a reality. Somehow his life would have to continue without her, or so he thought.

The last comment she blurted out to him nearly caused him to stop breathing. Ada had decided to accept an offer from Oscar Wells and run the art gallery and would be staying right here on Hartlyn Island. Jason would have to forgo his job offer as the official baseball coach at the University and move somewhere far away from her. He knew in his heart that he couldn't bear the sadness in seeing her all the time, most likely moving on with someone else. Jason watched her walk away until she turned the corner to her street. Ada was probably right. He didn't want her to go sailing and enjoy herself. The weather excuse was just that, an excuse.

The following morning Jason awoke startled with a knot in his stomach. He got out of bed and went to the kitchen determined to make this a routine day. He'd be meeting the guys for practice in an hour. That would take his mind off of her. While fixing himself breakfast the television was on in the background. He wasn't paying much attention until they broke for a special announcement.

"Due to gale-force southwest winds, a storm surge and large waves are possible today. Unless you are heading in the opposite direction, it's best to keep your boats secured at the docks," the broadcaster said.

So, it was more than an excuse for not wanting Ada to go sailing. She and the crew were possibly going to run into trouble out there. On the way to practice Jason tried getting through to the coastguard but the lines were busy. Next, he called Robert and Susan to let them know what was going on. They were very worried for both Ada and Jason. Jason met with the baseball team briefly and asked two of the seniors to hold practice for him. He hurried down to the dock and hopped on his boat. Fortunately, he had just gone fishing the day before and had extra clothing and food on board.

The dock was unusually quiet as he pulled away. Only one boat was being secured by a couple across from him. They shouted something, but he couldn't hear and only waved. Jason was certain that it was a warning about the weather. He put the gear in full throttle and raced toward the island. The waves were too much for his boat, and he was forced to go back.

Jason tried the coastguard again. They informed him that some of them were out looking for small craft boats who may be struggling. He described the sailing vessel and gave them approximate location of the island. Once Jason had his boat tied to the dock, he decided to stay until the winds settled so he could make another attempt to find them. His heart was racing and he was near panic thinking about Ada. If something happened to her, he would never forgive himself. The winds increased quickly, and the rain pounded the roof of his cabin. All he could do at this point was hope and pray that Lee could guide them away from the storm.

Several hours passed as Jason listened to the radio and the rescues taking place. There was not one mention of a sailboat that fit the description of the sailing vessel. The skies were dark from the storm, but it was nearing eight o' clock in the evening. It was almost impossible to control a boat in the dark during a storm.

Another hour went by, and the movement of his boat had settled, and the rain had stopped. Jason went upstairs to check things out and could tell that the waves had calmed down to almost a stillness. He started the boat and steered in the direction of the crew based on Ada's itinerary that she had shared with him when asking him to go.

Jason noticed that he kept holding his breath and reminded himself to breathe. He really was scared as to what he'd find or not find for that matter. The ocean was eerie at night and made you feel so small. Jason had purchased some high-tech equipment for his boat recently which helped immensely. The screen showed the island approximately twelve nautical miles off shore.

"Hold on, Ada, I'm on my way. Please hold on."

As he approached the tip of the island, Jason steered the boat as close as possible and slowed down in order to shine the lights on the shore. He was traveling parallel to the island and was near the end but didn't see any sign of the sailboat. His brow furrowed, and he blew nervously.

Think, Jason, think. Where else could they have gone? If the sailboat was pushed out to sea during the storm . . . oh please dear God, no.

He suddenly remembered that there was another island ahead. It was much smaller but frequented by boaters for the nice beach. Jason looked at the screen more closely so he could navigate safely. The waters were still extremely choppy.

Another thirty minutes passed before reaching the small island. Foliage came right out to the water's edge, and Jason thought the beach area was closer to the other end. He thought he could see some lights ahead. Maybe it was the coastguard out searching, and he could check with them on where they had looked.

Getting closer, Jason could see that it was two coastguard boats, and they appeared to be anchored close to the island. That's when he spotted the sailboat. It had been run ashore and leaning off to one side. He could barely make out the letters, but that was it! Ada had told him the name was "The Beginning of Us."

Jason's heart raced again, more in fear. He wasn't near enough yet to see anyone or what was happening. The coastguard vessel noticed him and shined a light in his direction. Jason held up his hand to block his eyes from the bright light, but took his hands off of the wheel long enough to wave his hand back and forth. As he approached and threw his anchor overboard, he could hear a lot of voices. Without so much as a thought, he opened the storage container on the deck and lowered the dinghy, used the ladder to step inside and then flung the rope back on board. The small motor was enough to get him the few meters to shore. He jumped out before the water was knee deep and dragged it into the sand. Then he began running towards the group shouting her name.

"Ada! Ada!"

Then Jason saw her. She was by the firepit and stood looking in the direction of his voice.

She looked so exhausted, and her hair was matted and clinging to the sides of her head. She smiled when she saw him. As he drew closer, he could see that her head had been bleeding. That's when he decided to pick her up and take her aboard his boat. He had seen the others being helped toward the coastguard vessels, and Lee had looked up in time to see the two of them and yelled over. At least he could pass the word to the rest because Jason wasn't waiting one more minute to get her home. All he wanted to do was protect the woman he loved.

Jason got Ada settled in down below and convinced her to lie down and rest while he piloted the boat back home. He could hardly take his eyes off her as she closed hers but reluctantly went upstairs. They had made good time when he pulled in and got the boat tethered. Surely Ada was hungry, so he quietly descended the stairs with some bread and ginger ale since she had been queasy earlier. She was sitting up looking around with the only the glow of the gas fireplace and gladly took the offering.

At the end of a brief conversation, she had referred to her

"late husband, Troy," and it was enough to cause Jason to turn his head for a moment. Thankfully, Ada hadn't noticed and quickly added that she would really like to get a shower. Jason didn't want to leave her side and sat down at the kitchenette to wait for her.

He was in deep thought until soft crying brought him back to what was happening inside the small cabin. Without hesitation, he knocked and entered the bathroom at the same time. The next thing he knew, Jason kicked off his deck shoes and opened the shower door. She hadn't turned any lights on and all that was glowing was a night light. It broke him to see her sitting on the shower floor, so he lifted her to him.

She expressed her difficulty in getting her shirt off, so without saying a word Jason pulled it gently up and off. He washed her hair as she stood while the silent tears and water fell. After he was done, Ada looked up at him so innocently for what seemed like several minutes. Then, she slid off her panties and bra without taking her eyes off of him. Standing before him was the woman he had loved from the time he was a teenager. There had never been anyone like her.

What the hell, Jason thought to himself. *I can't take one more minute of this torture.*

He took off his clothing, and in an instant had them both

covered with soap and water. They were skin to skin and kissed deeply and desperately. He wanted her more than ever and let any thoughts of hesitation or question dissipate with the steam of the shower. In one move he took her from the shower to the bed. Their lovemaking was intense and beautiful at the same time. He lost count of the times they soared together in ecstasy until at one point both had fallen asleep in each other's arms.

Even his dreams didn't let him rest, but he was happier than he remembered being in a long, long time. She was kissing his chest and moving lower. Jason heard himself moan but was soon awakened by a crash of some sort. He was still in a dream state when he sat up and saw Ada moving toward the stairs quickly and he could sense something had happened.

"Ada?" He called out to her. "Ada! What . . ." That's when he looked down and saw it. "Dammit!"

Why hadn't he thought of it? Then again, how could he have when what happened wasn't supposed to happen?

Jason threw on a pair of shorts and a t-shirt before darting after her up the stairs. She was running as fast as she could on the dock towards the beach. He had to catch her. There was so much explaining to do.

Chapter 34

Jason was calling out to her as they both ran, but Ada didn't stop until she reached the end of the dock where she tripped and fell. He had made it to her and was bending down to look at the blood running down her knee. Ada ignored the reason she had fallen and looked into Troy's deep blue eyes with tears streaming down her face.

"Why? Why?" She struggled to ask.

At first Ada pounded her fists into Troy's chest when he tried pulling her into him, but then she gave in and allowed herself to be held by the husband she missed and loved more than life.

After a few minutes he helped her stand up and with one swift move he had her in his arms carrying her back to the boat. She closed her eyes because everything was spinning.

Ada's initial anger and confusion dissipated and replaced by sheer joy that she had her husband back. It seemed like a dream since things like this rarely happened in life. She didn't want to let go of him for even a second for fear that she would awaken and find out it was not real.

They made love without speaking a word and then she laid in his arms afterwards while he told her the entire story of what had happened. At one point Ada sat up abruptly and gripped her chest.

"Oh Troy, you had to be in so much pain! I'm so sorry that I wasn't there to help you through the trauma."

He laid a hand over her leg and looked at her. "Honestly, Ada, I have no memory of the entire ordeal, just flashbacks at first and then I had to piece things together. I wasn't in a panic about my amnesia until I saw you in my dreams and could never reach you. By the time I realized you were my wife after almost a year had passed, I had no intention of revealing to you that I was still alive. How could I when . . ." He turned away from her, "when I don't even look like the same person you married. Plus, I thought you had most likely gotten on with your life.

"Oh, my love." Ada reached up and held his face in her hands. "Your eyes, your heart," she patted his chest with one hand, "the way you hold me when we make love. It is you. The face doesn't change how I feel about you or how much I love you. I'm beyond grateful to have you back in my life. Nothing was as good without you. I was empty inside like a part of me was missing. And it was, but now I'm whole again."

The sun was setting by the time they finished their conversation, among other things, and they were starving.

"How about some pizza and beer like old times?"

"Yes! Sounds perfect," Ada said as she reached over to give Troy another kiss. "I should go by the bungalow and get some clean clothes."

"I don't know. I kind of prefer you in one of my shirts or just as you are now."

Ada giggled and rolled on top of him again. "Oh my gosh! Who are we going to tell first? My parents? Daisy and Jackson?"

"I think the first people should be Robert and Susan. He's the reason you're here for the summer, by the way."

"Really? How's that?" Ada sat up, curious.

"He didn't tell me at first, but I guess he sent you a brochure on the summer courses. It has been his wish all along that I tell you. Susan doesn't even know."

"That it explains it then. I had no idea why I received the information but sure glad I did! Okay, let's go!"

Troy laughed. "I missed you so much. I can hardly stand to have you out of my sight for a minute!"

"No problem, I want you right next to me every minute! And we'll continue this later." Ada motioned her hands over the bed and winked.

After Ada changed clothes at the bungalow, they crossed the street. They could hear Maisy in the backyard.

"You picked out the perfect dog for us. She's a sweetheart."

"Yes, she really is, and I can't get over how much older she acts than a year." Troy opened the gate for her, and Susan saw them first and began running toward Ada.

By the time Susan reached her, and the two women had collided in a hug, both were crying. "Robert filled me in on everything," Susan said. "Well, at least the part he knew. We only guessed that the two of you were together since the coastguard gave us descriptions. What an incredible journey you have been on,

Jason. I mean, Troy." She hugged him as well.

Maisy was jumping up on Ada, so she sat down in the grass and romped with her a while.

Robert put his arm around Troy as they walked to the patio. "You have no idea how relieved I am that Ada is okay and the two of you found each other again," the older man said.

"You and me both," added Troy.

Susan had come back out with a bottle of champagne and four glasses. "This calls for a toast!"

The alcohol hit Ada fast, and she was feeling a bit dizzy. "We were going to grab some pizza. Would you two like some?"

"Oh, sur—" Robert started to say until he was cut off by Susan's hand on his arm.

"How about we keep Maisy another night and let you two kids get something to eat! We'll see you tomorrow!"

"Right, right." Robert stood up and escorted them to the gate. He had to hold Maisy because she was planning on going along.

"You can come home tomorrow, girl." Troy patted her on the head, and she seemed satisfied. Ada bent to kiss her pup on the nose.

They held hands as they crossed the street to Ada's car.

"Home. I like the sound of that," said Ada, smiling.

Troy opened the driver's side door for her. "Oh no, I want my husband to do the driving from now on!"

"You got it!" They both laughed.

Once they were buckled into their seats, they looked at one other and said at the same time, "What do you feel like listening to?"

Ada laughed. "I've got the perfect playlist!" She connected her phone to the car. It was the collection of favorites the two of them had created together.

"Oh yeah!" said Troy. Then they headed to the local pizza spot.

Once back at the house they decided to sit on the porch for a while and swing.

You have no idea how many times I dropped by Robert and Susan's and saw you over here. It was incredibly difficult to be around you without longing to kiss you.

Ada reached over and kissed him gently. "I'm curious, what kind of book are you working on together?"

"Robert is writing his third book on the subject of memory

loss and trauma, and I'm providing some firsthand knowledge about the process of regaining memory.

"Sounds fascinating. I can't wait to read it!" Her cell phone was ringing inside her purse.

It was Ada's parents calling back. "Mom? Dad?"

"Yes, we're both here darling," her father said. "We couldn't tell if you had something dramatic or exciting to tell us by the sound of your voicemail."

"Actually both," Ada said and looked at Troy who shook his head in agreement.

Both of her parents were speechless. "Troy, we can't express to you how happy we are that you are in our daughter's life again. She has been so sad. Well, we all have, son," said her father.

"Yes, Troy, this is the best news we could ever have hoped for! We can't wait to see you both!"

Ada was surprised at the sincerity in her mother's voice. It made her happy.

After they hung up the phone, Troy suggested they go inside and continue their celebration.

"What about Daisy? I promised that I would call and give her details of the sailing disaster after we got home from dinner.

You know what would be even better? What if I asked if she and Jackson could come up this weekend? We could surprise them!"

"Seeing me isn't going to surprise them. Troy's hand made a circular motion in front of his face."

"Listen, when they find out that you're alive and well, it's not going to matter who you look like!" Ada squealed with delight just thinking about it!

"Of course we'll drive up to see you tomorrow! I'm detecting an air of excitement in your voice," said Daisy on a call just a few minutes later. "Did you get more good news added to this new chapter of yours?"

"You could say that!" Ada laughed.

"It's so good to hear the happy Ada again, my friend."

"Something tells me that she's here to stay," said Ada.

Ada and Troy spent the rest of the day discussing the best way to reveal the news. They decided that Ada would greet them alone and explain what happened. Then, she would ask Troy to appear. No matter what the approach, this was going to be a shock for both Daisy and Jackson. The four of them had been inseparable for years.

That night Ada and Troy lay in bed recalling the plans that the four of them had made, like living nearby each other, having children at the same time and raising them together.

"Oh! And Daisy is pregnant!" Ada was so excited to share the news with Troy. "No way! That's awesome. I bet the two of them are psyched beyond belief!"

"They are for sure. When Daisy was here recently, she and I were adding to the list of possible names." Ada smiled sweetly at Troy.

"Hey, you know what? That's going to be us soon." He reached over and put his hand on her belly.

"I can't wait."

The morning came fast as the two of them had the best night's sleep together. The reality of what had taken place kept hitting them over and over. It was hard to believe. They quickly dressed and Troy took Maisy for a walk after he fed her. Daisy and Jackson would be arriving around eleven this morning. Ada planned to meet them on the front porch and Troy would stay inside until he heard Ada call his name.

At twelve minutes until eleven, Ada's heart started racing. She probably shouldn't have had that second cup of coffee.

"Breathe, Ada, breathe," she whispered to herself. She

was standing near the front window staring out to the street.

"Yes, breathe, baby." Troy wrapped his arms around her and squeezed.

Ada allowed herself to sink back into his chest and felt herself relax. They stood for a few minutes like that until she recognized Jackson's gray truck approach the front of the house.

"Oh my gosh, they're here!" She almost screamed the words.

"You're too cute," Troy said and kissed her on the top of the head before walking back to the kitchen. "Make sure I can hear my cue!"

The front screen door slammed and made Troy jump and turn around. Ada was already running down the front porch steps toward them.

"This shouldn't take long," Troy said to himself, laughing.

Ada practically threw herself into Daisy to hug her, and then stepped back quickly to apologize. "I'm so sorry little one," she said patting Daisy's bump. "Your Auntie Ada is a bit excited to see your mommy and daddy."

Daisy laughed and pulled Ada back over to her. After another minute she glanced over at Jackson standing against his truck and smiling at the two of them.

"Hey you! I've missed you, too!" Ada gave Jackson a big

hug. "Come sit on the porch and we'll chat. I made some fresh lemonade. Let me go and get it!"

"Sounds perfect, but first I have to pee! This little one sends me to the bathroom constantly!"

For a minute Ada panicked. She held the door for Daisy and said louder than necessary, *"And now I'm going to get you a drink, so you'll have to go again."*

Daisy didn't seem to pay any attention and headed straight to the bathroom. Ada went to the kitchen to get the tray with glasses and a lemonade pitcher. Troy was over in the corner by the back door petting Maisy.

Once they were settled on the front porch, Daisy took a sip of her lemonade, sat it back on the little table and turned to Jackson.

"Can we tell her now?" Jackson smiled and shook his head while crunching a piece of ice.

"Tell me what?" Ada sucked in air and said slowly, "Are you having twins?"

"What? Oh, no." Daisy laughed and Jackson nearly choked on the ice. "I got a teaching job, thanks to your neighbor Susan and her connections. I'll be teaching 3rd grade right here on Hartlyn Island."

"You're kiddi—" Ada stood up, clapping her hands and squealing.

"And that's not all. Jackson has decided that this would be the perfect place to start his new business! We're moving here, Ada. Can you even believe it?"

The girls were hugging and practically jumping up and down like they had often done as youngsters. Jackson had to laugh at them. They were acting like schoolchildren who just received some juicy gossip.

After things had settled down a bit, Ada sat on the edge of the wicker chair. "Now . . . it's my turn."

Ada began from the beginning of her arrival on the island and how she was immediately drawn to Jason. Daisy looked at Jackson and shook her head to affirm. When Ada made it to the point of the story when Jason rescued her from the storm and having to run the sailboat ashore, she was fairly certain that her two friends were assuming she'd announce the two had fallen in love. Jackson and Daisy had glanced at each other and smiled at one point.

They have no idea, thought Ada.

Since Jackson was present, she decided to spare the intimate details, but would tell her friend when the two were alone.

It was too romantic not to tell. But she did have to explain the reason she ran out of the boat. Daisy knew right away and let out a gasp. Her hands went up to her mouth, and she laid back in the swing. It took Jackson a minute to catch up, but then he recalled the four of them deciding on tattoos prom night and Daisy chickening out at the last minute.

Jackson was on the edge of his seat and brushed a nervous hand through his hair. "What are you saying, Ada? Is ...is he?"

Ada started crying and shaking her head.

"How is that possible?" Jackson was near tears himself, and Daisy began sobbing as soon as Ada did.

After she composed herself, Ada said softly, "I'll let him explain everything."

At that, the door opened, and Troy stood with a slight smile on his face. "Hi, guys, it's been a while."

Daisy stood up and ran to him, almost knocking him over. He hugged her, and then looked at his best friend.

"Man, I . . . I just . . ."

Daisy moved to put her arms around Ada. The two guys embraced each other and kept slapping each other's backs. When they finally pulled back, both had tears in their eyes.

"Hey, Babe, do we have anything stronger than lemonade?

I think we could all use a drink!"All four laughed.

"I have an idea," said Ada excitedly. "Let's grab a picnic basket and throw some food and drinks inside then head to the beach. I'll grab some Dr. Pepper for Daisy!"

"Yes! Just like old times!" Daisy chimed in.

After spreading out a couple of quilts, Troy spent the next hour relaying his story to Daisy and Jackson as he had told it to Ada. There were lots of questions and he did his best to answer them. Daisy and Jackson were in disbelief and kept repeating they just couldn't believe it.

Troy raised his beer bottle saying: "To lifelong friends, celebrating old times, and making memories . . . together again."

They clinked their drinks. "Hear, hear," they each said.

"What I really want to know is," the three of them looked at Troy intently, "did you take my suggestion of naming your first baby Charlie, whether it was a boy or girl?"

They all fell over laughing.

The sun was beginning to set, so Jackson and Daisy decided to go for a short walk on the beach. Ada sat between Troy's legs, and he wrapped his arms around her. They sat in silence for quite a while and watched the setting sun dance off the water.

Contentment, gratitude, and love filled every space in her heart. It was as though Troy was reading her mind and acknowledged the same feelings with a gentle squeeze. She kissed the palms of his hands and then reached up to place them on either side of Troy's face, her own holding them there.

No words were needed.

Epilogue

Ada sat on the front porch in a wicker chair with Maisy beside her. "We're home," she said aloud.

The words brought so much joy to her heart. The plans that the four friends had made long ago were now coming to fruition. Not in her wildest imagination could Ada have envisioned this two years ago.

The last four months had been a whirlwind of activities including Daisy and Jackson moving into their new home two streets over. Daisy loved her new teaching job, and she and Ada were decorating the nursery. Her best friend's baby boy would be born in a little over two months, and she couldn't wait! Jackson had standing room only at the grand opening of his new business downtown. Troy decided to pick up where he left off on his counseling degree and accepted the official offer as the University baseball coach. Ada settled into her new role as the art gallery manager of Pacific Cove. Oscar promised to visit at least every three months. Robert and Susan were enjoying having the four young people over for cookouts, and he and Troy were wrapping up their book. There were some changes made to the bungalow after she and Troy had purchased it from Marilyn. They started by returning the layout of the home to its original design before there was a rental unit.

Troy would be home from his class soon, and Ada had something important to share with him. Maisy followed Ada back inside to a bedroom adjacent to the primary. There was a butterfly bush just outside the window that was often visited by colorful butterflies and hummingbirds. Ada stood near the window looking out as the sun shone through and warmed her body.

"This will make a perfect room," she said aloud.

"A perfect room for what, Babe?" Troy came up behind her and kissed her lovingly.

Ada turned towards her husband, took his hands and placed them over the lower part of her belly.

"For our baby girl." She smiled, and so did he.

Acknowledgements

Thank you to Taylor Miller, my incredible book editor; to Abby Thrash, my amazingly talented daughter-in-law and book cover designer; and to my family for your continued encouragement, especially my husband, who is always my biggest fan.

A special thank you to my former students on the 2017 yearbook staff at Jackson Middle School for voting me "Most Likely to Become a Published Author," even though I never mentioned my dream of writing a novel.